What's it gonna be?

D1662328

by Cassandra Piat

Printed by ELP Mauritius

ISBN: 978 99949 – 0 – 137 – 1

DEDICATION

To Mame & Pape, Christine & Patrick – thank you for always believing in me...

To my wonderful hubby, who will probably recognise himself somewhere in the book!!

To my 3 gorgeous children who keep me on my toes, but fill my life with happiness.

To Cecile – thanks so much for sharing my excitement as if it was your own book.

To Jo and all my other crazy and wonderful friends!

And finally, to Grand-mère Laurence – I miss your 5 minute, bum-on-the-edge-of-the-seat visits so much...

Love you all – this one's for you…

ACKNOWLEDGMENTS

Many thanks to my Editor, Jenny, for her valuable advice and guidance and to my Illustrator for her wonderful cover.

A huge MERCI to Vincent & Cecile for giving me the first 'live' copies of my book. What a precious gift… Thank your for being the amazing friends that you are.

Chapter One

I jumped in surprise as I heard my mobile phone ring. Picking it up distractedly, I was roughly shaken back to reality at my boyfriend's voice on the other end of the line, sounding none too pleased.

"Lucy, where *are* you?!" he asked impatiently.

Oh Blast! I looked at my watch and realised that it was already five past eight! I was meant to be meeting him at the movies at eight and I was late… again!

"I'm on my way! Just out the door," I stammered, bouncing off the couch and throwing my book on the table.

"Lucy, will you ever be on time - *ever*?" He replied tersely, clearly exasperated. "Hurry up, *please*."

"Be there in 5 minutes!" I exclaimed, as I raced to the bedroom. I flung open the cupboard doors and my heart plummeted - finding something to wear in this mess was a challenge equal to climbing Mount Everest solo!

I groaned in despair. I had promised, no make that, 'promised, promised, *promised*' Matt that I wouldn't be late this time. I scavenged my way through the pile of clothes on the floor like a dog digging a hole in the sand. Why was it that every time I was in a hurry, all my decent clothes were either dirty, un-ironed or had done a runner on me? I mean, just ask me "What clothes *don't* you want to wear tonight Lucy?" And ta-daammm, you'll find those clothes clean, impeccably ironed and neatly folded or hung up in my cupboard. But what I would like to wear - nowhere in sight!

I suddenly remembered the jeans I'd worn the previous day and raced to the bathroom where I had seen them last.

Got'em! I exclaimed happily to myself and started pulling them on. I stopped half way at the sight of a coffee stain on the left leg. Damn! Now I remembered why I'd thrown them on the floor yesterday!

What now? I looked around desperately trying to spot something else suitable, but realising that it was a lost cause and that the dirty jeans would just have to do, I pulled them on, grabbed my keys in one hand, my shoes in the other and raced out the door. At least the movie theatre would be dark and everyone would have gone in by the time I got there, I tried to reassure myself.

Luckily Curepipe isn't very big and I lived only a few minutes' drive from the cinema complex. As I parked my car, the smell of pizza emanating from Pizza Hut made my stomach rumble and my mouth water. No time for that now, I thought sadly as I climbed the stairs two at a time. I spotted Matt straight away. He was pacing up and down near the entrance, looking around - glanced at his watch ten times in the five seconds it took me to reach him! He didn't look happy. He finally saw me and, although my unrealistic self was hoping for a little smile, even just a fake '*yuck, I've eaten a bitter lemon*' one, all I got was a glare as he heaved an exaggerated sigh.

As I reached the big glass entrance doors of the cinema - the one where everyone flashes those discreet looks at themselves to check that everything is all in place before entering - I snuck a quick glance at my reflection and realised that I had completely forgotten to brush my hair, and that the pencil I had stuck in my ponytail while reading was still proudly sticking out!

Oh well, no time to do anything about it now. Matt looked me up and down, clearly unimpressed by my fashion statement. He remained unamused as I jumped up, ignored his icy stare and planted a kiss on his cheek.

"Hi! Sorry I'm late," I said cheerfully, grinning mischievously up at him.

"Is the un-brushed, just got out of bed, pencil sticking out hairstyle the new 'in' thing?" he asked irritably, giving me another once-over. I rolled my eyes at him, taking the pencil out and making a feeble attempt at straightening up my hair.

Matt has been my 'significant other' for the past four years. He's older than me, not the 'you could be my father' type of older, but still, eight years older. We met at a party I had gone to with my boyfriend of the time, Nick. Things between Nick and I had become as fizzy as a flat coke by then, but we were still together, I guess both not wanting to be the one to do the dirty deed and leave.

When Matt and I had met, he had looked towards me with his beautiful blue eyes twinkling playfully and said, "Hi! I'm Matt. My friends call me Matthew Carl James Riley for short."

"I'm Lucy," I had answered, giggling. "It's nice to meet you Matt."

"Oh, you can call me Matthew Carl James Riley," he had replied poker-faced, and I had burst out laughing.

As he had grinned back at me, I had felt something stirring deep inside, which had surprised me as he really wasn't my type physically. Not that I didn't find him cute, because I did, but let's just say he wasn't really the type I usually fell for. He has the most amazing aquamarine eyes, light brown hair which he usually keeps pretty short, a nice body i.e. muscles in all the right places and a smile to die for – his eyes light up and they crinkle up on the sides, and basically it just does all sorts of strange things to me. The downside is that he isn't that tall – he's only about five foot nine which makes him only a few inches taller than me and therefore much shorter than the men I am usually attracted to. But he has an undeniable charm and has always been quite popular with the ladies.

Our stubborn and highly independent natures have led to many pointless arguments, some break ups, but we have always ended making up again. We have a lot of fun together, are like best friends and more importantly, he makes me laugh like no one else can.

The only problem is that, despite all this, I really don't see us ever getting to the altar, as he has a major 'commitment phobia' - an irrational fear of the "M" word. Even the word 'wedding' sets him off and makes him start to hyperventilate – it would actually be hilarious if it wasn't so frustrating!! Seriously, it must be the scariest thing a man can hear these days. Instead of shouting "BOO" to a man, try shouting "MARRIAGE" and see how high he jumps and how loud he screams!

Matt's already thirty-four years old, and although there's really nothing wrong with being thirty-four and I love him very much, I've decided I don't intend to wait much longer for him to make up his mind.

As we walked towards the ticket counter I realised that it was much lighter than I'd anticipated inside and that my coffee stain seemed to have tripled in size since I'd left home! Just as I was putting my finger in my mouth to rub it on the stain, hoping it might look like it was actually water that had wet my jeans, I heard a woman's voice saying hello to Matt. Although I didn't recognize the voice straight away, the little chill that ran through my body gave me a pretty good idea. Surely not? I glanced over Matt's shoulder to have a look, finger still in my mouth. And there she was - Jessica!!

OH MY GOD! She was back! My finger fell out of my mouth as my mouth fell to the floor.

I leaned my face on Matt's shoulder realising it was the only way to get my mouth to stay shut, and tried to force a smile with my deformed lips. She said a cheerful hello and I let out something sounding like a cross between a bark, a groan, a squeak and a grunt! I glanced at Matt to see how he was reacting to her and his smile was doing at least three laps around his face. I could have strangled him there and then!

Jessica was an ex-girlfriend of course, but not just any ex - she was *the* ex! She was the love of his life, the one who had broken his heart. Although it's been over four years, I just know that he still thinks of her and probably wishes I were more like her. I mean who wouldn't? Just look at her, with her long blond hair, her big blue eyes, her sparkling (very clean) white jeans and her Pamela Anderson sized breasts! Perhaps she isn't beautiful but there's something about her, a *je-ne-sais-quoi* that makes you look twice.

My eyes travel down to my stained jeans and I cringe in embarrassment. Ha! So much for a dark theatre, I grumbled inwardly. Then, as I once again gaze at her beautiful, immaculately brushed hair, my hand unconsciously rises up to smooth down my own very scruffy look.

Luckily she's been living abroad since they broke up. I hate her! I thought darkly.

Just look at the way his eyes are sparkling at her. Look at his smile - it's almost covering the bald spot on the top of his head! And, hang on! Is that drool I see at the corners of his mouth?!!

I suddenly realised that she and Matt had turned towards me and were both looking at me expectantly. I looked from one to the other, before mumbling a lame, "Umm…Sorry, I didn't quite get that…"

Making a special effort to come back to the land of the non-idiotic people, I asked her what she'd been up to and how long she was back for. Holding my breath, I waited for her answer, which with my luck, would be; "I'm back for good". But it seems that the moon was in the 7th house and Jupiter in line with Mars, because it turned out that she was only back for a few days.

As she went on to tell us about her new job in Paris, my gaze swept down to her chest. That sure is a major thing we don't have in common, I thought despairingly. She really has a HU-GE pair. I stared sadly down at my own flat chest… I have a serious case of 'fried-egg syndrome' and its quite depressing when I have Miss Baywatch in front of me. I couldn't help feeling sorry for Matt to go from those to mine!

Suddenly frustrated, I decided that I had had enough

of playing gooseberry and nudged Matt gently on the arm. "The movie's about to start, we'd better get some seats."

"Why don't you join us?" Matt said to Jessica as my head did a 360 pivot on the spot and my mouth fell open again. I couldn't believe him! I pinched him hard, keeping a big fake smile on my face. I felt him wince and she probably caught on, but I didn't care. I mean how much could one take? I know I can be a walkover at times but honestly, this was too much.

As she smiled and told us that she was in fact with friends and they were watching the other movie, I grabbed Matt's arm and pulled him towards the cinema. I smiled, another fake one - they were starting to come pretty naturally to me now - and said goodbye to Jessica. She smiled back and I felt a bit guilty when I realised her smile actually looked genuine.

"Oh Lucy!" she called out to me just as we started walking off. I stopped and looked over my shoulder expectantly.

"I think you must have spilt something on your jeans, there's a brown patch just above your left knee," she said, her silky smile making my guilty feelings disappear as fast as they'd surfaced.

Gee, thanks for making sure everyone heard that! Write it on the front page of the newspapers why don't ya! Better still, how about broadcasting it live on National TV, you stupid cow! I thought angrily as I felt myself fuming inside. But I just forced another one of my fake smiles and feigned great surprise.

"Oh gosh," I exclaimed, looking down at my jeans in mock surprise. "I hadn't noticed... oh, how embarrassing!" and I scrubbed the stain pretending that I was trying to remove it.

I looked up and caught Matt's gaze – his blue eyes were sparkling with mirth as he stood there watching me and he was clearly having a hard time stopping himself from bursting out laughing. I narrowed my eyes at him, daring him to say a word and stormed off ahead of him, seething. He knew me too well and knew that I had worn the jeans knowing full well that they were dirty. I felt so humiliated, but then again, it was typical of me to put myself in such situations. Miss Perfect white jeans would never have left home with dirt stained jeans!

To top it off, the film was pretty much a disaster, especially for a 'happy ever after' type of person like me - it was about a fishing boat caught out in a storm and in the end they all drowned (took two whole hours!).

They should have saved us the time and drowned after the first huge wave hit them, if you ask me!

"Next time I choose the movie Matt!" I grumbled as I stomped ahead of him out of the cinema, still not over my humiliation. He just looked at me and chuckled.

"Sure Luce, next time they're showing Bambi or Cinderella…" he snorted and I playfully slapped him on the arm as I felt a reluctant grin tug at my lips.

He'd made a lot of effort to get back into my good books during the movie, holding my hand, getting me chocolate in the middle of the movie and whispering stupid remarks in my ear, managing to make me laugh despite my firm intention to sulk for at least a week. He didn't even complain when I grabbed his arm, digging my fingers painfully into it every time there was a tense moment – which was pretty much throughout the film, as wave after wave threatened to make the boat capsize.

As we walked back to the car, I glanced at Matt and couldn't help wondering if this film was some kind of sign telling me 'quit, while you're ahead – stop fighting the inevitable". Oh no, it's official, I'm becoming prematurely senile! Reading a sign from above about my love life in a ship-in-a-storm-and-they-all-die story! But then again… maybe that's exactly what our relationship was like, a ship in a storm, the question being whether we'd end up beating the storm or sinking…

Chapter Two

Matt dropped me off at the entrance to my apartment block and gave me an affectionate hug and a kiss. Still feeling put out by the Jessica episode, I pulled away when he tried to kiss me again. I was not in the mood.

Matt often stayed over but hadn't had the time to organize his work clothes before the movies, "because I, unlike you, was on time!" he had said jauntily before leaving. I switched the stair lights on as I walked up to the first floor.

Home is a small block of apartments, eight flats in all, near the center of Curepipe, a small town which is situated on the central plateau of the island of Mauritius.

The apartment actually belongs to my parents, and was built on the land where my grandparents' house used to be and in the neighbourhood where my mother grew up. It is surrounded by houses owned by family and extended family, and they have all been living here forever. My family left Mauritius to live in Australia eight years ago, but I moved back here five years ago. There aren't many young people in the complex, actually none except me, but I'm really happy here as there are plenty of lovely old people who are mostly friends of the family, and they make me feel cared for.

Curepipe itself is a very dreary looking town with heaps of ugly grey buildings, although a few modern buildings are starting to rise up here and there adding some much needed colour. There are a lot of shops in town, not shopping centres as you see in big cities, just small shops one next to the other which, for the most part, run parallel to the main roads, with a few grouped together forming "arcades" as we call them here. Basically you can find pretty much anything you need around town. Not much nightlife on the other hand, although there are a few Chinese restaurants, one or two trendy cafés, a steak house, one gastronomical restaurant and we even have our very own Kentucky Fried Chicken and Pizza Hut!

There are two apartment blocks and my maternal Grandmother lives in the block just next door and comes to visit every two days. She's a socialite who spends every afternoon from four to six o'clock visiting friends, family and neighbors, all living at a walking distance from her apartment. She is therefore a great source of gossip. She pops in for not more than three to five minutes at a time, bum on the edge of the sofa, bag held firmly under her armpit in a 'I'm about to go' position, filling me in on all the gossip of the day. She always ends "but of course I'm really not interested in gossip, my dear".

I unlocked my door, happy to be home. My head was still racing with thoughts of the evening; Jessica, Matt and the stupid movie. I just wanted to fall into bed and sleep it off. Pity Matt hadn't stayed the night - it would have comforted me to have him nearby.

Matt lives five minutes away in a bachelor pad that I try to avoid as much as possible. Mine is not luxurious but his apartment is just the worst. It is five floors up with no elevator and is tiny i.e. two large steps get you to either end of the apartment. To top it off there's a bus stop just underneath his window, well five floors and a wall down, but it might as well have been in his room. At six o'clock every morning you get shaken up by the screeching brakes of the first bus of the day - and let me tell you that Mauritian buses are quite something - its gear box sounding as if it is just about to collapse right there, not to mention the banging of the metallic doors, the accelerator being revved up by the driver and the shattering noise of the whole engine. Overall, definitively not a very soothing way to wake up!

Then there's the food thing. There's never anything there! Matt's cupboards are completely devoid of food apart from an expired can of tuna and an old packet of 3-minute noodles (which have both been there since I met him four years ago) and a cockroach or two. His fridge usually has a few beers in it, but that's about it. Pretty much the typical male-living-alone fridge - well one who has a girlfriend to run to for food, that is! If I do sleep over I have to bring dinner, coffee, milk and anything else I'd want to eat or drink. Basically, it's much simpler for him to come to me, and besides, my apartment is really spacious and much more comfortable for two.

I showered and got into bed, feeling restless. I wasn't sure why, but I guess seeing Jessica had shaken me up a bit. Images, thoughts and questions raced through my head. Why couldn't he glow like that when he looked at me? Why couldn't he think *I* was the most amazing thing since rugby?

I mean look at me - I'm tall with shiny long brown hair, green eyes which are apparently quite striking and overall I guess I'm not bad looking. I'm actually quite smart, not fat - Ok, so I admit to a bit of cellulite on the slightly non-muscled thighs, but still - I'm friendly, outgoing, fun loving - what else did Matt want? Ok, if I'm really honest, I'm a real scatterbrain, I'm always late, I'm super messy and I tend to be rather stubborn. But nobody's perfect surely?

I guess deep down I know that he loves me, not like he seems to worship Jessica maybe, but he is good to me and we are great together. But is that enough?

Then again, why am I staying with someone who doesn't want to get married, or even worse, who doesn't want to marry ME? After all, what's so great about him? Ok granted, he has an amazing sense of humour and makes me laugh, he's super generous, he's kind and thoughtful and would make an amazing dad, but he's also so bloody stubborn half the time that it drives me crazy. And how about his complete inability to make a decision! Not to forget the fact that he always spreads out the newspaper on the toilet floor and then just leaves it lying there when he's done! Or that he never puts the lid back on jars after opening them - then tells me off if I do the same! I scold myself in frustration. So, why don't I just leave him?

Could it be the 'comfort zone' thing that's making me stay with him despite wanting more from him? I wondered wearily. Not having the courage to find myself on my own again after four years with him and at twenty-six years old? Is it the fact of not having the courage to start again with someone else? Or am I scared of being left on the shelf and becoming a bitter old maid, eating microwave dinners for one alone in front of the TV with only a cat as company, knitting endless booties for grandchildren I'd never have...

I sighed and shifted positions again - I've never really known what I wanted to do professionally (although recently I've started wondering whether I shouldn't try to do something like Copywriting, as I love writing) - but one thing I've always wanted was to eventually find myself a Prince Charming who would seek out the sun, the stars and the moon for me, marry him and have lots of children. Surely that's not too much to ask, right?

I sighed loudly and pulled the sheets off the edge of the bed so that my toes stuck out on the other side. I felt less trapped like that - it seemed to reflect my feeling on my love life at the moment. I felt trapped, in a rut and I just didn't know how to get myself out of it. Or did I even want to get out of it?

Chapter Three

When my alarm went off at seven the next morning it felt as if I hadn't been sleeping for more than a few minutes. I snoozed until about half past seven, then realising the time, sprang out of bed and fell straight back down again as I saw little twinkly stars buzzing around my eyes. I decided to lie down for a few more minutes just to make sure I recovered from my head rush. The next thing I knew it was eight o'clock and I was late – AGAIN!

I rushed into the shower, brushing my teeth at the same time and thus benefiting not only from a soap wash, but from a toothpaste-dribble wash too! They really should invent a soap and toothpaste 2-in-1 thing, and call it 'Dribble and Wash paste', as I'm sure I'm not the only person who brushes their teeth in the shower! I ran around the room once again trying to find something to wear in the bomb debris of my apartment. Clothes were lying around everywhere, piled high on the desk, overflowing over the chair, stuffed under the bed. There were dirty coffee cups around the place, one on the bedside table, another on the desk, another in the bathroom and I even found one in my knickers drawer.

I'd had a really lazy week cleaning wise, but it wasn't always like this. Ok, so maybe most of the time clothes-wise, but the dirty mugs usually found their way to the kitchen at least. The lounge and TV room were relatively tidy, except for magazines lying around on the floor and the sofas, videotapes littered all around the TV and a plate or two from my TV dinners of the week. I really hoped that one day I would grow up and become tidy. Surely the older and wiser thing could also apply to older and tidier? I for one really hoped so! Having covered the four corners of my apartment, I groaned as I realised that I had no choice but to iron something, and looked at my watch in despair. When, oh when, would I ever be early, or let alone on time anywhere?

I arrived at work twenty minutes late, after having driven as if I was giving Michael Schumacher a run for his money! Luckily I knew the road with my eyes closed, because at the speed I was driving my eyes pretty much felt like they were closed - which was a pity as it was a beautiful day and the Moka mountain ranges in the background were spectacular.

I gazed around the parking lot, and heaved a sigh of

relief as I saw that there was no sign of a white Mazda anywhere. In other words, my boss hadn't arrived yet!

Work is at Trends, an Advertising Agency, found in the town of Moka, a fifteen minute drive from Curepipe. An office full of wacky individuals, ten in all, which made it a completely riotous environment to work in. Granted, my job is the most boring one there - Secretary to the Big Boss - but as I spend as little time as possible at my desk, or working for that matter, I love my job!

I raced from my car to the office and fell into my chair, switched on the computer, took the 'Things to do' pile of papers from my basket and proceeded to spread them out all over my desk. "There!" I said aloud with a big smile, as I looked at my messy desk with pride. It had the desired effect of making it seem like it'd been hours since I'd arrived.

My office was a mess anyway, piled high with props of press ads already presented or yet to be presented to clients, reels of our commercials and cassettes of our radio ads piled up, some on the shelves, others on the floor, and all waiting to be filed and stored in alphabetical order. The walls were covered in our best print Ads ranging from baby nappies, to cars, to dog food, to Hotels, to soft drinks - which made for quite a bizarre mix and match. Files and newspaper cuttings of both our campaigns and our competitors' campaigns brimmed over all sides of the other shelves. There were piles of magazines all around the periphery, as I tried to keep a minimum amount of space in the center in order to be able to get from my desk to the kitchen and Olivia's office!

Basically I guess, my office resembled my apartment – it looked like a bomb had been dropped in it. That's why I felt so at home here. And funnily enough, I can find pretty much anything asked for relatively quickly, which is probably why my boss, John, hasn't actually realised, or commented on the fact that it had been six months since he'd asked me to sort it all out.

I headed to the kitchen to make myself a cup of coffee on my way to Olivia's office down the hall. Sarah and Phoebe, our two copywriters, were standing in the kitchen chatting away. As Sarah is eight and a half months pregnant and really, really huge and the kitchen is extremely small, there was no way I would get past her to reach the kettle and cups.

"Hi girls!" I said cheerfully, "Umm…"

I grimaced as I wiggled exaggeratingly, trying to squeeze myself between the wall and Sarah. It was definitively a no-can-do situation and I grunted loudly to tease her.

Sarah gave me an evil glare causing me to burst out laughing.

"This is no laughing matter, Lucy. Wait till you're nine months pregnant and look like a sumo wrestler!" she muttered pretending to be angry, although I could see the mirth in her eyes. She wasn't in the least hung up on the fact that she was really huge.

Phoebe is a slightly plump brunette with short unruly hair and is completely spaced out. Although at times I seriously doubt that she's mentally stable, she's just hilarious.

I finally grabbed my cup of coffee, leaving the two copywriters discussing the latest radio commercial and headed to Olivia's office. I envied them, as their work always seemed so exciting and such fun. They were forever bouncing ideas off each other and I often heard them in fits of giggles while working.

Olivia is my best friends as well as my colleague, except that she's an Account Manager and is pretty busy and stressed out with work most of the time, unlike my lazy self. She's ambitious and does a great job but always finds time for our gossip sessions, which are as essential to her as they are to me.

Just as I flopped down into the chair opposite Olivia's desk, opening my mouth to start my verbal diarrhea, we heard yells emanating from the artwork area, the voice sounding oddly like my boss, John, the one who wasn't supposed to have arrived yet.

"WHAT DO YOU MEAN THE PRINTER'S NOT WORKING?" We heard him yell – in fact, I'm pretty sure they heard him up in the Himalayas. "I HAVE A PRESENTATION AT TEN O'CLOCK AND IT'S ALMOST NINE O'CLOCK. WHAT DO YOU SUGGEST I DO NOW?"

As I peeped through the door I could see poor Yann, who just happened to be the Mac Operator working on that particular campaign, shaking like a leaf in a very gusty wind, his dark skin turning the same color as the new brand of white toilet paper on his desk. As if it was his fault that the printer had decided to pack up! John turned around and stomped out of the artwork and headed back to his office.

I snuck behind Olivia's door waiting for him to go by. Just as I thought that the coast was clear, I heard him shout;

"LUCY! If it's not too much trouble, would you very much mind coming out from behind Olivia's door and heading back to your office, and maybe for once, actually getting some work done!"

I rolled my eyes at Olivia who was grinning, and

whispered a quick, "See you later" and headed back to my desk.

John, the big boss at the Agency, is thirty years old and started the agency three years ago with just himself and two others. Now there are ten of us and we're the best agency around. He's a creative genius and a great businessman too. Physically he's not very impressive with his tall, thin silhouette and short dark hair, slightly slanty eyes and freckles, but he's got the gift of the gab and has the clients eating out of his hand. Although he's young and pretty OK much of the time, most of the people working here are pretty scared of him because he's got a really short fuse; can be all smiles one minute, and blow up sky high the next.

I don't mind being his secretary though because, to his amazement, he doesn't scare me in the least! If he screams at me, I just answer right back! I think that's probably why I'm still around. All his previous secretaries were too terrified of him and ended up leaving. The fact that he doesn't instill any fear in me annoys him no end, but I have actually come to the realization that it is probably a relief to him too.

I returned to my desk and proceeded to sort out the printer crisis and get back into my boss' good books. As soon as he left at a quarter to ten, with the presentation boards ready and in hand, I went straight back to Olivia's office for our gossip session.

"So here goes the inevitable question Olivia - how's the love life going?" I asked, grinning.

Chapter Four

Olivia hasn't had much luck on the love side; one boyfriend leaving her suddenly when everything was going just fine (well, except for the little her-kissing-another-guy incident!), then there was the one who was embarrassed to be going out with her so didn't want it to be known by anyone (which in a tiny place like here, is rather hard - unless you just don't see the other person at all, which is kind of what happened!), then there was the one who kissed another girl after expressing his undying love for Olivia ... do I need to go on?!

So, now it's been a while since the last guy and she's getting worried about finishing up "on the shelf" as the expression goes. We're both 26 years old, and let's face it, we're not getting any younger and with absolutely no potential male prospects in sight, she's starting to panic.

I have to tell you here that Mauritius is a small island and that meeting someone new and unexpected is, I'd have to say, quite unexpected!

Ok, so there are over 1,3 million people on the island and that doesn't sound so bad, but in fact Mauritius is a really multi-cultural society and although we all live in harmony, there are not a lot of inter-marriages. It's not a black/white thing, but more a religious and cultural thing. We all basically end up marrying within our own culture, and we, the European Mauritians, happen to make up a tiny 2% or so of the population… and even that wouldn't be so bad if that 2% was made up of handsome and eligible men between the ages of 25 and 35 years old! But that is not the case and to top it off, in Olivia's case half of the 2% male potential are actually related to her in some way and as she already knows most of the other half – well, you can understand her problem. Let's just say there's not much room for surprises!

It's actually pretty hard to go anywhere here without bumping into someone you know or are related to. At social gatherings for example, there's always the traditional questions asked by the older generation, "Lucy Evans? Oh, and your parents are?" "Oh, Harry and Teresa - of course I know them! We were at school together" or "But we're related! My mother's sister married your father's mother's cousin!" or "Oh, but of course! You look exactly like your father!".

In a way it's all kind of endearing as you really never feel alone, but it is sometimes exhausting not to be able to just fade into the background. Even when you're driving, one hand seems to always be up in a sort of Queen's salute as you're forever seeing someone you know. Basically, all the bad hair days and hormonal bad mood days cannot go unnoticed in our part of the world!

Anyway, back to Olivia and her non-existent love live…

"So? Anything to report?" I asked as I watched her signing off a few letters.

"No, nothing at all," she said with a sigh, putting the pile into her 'out' basket and glancing up at me.

"Well, apart from my family still trying desperately to set me up with guys they are sure would be just perfect for me... And let me tell you, it's pretty scary seeing the guys they come up with! I'll seriously need to re-evaluate myself if they really think those guys would suit me," she said, her dark eyes sparkling at me.

Olivia has blond hair cut into a severe bob above her shoulders, brown eyes with really long eye lashes and a really cute small rosebud mouth. She is slim and quite tall and is always really well dressed. She has a sophisticated look about her which may have scared off a few potential suitors in the past.

"So who's the latest catch?" I said, unable to hide the amusement in my voice.

"Well let's see… after the dentist, who just happened to be at least 45 and not married - which pretty much speaks for itself - they're now trying to throw me onto Philip, who's sweet enough but really too sweet and 'goody two shoes' for me."

I scoffed, "That's for sure!" I knew Philip and he was just too nice and also just not her style.

"Anyway, just wait till you hear just how desperate they are," she continued. "On Sunday, I was at my brothers' place and he told me that he thought I should subscribe to Match.com on the internet - can you believe him!" she exclaimed, clearly outraged.

Match.Com! It's one of these *'We'll help you find your soul mate'* type of things where you answer a whole lot of questions about yourself, what sort of person you are and what sort of person you're looking for, then you wait for all your potential soul mates to reply! Totally not my kind of thing – you never know who you may end up with, there are so many psychos out there. For all you know, while you think you're corresponding with a 6ft tall, brown hair, brown eyed, athletic guy it could actually be a 5ft2, brown eyed, blue haired, 200kg reclusive woman! It's true, how could you possibly know?

"You're joking?!" I exclaimed, in astonishment.

"No, I'm dead serious! I said 'no way' at first, but then he offered to give me the pair of sunglasses I'd been begging him for, if I agreed. So I gave in; and that's when he confessed that he'd actually already signed me on and that I'd probably be getting replies soon!"

"That's hilarious!" I said, shrieking with laughter. It just didn't seem the kind of thing any normal person, and my best friend at that, would do!

"Hilarious! For *you* maybe! I was furious at first, but then I guess I saw the funny side of it, and thought 'why not'? After all, I don't have to reply to anyone if I don't want to you know, it's all anonymous."

"It's such a spin out! Just imagine if you end up meeting someone that way…" I said, my thoughts drifting off imagining Olivia getting married to a gorgeous, dark haired man...

"Stop right there you romantic old fool!" she laughed. "These things only happen in the movies, and you obviously really should get down to watching more action movies or real life dramas to get back down to earth!"

"Hey! That's not very nice!" I replied pouting, before

breaking into a huge grin, as we both knew she had a point there.

"I haven't told you the funniest bit yet!" she said. "Get this! My code name is 'Island Duchess' chosen with the compliments of my adorable brother!" and she flicked her hair theatrically in an 'aren't I so gorgeous' way.

I laughed. "I can't wait for you to get replies - they'll all probably be lunatics, I mean, what normal person would subscribe to Match.com in the hope of actually finding love?"

"Speaking of love," she interrupted, looking up from her letters. "How are things with you and Matt these days? Any signs of an upcoming engagement?"

"No, I just don't think that he'll ever summon up enough courage Olivia…" I replied forlornly, picking up a pen and fidgeting, suddenly needing to do something with my hands. "I honestly thought he was so close at one time, but I think the moment has passed, and now I just don't know anymore…"

"That really sucks - I just can't understand the guy at all. I mean, it's obvious that he's crazy about you, so why can't he just do it? Where does his fear of commitment come from?" she asked.

"I just don't know. His pessimistic nature maybe…I think he just doesn't believe he can make someone happy. Oh, who knows? Maybe he just doesn't love me enough…" I answered despondently, forcing myself to face the hard truths. It was something I was considering more and more these days.

"It must be so frustrating for you," she said gently.

My shoulders slumped and I let out a huge sigh. "It sure is Olivia, and it's really starting to get me down. I know that for my own good I'll have to give him an ultimatum soon, but I guess I know it'll just scare him off, and I'm not sure I'm ready to handle that yet."

"You have to find the strength Lucy, he'll come round. If he doesn't, it's better that you find out now, instead of spending another five years with him, before realising that he'll just never commit anyway - and by then your biological clock will have ticked way past its use by date, and you'll find yourself an old maid with Disney Channel being the closest thing to having kids in your house."

"I know, I know, I will get round to it but it's just so hard," I replied wearily, as I spun the pen through my fingers. Suddenly, my head flew up as I realised that I had completely forgotten to tell Olivia about the movies.

"Guess who we saw at the movies on Friday night?" I blurted out.

"Umm… Sam and Vic?"

"No…" I said, bursting with impatience to tell her but wanting to see if she would guess.

"I know!" she exclaimed, her face lighting up. "Nick!"

"Ok, let's just pretend that it was a rhetorical question then shall we?" I said, not having the patience to wait any longer to spill the beans.

"Ok, tell me then!" she said sounding intrigued.

"JESSICA!" I exclaimed dramatically.

"NO!" she said in disbelief, her eyes popping out like Hugo her goldfish.

"YES! And of course Matt was drooling all over her - it makes me sick! I had to control myself not to knock the silly smile off his face!"

"What about *her* face?" she said, grimacing.

"Well, it's not her fault he's so gaga for her; it's no use hating her!" I said resignedly.

"You're exaggerating surely?" she asked, looking concerned.

I ignored her comment and went on.

"You should see the size of her breasts! It's so bloody depressing. I mean, she's just like those gorgeous actresses in Baywatch, running along the beach with their huge boobs flying through the air."

Olivia burst out laughing. "It really sucks doesn't it..." she said sympathetically, having the same size problem as me. Who said size was only a man thing?!

"Well, to be honest, I have a tendency to exaggerate Matt's obsession with her - jealousy of course," I said grimacing at Olivia. "But I just know he loved her more than he loves me…"

"Don't be ridiculous Lucy! Besides, you never even saw them together when they were going out."

"I know – I just feel it that's all…" I replied glumly.

"Well, just dump him then!" she replied, exasperated.

"Easier said than done," I wailed. "I can't throw four years away just like that!"

"I know. I'm sorry. I'm not being much help here – it's just so frustrating because I just don't get him at all," she said sympathetically, as she turned to answer her phone.

"I can understand, because I'm pretty lost too..." I sighed.

She looked at me and mouthed, "Sorry, I've got to take this call".

I strolled back to my desk feeling frustrated. What the hell was I going to do about Matt? I wish someone would just shake him up and tell him to stop being such a coward. It makes me so angry! How can a 34-year-old guy be so scared of getting married when the thing he's always wanted in life is a wife and kids?

Chapter Five

"Lucy! There's someone here to see you!" Léa, our receptionist, called out from her desk. Once again I was sitting in Olivia's office having a coffee and a chat and I wasn't in the least motivated to move.

I called out lazily, "Who is it?"

"Says he sells office supplies," she answered loudly, not caring if the person could hear her or not. I sure was glad John wasn't around to hear us being so rude!

I frowned.

"Hey, call me if he's cute and I'll come and have a look," Olivia said mischievously. I laughed and sighing loudly, headed back to my desk.

As I walked in I saw a short, reasonably muscly man, with spiky dark hair and grey eyes. He actually wasn't too bad looking, I thought. But then he spoke. Oh-My-God! What was *that*?! The poor guy sounded like someone who had just sucked into a helium balloon!

"Hello Ms. Evans," he said, giving me a suggestive once over. Crikey, he could at least try to be discreet about it – we were in an office after all!

"Hello, Mr….?" I said.

"Mr. Delano," he smirked.

"So, what can I do for you, Mr. Delano?" I asked, smiling with determined politeness.

"You can't even begin to imagine…" He grinned at me as my eyebrows rose in shock.

I stared at him frostily but didn't say anything. His grin widened, and then he changed his tone into a more professional one, and began telling me about the products he sold. His prices were really competitive and it would definitively be interesting for the company to do business with him.

"Ok, thank you for your time Mr. Delano. I'll have a chat to my boss about it and will get back to you soon," I said getting up, hoping he would do the same.

"Isn't he here now?" he retorted petulantly, not moving from his seat.

"No, and even if he was I couldn't just barge in to discuss this with him now," I snapped, and then added a smile remembering that I had to be professional here.

"And why would that be?" he asked rudely.

"Because that's the way it is," I said smoothly, the fake smile plastered on my face.

"Ok then," he said as he finally stood up to leave. He extended his hand for me to shake and I grimaced at its wet grip. As I tried to remove my hand from his sweaty palm, he squeezed it tightly before letting go, laughing as he registered the shock on my face.

"See you soon then Ms. Evans," and to my relief, he turned and left.

What a creepy guy, I thought as I looked through his prices again. They really were interesting, especially since we had a high turnover in ink cartridges and paper. I wasn't overly enthusiastic about doing business with him as there just seemed to be something not quite right about him, but I knew John would be. Oh well, maybe it was just a bad first impression.

When I got home from work, I went up to see my grandmother but she wasn't back from her visits yet. I had missed yesterday's episode of "Drop Dead Diva", and as she was a fan of the series, I knew she'd be able to fill me in on it. I loved the way she told me about the details and how shocked she was as soon as someone cheated on someone else or when a woman would flirt or come on to a man instead of it being the other way around.

As I was walking back towards my apartment block, I saw her car turning into the driveway. I watched her drive past in her little red and white VW and grinned as it looked as if the car was driving itself. All I could see was the very tip of her head peeping over the steering wheel. It never ceased to amuse me. I waited for her to park then went in for a quick chat before heading back to my apartment.

I walked past the row of letter boxes at the bottom of the stairs and noticed a few letters sticking out of my letter box. Endless bills or reminders as usual, I thought, but decided I'd better get them anyway. I was pleasantly surprised when I saw a postcard in the middle of the bills - must be either from my brother or my sister, both in Europe at the moment. My younger brother, Mark, was backpacking around for a few months and my elder sister, Natalie, was on her way to a traineeship in Slovakia.

Natalie is two years older than me and an eternal student. She has done never-ending degrees and postgrads and was now heading to Slovakia.

She had asked to be sent to Europe, hoping for somewhere fun like Spain or France, but ended up finding herself in Eastern Europe. She wasn't too excited at first, but her adventurous spirit took over as she read all about the place and prepared her departure.

I looked at the postcard and admired the beautiful city of Prague. I turned it over and began reading.

Hi Sis!

I'm sitting in the Hdezovice train station waiting for my train to Zilina wondering why the hell I'm doing this!!! This morning I went walking around the 'Old Tower' of Prague, it's very beautiful, the buildings are so old. Bit of a problem with the language thing though – if it's like this here then what will it be like in Zilina where there are hardly any tourists passing through? Anyway, I guess I'll soon find out!

Dobry den

Natalie

P.S. What's up with that boyfriend of yours? Still being his same old cowardly self? Get that glittering diamond on your finger once and for all or DUMP him!

I grinned as I read her P.S. - I wish I was as strong willed as her. But I wasn't. Even going off to a third world country alone and not speaking one word of the language… no way, just not for me! My sister was the sort to speak her mind and she just couldn't cope with Matt's indecision. They got along really well and he always knew what to say to make her laugh but she always got annoyed at his lack of self-assertiveness, as she called it. Being a black and white type of person, she kept telling him 'either you love her or you don't!' to which his eternal answer was 'it's not that simple'.

Matt came over later and we ordered a pizza, as neither of us felt like cooking and my fridge was empty anyway! We sat outside on my little balcony which had just enough room for two chairs and a little table. Although the view only looked over the rooftops, it was peaceful sitting out looking at the stars. I could also see the top of the old Catholic church lighting up the sky not too far off in the distance. I loved listening to its bells toll every hour.

I couldn't resist asking Matt if he'd been happy to see Jessica again.

He shrugged and said, "Sure."

"Matt, you were practically drooling over her!" I exclaimed, exasperated at his nonchalance.

"Don't be ridiculous. It was nice to see her and catch up, that's all. Where's the problem?"

"You're still in love with her. That's the problem!" I cried, jealousy surfacing from every pore.

"Lucy, you're being ridiculous! I'm with you now, she's history. It's O-V-E-R. I did love her once, sure, but I've moved on now."

"If you'd seen your face last night then you'd understand my reaction." I insisted, pouting some more.

"Oh, stop it will you," he said impatiently, getting up and heading back into the lounge, where he switched on the TV. I followed him in, grabbing the remote from him and switching it off again, determined to continue our conversation.

"Why did you ask her to join us? Don't you realise how humiliating it was for me?" I said in exasperation.

"I just thought it was the polite thing to do. I'm sorry if you took it that way," he said, looking surprised.

"Well how else would I take it Matt? You really don't think sometimes do you?"

"I think men and women just think differently," he said lamely.

"Yeah right! Men are from Mars, Women are from

Venus, blah blah blah!" I said annoyed. "And besides, that's usually *MY* line!"

He rolled his eyes at me and was about to say something when I cut him off and said, "I bet you had a good look at her boobs though didn't you?"

His face broke into a Cheshire cat grin. "Well… Ok, I have to admit I'd forgotten how big they were."

"Do you miss them?" I asked cheekily, suddenly finding the situation funny.

"What? Miss them, when I have your pancakes in compensation? No way!" he said laughing, as his hands caressed my breasts teasingly. I pushed them away as he chuckled, leaning over and giving me a kiss on the cheek before grabbing the remote from me and switching the TV on again.

That was the end of it then, but I did feel better about Jessica and he did sound sincere, so I guess I had to stop being jealous of her. I don't know why I always feel second best in his eyes. I keep wondering if he'd have married Jessica if she hadn't broken up with him… but I'll never know, will I?

Chapter Six

The weekend arrived and we headed down to Matt's beach cottage. It is situated along the south-east coast in a remote and tranquil area with beautiful white sandy beaches and a wide lagoon. Matt's family, and extended family, all have cottages down there along the same stretch of beach. The grandfathers had bought the land way back and had eventually divided and sub-divided it to give each child a piece of land on the beach.

Most weekends we all go down for a bit of fresh air, sun, sand and sea. The cottages are right on the beach, a luxury not found in many countries and it is really beautiful - just like on the postcards. Sometimes the places on postcards look so magical that you think the photos are obviously not real, but that's what this is like: a real life postcard in all its splendour.

I love the smell of the sea, a mixture of salt and algae, and I inhaled deeply through my window, feeling a sense of total relaxation spread through me as we neared our cottage.

When we arrived we changed into our bathers and headed straight to the beach. It was a gorgeous day. Matt's nephews and nieces had already arrived and were playing on the beach. There was a united "MATTTTTT" and "LUCYYYYY" scream when we arrived and all eight ran up to us and jumped in our arms, a few on each side. They adored Matt and I think they liked me a lot too. He was absolutely besotted by them and spent hours playing with them, taking them out in the boat, playing games, having races and just fooling around. As they dragged Matt into the sea, I declined and went to settle myself in a deck chair on the beach.

Matt was born to be a father. He had such a way with kids. He always knew exactly what to say to make them warm up to him and entertain them, and he had so much patience with them, it was completely endearing. I fell in love all over again every time I saw him with his nephews and nieces.

I rubbed on sunscreen and looked over to where they were in the sea. Matt was in the process of dunking one of his nephews while throwing one of his nieces over his shoulder. They were all screaming and laughing. He really would be such a wonderful dad…

It's so hard to understand how people function sometimes, what drives them, what scares them and how to reach their innermost selves. I just didn't understand why he was so scared of marriage. Ok, granted, maybe his parents don't have the greatest marriage of all times - he reckons it's a bit of a 'loveless marriage'. But then again, they aren't at each other's throats or anything. I just wished I understood what his problem was…

I was suddenly hot and bothered and no longer felt like lying in the sun. I sat up and looked at the sparkling turquoise blue sea stretching out before me, but was too restless to stay, so decided to go back to the cottage to get something to drink.

Matt's cottage was a really cute one-bedroom house with a lovely thatched roof and coconut trees growing on either side of the veranda. Half way up, I heard that the phone was ringing and ran the rest of the way.

"Hi Lucy, it's Olivia!" she said cheerfully.

"Hey you! What's up?" I answered, already feeling much better just at the sound of her friendly voice.

"I got my first reply!" she exclaimed, and sounded so excited I was wondering if she'd sent a CV out or had some major event which I had forgotten about.

"Reply to what?" I finally asked, puzzled.

"Match.com!" she cried impatiently.

Of course! I'd completely forgotten about that. I told her to tell me about it as I lay down in the deck chair on the verandah with the portable phone, enjoying the warmth of the sun on my skin. It really was a beautiful day.

"Well, as expected, it's a total loser; I mean get this, his email address is 'buzzmehoney'!!"

I burst out laughing.

"Listen to this; If you'd like your back rubbed, your toes tickled, your legs massaged, you'll love my softer touch…" Olivia read in a husky voice, trying to control her laughter.

"I think you've found the man of your dreams, Olivia!" I laughed into the phone.

"Hope that'll teach my brother a lesson and he'll finally just leave me alone and let me find my own man now!"

After my conversation with Olivia, I grabbed a diet coke out of the fridge and headed back to the beach. Matt was still in the sea and the kids were still joyously screaming away. I lay back under the coconut tree, sipping my diet coke and watching them.

I thought of Olivia trying desperately to find someone to love and me who supposedly had found someone… but then again, maybe I was as far away from love as she was…

Chapter Seven

After lunch, Matt said that he wanted to have a nap, but as soon as we lay down he started nuzzling my neck and I realised that it wasn't a 'let's sleep' nap he was after! His lips covered mine in a seductive kiss that sent sparks exploding through my body...

I was down to my knickers and bra when we suddenly heard Damian's voice calling out for Matt as he walked into the house.

"Oh shit!" I muttered in panic, as Matt's lips tore away from mine. I bolted out of bed and shot into the bathroom, hiding behind the door.

As I heard his footsteps by the bedroom door, I held my breath.

"Oh there you are Uncle Matt," he said, as I heard him fall down onto the bed next to Matt.

"Hi there squirt!" Matt said affectionately, clearly trying to seem unflustered.

"I'm so bored. What are you doing?" I heard him ask.

"Well, I was just relaxing in bed," Matt replied innocently, making me grin.

"Uncle Matt, are you naked under there?" I suddenly heard Damian exclaim after a moment's pause.

I froze and waited for Matt's answer but he just laughed and said, "Yep! Sure am buddy!"

"But *why*?" Damian asked, clearly perplexed as I tried to suppress a giggle.

"I was hot," Matt answered, as I swallowed my laughter thinking just how hot we had been about 3 minutes before being so rudely interrupted!

"But it's not really hot," Damian said sounding skeptical.

"Hey! Don't do that!" I heard Matt shout out, before he burst out laughing. I wondered what was going on but soon found out as Matt said loudly, clearly for my benefit; "Hasn't anyone ever told you that it's rude to lift the sheet off someone naked?"

"Is *that* what my willy will look like when I grow up," I heard Damian ask Matt, sounding rather concerned.

Matt snorted, masking my burst of laughter and

replied, "Well…not exactly. But pretty much I guess - although everyone's is different actually."

"Oh *GOOD!*" Damian replied with a huge sigh of relief as Matt roared with laughter.

"What do you mean *GOOD?*" Matt exclaimed in faked indignation.

"Well, it doesn't look so great you know," Damian replied seriously. "It's all hairy and shrivelled up."

I felt a wave of uncontrollable laughter make its way up and desperately tried to think of something really sad to push it down again.

And just when I had got myself under control again, Damian asked,

"Has Lucy seen it?" and I spurted with laughter.

"What kind of a question is that?" exclaimed Matt, probably tickling him as I heard Damian scream begging him to stop. Matt was clearly trying to change the subject, but Damian was having none of it.

"It's just that if you really like her, I really don't think you should show it to her, you know. It's really kind of ugly and it will definitely scare her off."

Matt guffawed and said, "That's it!" and then I heard

the sounds of scuffling on the bed.

"Hey Mr. Indiscretion!" Matt finally said. "Why don't you grab yourself a drink from the fridge while I get dressed and then we can play a bit of football?"

"Indiscre…*what*? I don't even know what that means! But yeah, a drink and football sounds cool to me!" he said as the bed creaked and I heard his footsteps head out of the room.

"I'll be right there," Matt told him as I peeked out of the bathroom to make sure all was clear. Matt and I looked at each other and both doubled up with laughter, me quickly taking a pillow to drown out my hysterical giggles. I didn't even want to imagine him recounting the story to his cousins and parents later on.

Matt walked back out, now dressed in shorts and I whispered, "Ugly, hairy and shrivelled up huh?" and fell back down onto the bed, shrieking with laughter.

"Did you just call my main man *ugly, hairy and shrivelled up*?" Matt asked, standing over me with a mock menacing glare which only made me laugh harder.

"Um…yeah. I did actuall–", and the end of my sentence caught in my throat as he pinned me down on the bed. I laughed uncontrollably as he held me down, cocking his eyebrow at me.

"We'll see about that later young lady…" he said huskily as he bent down to give me a quick kiss on the lips before heading outside.

I giggled and wished he could have stayed with me… I stretched out on the bed smiling to myself. Matt had handled that really well I thought. He really had a way with kids. I think I would have lost the plot completely in his place. At times like these I knew exactly why I was holding on so tight to Matt…

That night, while we were on our way to meet our friends for dinner, Matt recounted the whole story for me, describing in detail Damian's expressions. We were in hysterics. I'm sure the whole beach had now heard about Uncle Matt being naked under the sheet!

We were heading to Grand Bay, an extremely touristy beach town in the North, full of shops, restaurants, bars and nightclubs. If you wanted nightlife in Mauritius, then this was the place to be.

We fell into a comfortable silence and Matt began singing along to the radio.

"Has anyone told you that you're a really terrible singer Matt?" I said, teasing him. He just grinned back and sang even louder, making me laugh.

I looked over at Matt tenderly and thought how well things had been going. I looked at him again and my heart did a little flip as I took in his face, the crinkles on the corner of his eyes, his strong muscly arms and even the hairs sticking out from the top of his shirt... Did he feel it too? I wondered.

I jumped in surprise as I heard myself blurt out, "Where do you see yourself in five years Matt?"

He did a double take before breaking into a smile.

"I really have no idea actually."

"Go on," I urged. "Humour me. Just think about it hypothetically."

He thought for a while, then answered, "Well, I'd like to think that I'll be married with at least 2 kids by then!"

I was just taking it in when he looked at me, smiled and winked!

Oh my *god*! Could that actually mean that he could see himself married to *me* in 5 years' time?!

Chapter Eight

I had just finished preparing some toast, when I heard the doorbell ring. I took my piece of peanut butter toast and went to open the door. And there was Vic.

Vic, short for Victoria, was one of my best friends; we'd known each other since we were knee high to grasshoppers. She was the complete opposite of me, both physically and character wise, but we'd always got along wonderfully well. Her wild eccentric ways balanced out my pretty straight-laced personality and visa-versa.

"Oh yum… peanut butter, my favourite," she said as she grabbed the toast out of my hand and took a bite. I grabbed it back and told her to come into the kitchen to make some more. When we were at school, we'd go back to her house after school and we'd eat at least six pieces of toast each, loaded with peanut butter.

"So how are your three monsters?" I asked, munching on my toast.

"Oh my angels…" she answered, her eyes glazing over thinking of them as she flicked her long blond curls over her shoulders.

They were so far from being angels that I burst out laughing.

"What?" she said, taking her toasts out of the toaster.

"ANGELS? Yeah sure!" I grinned, rolling my eyes at her.

"You don't like my kids very much do you?" she said, pouting.

"Sure I do… when they're sleeping!!" I replied and giggled at my own joke.

"Ha! Ha!" she said narrowing her eyes at me but I could see her lips twitching until they finally broke into a smile. Vic was wearing a pair of tight jeans which hugged her curves sexily, with a long white slightly see-through tunic and a long necklace from which hung a turquoise blue pendant in the shape of a star, and brown boots. She always dressed to kill but wasn't in the least vain and I doubt she even realised that she looked stunning most of the time. Although she didn't have the body of a model, she had the curves of a real woman.

She had three children; Tim, three, Jessie, four and

a half and Christopher, six years old. On the best of days, the trio are impossible to control, and on less good days they are enough to drive the sanest person crazy! But Vic never seems fazed by their endless fights, screams and the mess they leave in their wake.

"So how's Sam?" I asked, he being the husband.

"Oh, he's Ok, but I don't see much of him these days with his new job," she said glumly. Sam had just taken a new job as Manager of a big finance company. "He loves the challenge but has loads to learn still. He's off to Singapore and Pakistan for conferences later on in the year."

We chatted on for a few hours, or rather, she talked and I said a few 'yes, no's and 'mms' now and again. She was one of life's talkers. She was very funny with an endless stream of gossip and stories, all exaggerated by at least 200%, that's if they weren't completely made up in the first place! But one thing was certain, you could never be bored in her company and if I feel down and in the dumps, no one can make me laugh like she does.

Suddenly she asked me how Matt was and if we were any closer to getting engaged. She wanted me to hurry up and have kids so that our kids could play together. However, it wasn't looking like it would quite work out that way...

"Well…" I said, not really wanting to get into that conversation with her.

"That's a definite 'no' in my books." She sounded exasperated.

"Just give it time," I said weakly. "I mean, just the other day he mentioned that he imagined himself married with kids in the next five years."

"Five years! You'll be all dried out by then girl! I don't get you – I mean, look at you. You could have any guy you want and you're staying with someone who hasn't got the guts to commit. Get rid of him!" she exclaimed defiantly.

"Oh don't you start!" I said, annoyed at her interference. I was sick of people asking me the same questions, especially as I didn't have the answer.

"Well someone has to knock a bit of sense into you!" she said dramatically, flicking her long curls back over her shoulder.

"And that person would be you?!" I scoffed. She was the least sensible person I knew, impulsive and eccentric yes, but sensible, definitively not.

"Of course!" she said joyfully, not realising or choosing to ignore the fact that I had been sarcastic.

"I know just the thing you have to do…" she said grinning widely, "FALL PREGNANT! That way he'll have no choice but to marry you!"

I stared at her in horror. "I could never do that! How could I live with myself knowing I had trapped him into marrying me?"

"Don't look at it that way, he loves you and it wouldn't be trapping him, just giving him a little push of encouragement!" she said, obviously very pleased with herself.

"No way!" I retorted. "I would wonder every day of my life whether he had married me out of duty because I was pregnant, or if it was out of love. I couldn't live with that."

"Ok, Ok… *fine*!" she said, raising her hands in surrender. "But you know, if it doesn't work out, Sam and I can find you someone special."

"Oh please!" I said shivering at the thought of her setting me up with someone, although I couldn't help being curious as to who they had in mind.

"Like who?"

"Ah-*ha*, so you are thinking about leaving him then!" she exclaimed gleefully, rubbing her hands together in anticipation.

"I never said that" I said, chuckling.

"You didn't have to. I can just *feel* these things." She put her hand on her heart, theatrically. Might as well humor her I decided, she wouldn't listen to me anyway.

"Of course you can," I said trying to hide my smile.

"I knew you'd agree!" she exclaimed excitedly.

"I didn't say I agreed with anything," I sighed. Once she got her teeth into something, there was no letting go. "Besides I'm still with Matt and very much in love with him."

She pulled a face at that, and then suddenly grinned as a thought obviously occurred to her. "Yes, but the important thing is that you didn't *disagree,* so it's a definite *maybe.*"

"So who is it anyway?" I asked, not bothering to argue with her. "Beside you can't possibly know any single men that I don't know."

"Well I do - but I can't tell you who it is because you don't know him anyway," she said smiling wickedly.

"What do you mean you can't tell me?!" I exclaimed.

"No, it would be a bad omen," she said melodramatically. "I can't risk it – but when you meet him, you'll just *know*..."

I looked at her and shook my head in amusement, as she carried on.

"We'll make sure you two meet and that's all you need to know. The rest will take care of itself," she said mysteriously making me laugh despite myself.

The following evening I went to Two and Sixpence, a cozy little pub on the Waterfront, to meet Olivia for a drink. The Port Louis Waterfront had been built a while back and was a much needed breath of fresh air for the capital city, which was overcrowded with old buildings consisting primarily of shops and offices. Port Louis itself has no nightlife, apart from a few Chinese restaurants, but The Waterfront was built around the Harbour and has two business hotels, shops, restaurants, pubs and a casino, which makes it quite picturesque. It is always crowded on weekends – Mauritian families arriving by car loads to enjoy a meal, stroll along the quay or watch the boats in the harbour, basically just enjoying being out for the evening or for the day. Now that it exists I wonder how we all managed without it.

As for us, we often came to the Hotel's 'Thank God it's Friday' cheap drinks sessions on Friday evenings. A lot of the young businessmen and women of Port Louis and the surrounding regions meet here to relax after work. Spending an evening sitting on the terrace of a café, you could imagine being in Cape Town or even Australia.

Olivia had been attending a conference for one of her clients at the Waterfront Hotel all day and had left a message for me to meet her at six o'clock if I could, as she had some gossip for me. Needless to say, I wasn't going to miss that for anything.

I walked into the pub at ten past six and pushed my way through the jam-packed room, heading towards the bar and outside terrace. I knew she would be there and as soon as I reached the door, I noticed her sitting at a table outside with Phoebe, Yann, Andrew and a few other guys from another Ad Agency. I walked up and greeted everyone, before heading to the bar to get a drink.

Olivia accompanied me and we tried to talk above the noise and music inside. We finally got our drinks, me spilling half of mine down a guy's suit trousers after he bumped into me. Just typical, I thought glumly. I was so accident prone.

"Thank goodness for the terrace outside," I said to Olivia as we grabbed the last free table and sat down.

"So, are you going to tell me, or do I have to beg?" I asked genially as I admired the colours of the sunset reflecting over the water.

Olivia grinned, looking really pleased with herself.

"I got a reply from a really cool sounding guy!" she exclaimed, beaming. "His name's Pierre and his profile seems totally 'normal'. To sum it up he's 28 years old, has blond hair and brown eyes and is 1,82m tall. Apparently he doesn't smoke, has no children and has never married. He likes the movies, Italian food, skiing, basking in the sun, romantic evenings by the fireplace… It also says that he's open minded, intellectual and friendly."

"Wow! He does sound super normal!" I exclaimed, surprised.

"Doesn't he just! Oh yes, he's a Chartered Accountant – pretty impressive if I do say so myself," she smirked. "Anyway, that's all I can remember off the top of my head, but basically he screams normality and is looking for someone 'lively, positive and generous' which is exactly '*moi*' isn't it?" she exclaimed happily, making me laugh.

"So have you written back?" I asked, fascinated by the whole Match.com concept, all of which seemed so surreal to me.

"Yep, sent him an email saying thanks for his reply and told him something about my brother writing my profile but not to worry because it was all true, and I asked him if he was French. I mean Pierre sounds French doesn't it?"

"Definitely! So has he written back?"

"Well I only sent it just before leaving work this afternoon so we'll see tomorrow."

But where could it go really? I mean, it's all very well to meet someone on the internet but in an international situation like this neither one of them is likely to leave their job and their country for the other, or go over just to see if things can work out? I told Olivia my thoughts on the matter and she agreed with me, saying that anyway she was only playing along for the fun of it.

"And now to get back to real life…" she said, her eyes twinkling. "I met the sexiest man at the exhibition today…"

"*Oooh*, tell me all!" I said, taking a sip of my wine, loving the excitement of Olivia's single life. I had been with Matt for so long that I had forgotten what it was like to flirt and meet new men.

"He's quite old," she said. "But just oozes sexiness and has such an enigmatic smile. We actually flirted quite a bit, but all very innocent of course."

I was looking around the bar as she talked, when suddenly my eyes fell on someone who looked strangely like Sam. "Hey, Olivia?" I interrupted her. "Isn't that Sam over there leaning against the bar, talking rather intimately to a stunning brunette?"

Olivia followed my gaze and looked back towards me, eyes wide.

"Sure looks like it," she answered frowning.

"What the hell…" I mumbled. "I wonder who she is? She's definitely not from around here."

"Are he and Vic having problems?" Olivia asked, still staring at Sam.

"Not that I know of. All I know is that he's been working a lot since he got his new job. I wonder if this is what he means when he tells Vic he's 'working late'?!"…

Chapter Nine

"To what do I owe the honour of this early morning wakeup call? You do realize it's 6.45am don't you?" Matt said sounding amused. He knew that I never got up for at least another half hour. I quickly told him what had happened last night and asked him if he knew who the brunette was. He seemed surprised and didn't have a clue, although he said he was pretty sure that Sam had told him about overseas representatives being here for a week.

"Yeah, well, they sure didn't look like they were talking business!" I snapped.

"Luce, don't make a big deal out of this. I'm sure it's nothing. Sam wouldn't do anything stupid. But if it makes you feel better, I'll talk to him and see what's up."

I rang Matt up about ten times during the day asking him if he had talked to Sam or not. He kept telling me that Sam was busy in meetings and that he hadn't yet gotten through to him. After my tenth call, he warned me that if I called him again about it, he wouldn't tell me what Sam said if and when he finally did get to talk to him.

"You're so mean!" I grumbled and he chuckled, hanging up.

I was just about to head home when Matt called.

"Finally!" I said grouchily. "You sure took your time."

"Well, some of us actually have work to do and can't spend the day on the phone," he said teasingly.

"Whatever!" I muttered. "So? What did he say?"

"Well, he was busy and couldn't really talk, but I'm meeting him after work for a drink. Why don't you come and grab a pizza with me afterwards and maybe we can go catch a movie too? See if Olivia wants to join us if she's not doing anything."

Frustrated, I said I'd meet him there at 7.30 p.m.

We had just arrived at Pizza Hut on the Waterfront and I was waiting for Matt to return from the gents. As I looked out over the water, I thought of Vic and Sam once again and wondered if something really was up. The image of the brunette flashed in my mind. Sam had looked like he could swallow her whole! Then again, looking as she did I guess it was only natural for men to react that way, whether they were married or not; it's not as if they were really in control after all! Everyone knows that a man's penis acts like a remote control and temporarily removes all their brain functions when they are faced with the opposite sex, especially if they happen to be sexy and gorgeous - not that that's really a prerequisite when they've had one too many drinks!

I cringed, imagining Matt with the brunette but somehow I knew he'd never talk so intimately with another woman while still going out with me. He was really big on fidelity and respect and I loved him all the more for it.

"Penny for your thoughts," he said as he sat down opposite me.

"Are you going to tell me what Sam told you?" I asked, not being able to wait a second longer.

"On second thought, I think I'll take my penny back and leave you to it Ok?" he said, grabbing the menu and ordering a large Hawaiian pizza.

I pretended not to have heard and pushed on, "Matt?"

I realised that he didn't want to discuss the subject and it made me worry all the more as he usually had no problems telling me everything. I looked at him, waiting for him to answer.

"Well, he told me that he also agrees that the penalty against Giroud was completely unfounded and that the umpire was utterly against Arsenal and pro-Manchester as usual" he said, grinning mischievously at me.

"OW!" he yelled, as I kicked him under the table.

"*MATT*!" I wailed. "You said you'd tell me!"

We looked defiantly at each other for a few seconds before he finally gave in.

"Ok, fine Lucy! When I asked him how things were at home he answered that it was a bit tense and that Vic was always on his back these days. He said that she hated his long working hours. He also told me that he had had representatives over for a week but that it hadn't been all bad as he'd had to take one of the French reps out for drinks and dinner and that she was really hot!"

"What a bastard! Did you remind him that he has a wife and three kids?" I snapped back.

"Hey! Don't kill the messenger!" he protested, raising his hands in surrender.

"Very funny! So what did you tell him?" I asked, annoyed.

"Well, I asked him if he could introduce me to the French Rep…" Matt said seriously, before bursting out laughing.

"*Maaatt*! This isn't funny!"

"Ok, Ok! Well, I told him to be careful because people could get the wrong idea and Vic could end up getting hurt. He said he agreed and that he hadn't thought it was a big deal, but that he would be careful in the future."

"And that's it?" I cried in annoyance.

"Lucy, what do you want me to say? That he told me he'd had sex with the brunette in the pub toilet? Enough now! I really don't want to discuss it anymore. Oh good, there's Olivia, at least she'll be better company than you right now," he said, clearly frustrated.

"Hi there you two," Olivia said, sitting down next to me. "My, my, aren't we looking all happy and cheerful," she grinned, looking from me to Matt and back. "What's up?"

"Matt's being a pig!" I said, sulking.

"Lucy's being a bore!" Matt retorted.

"Gee, aren't I in for a great evening!" she said good-naturedly. Matt and I looked at each other and couldn't help laughing.

"Do you know who showed up at the office again, twice this week?" I asked Olivia as we walked back to our cars after the movie. "That strange guy I recently began to buy stationery from for the office."

"Who's that?" Matt said, suddenly interested in what we were saying. "How come I haven't heard about him?"

"Well he is just a short, average-looking stationary supplier. He has this awful high pitched voice though; poor thing sounds like someone is perpetually squeezing his genitals really tightly!" I said as Matt chuckled. "The first few times he showed up he was a bit flirtatious and annoying but I didn't make anything of it. But this time, he seemed to be ogling me all the time. I'm pretty sure I caught him looking down my shirt when I bent down to pick up a piece of paper on the floor! So far I've just ignored it and been falsely friendly, but it seems he might have gotten the wrong idea somehow…"

"Just stop buying stuff from him then," Matt said, unimpressed.

"I know I could. But then again, his prices are really good and I am meant to be doing what's best for the company. Besides, he hasn't done anything wrong really; it's just that he's being just a tad too friendly for my liking. I'll just see how it goes…"

"Hey! Isn't that Sam's car over there?" Olivia suddenly said, interrupting me.

Matt and I followed her gaze and saw his red Renault.

"What the hell is he still doing here – he left you at 7.30p.m. didn't he?" I asked Matt upset all over again.

"Yes, but I didn't ask him if he was doing anything afterwards. He told me that he wouldn't be able to stay long but I didn't think to ask him why."

"Probably entertaining long-legged brunettes again!" I snapped.

"Lucy, you're like a dog with a bone! Stop dramatizing and give the guy a break!" Matt said in exasperation.

"Guilty until proven innocent!" I retorted and heard Olivia giggle.

Chapter Ten

I patted my way around my bedside table, reaching for my alarm clock. It was a Saturday morning and we'd been out to dinner at a Chinese restaurant in Quatres Bornes the previous night with a few mates from Matt's work. I felt terrible, obviously due to all the cheap red wine we had indulged in. I heard something fall to the floor but couldn't really be bothered finding out what it was. There weren't a lot of options any way; either the lamp, a photo frame, the alarm clock or my glass of water. I heard Matt groan beside me as he rolled over and I grumbled an inaudible "orry" as my hand finally found the clock. I brought it round to my co-operating eye and saw that it was nine thirty. Wonderful! Not nearly time to get up yet, I thought happily, as I buried my head in my pillow and dozed off again.

We finally made it out of bed at about twelve o'clock, both swallowing a few neurofens for our headaches before heading to the kitchen for some coffee and toast.

We sat eating and reading the papers, well me just the movie and gossip section. We couldn't quite handle sentences at this stage, only the odd word here and there. We mumbled things like 'utter 'cffee' 'bread' 'anks' and 'no-anks'. Luckily being in the same hung-over state, we were able to understand each other! It was like a special telepathic jargon for hung-over people, only understood by those in an alcoholic trance. Actually, they should create a 'Dictionary of Drunken Jargon' as I'm sure it would help many people in their conversations on Saturday and Sunday mornings!

After showering and getting dressed an hour later, Matt hit me with a bombshell.

"Luce, please come shopping with me."

Shopping with Matt. The ultimate nightmare. The nightmare to end all nightmares. If you ever want to punish yourself for any really big sins you may have committed, going shopping with Matt will give you complete absolution!

"Shopping? Like, *today*? *Now*?" I asked, completely shell-shocked.

"Go on… *please*. I desperately need new clothes and we've got that drinks party next weekend. I'm really sick of wearing the same thing every time we go out."

I sighed, despondently. I really wasn't up to shopping at all, let alone shopping with Matt. I'm not a very clothes-shopping type of person. Must have a gene malformation somewhere in that womanly department! I only go when I really, really have to. Besides, anything I like always ends up being too big, too small or the wrong colour. My small chest, medium size hips and long legs make it rather hard to find clothes that are just right for me. I always come home completely depressed and with absolutely nothing, apart from chocolate, in my shopping bag. So I've officially stopped altogether.

But shopping with Matt was really the worst.

"So?" he asked me again, eyes hopeful and pleading.

"Ok, fine. Let's go," I said resigned.

We drove to the Bagatelle Mall which was halfway between Moka and Port Louis and had only recently been built. It was modern, with lots of restaurants, cafés, pubs, cinemas and heaps of designer stores. Basically a great place to hang out and shop for clothes.

Half an hour later, we entered Woolworths and my ordeal began…

"So what do you think of this blue shirt?" he asked me, holding it up in front of him.

"I like it; it looks really good with your eyes," I answered, admiring the effect the colour had on his eyes.

"But don't you think blue is a bit boring - I mean everything's blue isn't it?" he asked, looking at himself in the mirror. "Don't you think the yellow one would be more original?"

"Yeah, it would and it's actually really nice too," I answered looking at the light yellow shirt he held in front of him.

"So which one should I get?" he said, holding first the blue one then the yellow up in front of him.

"Just decide which one you prefer," I answered.

"But which one would you get?" he asked looking up at me.

"The blue one," I answered honestly. It really looked gorgeous on him.

"Why?" he asked looking quizzically at me.

"Because I like blue and you look gorgeous in it," I

said hoping that if I flattered his ego it would help him to make up his mind.

He stood in front of the mirror for a few more minutes trying first the yellow shirt, then the blue, followed by the yellow again, without saying anything. I watched and waited. It could take hours, days or even weeks before he made up his mind. Suddenly he walked to another row of shirts and took out a green one.

"What about this green one here?" he asked.

"No, I don't like it," I answered, my patience wearing thin.

"But why? It would go really well with my beige trousers wouldn't it?" He looked at me questioningly.

"Well get it then! Just choose the one you like, Matt," I answered as calmly as I could.

He sighed. "But it wouldn't go with everything like the yellow or blue one would."

"Well, get the blue one then!" I barked, now totally exasperated and got up to head to the till. I turned when I realised that he wasn't following me. I looked back to see him trying the yellow shirt on again.

"It's actually a little big on the shoulders isn't it?" he

said, looking over his shoulder at me.

"No, it looks fine," I said shortly not caring if he bought one with pink and red poker dots on it at this stage.

"Ok, I'll get the blue one then," he suddenly decided.

I heaved a huge sigh of relief as the shop assistant smiled her condolences at me.

"But..." he said, stopping halfway to the till as my heart plummeted. "Maybe I should just get a white shirt actually - at least it goes with everything."

This was often his reflection and he therefore had a cupboard full of white shirts.

"*Arghh*!" I cried in frustration. "You are the most frustrating man in the world!!"

"Oh, stop exaggerating!" he said nonchalantly. "Besides, you can't possibly have met every single man in the world."

I rolled my eyes at him. He sighed again as if the weight of the world was on his shoulders, then grabbed the blue shirt and the white one.

"I'll have them both," he said to the exhausted shop assistant.

We stopped off at McDonald's to get something to eat on the way back, both too exhausted to say a word to each other. To my great joy McDonald's had finally opened at Jumbo in Phoenix about four years ago and we often headed there for dinner on Sundays.

"What are you having Matt?" I asked glumly as we pulled in. I felt drained and just didn't have the energy to wait the half hour it usually took him to decide on his order. We couldn't even go through the drive through anymore because he just took so long to decide what he wanted that the cars behind us always ended up honking with impatience.

To my surprise he grinned sheepishly at me and said, "I think after our delightful little shopping expedition, it's best if I just say; I'll have whatever you're having Luce!". This, needless to say, made me burst out laughing helping to thaw the tension between us.

When we got back to my apartment, I headed straight to my bedroom and fell exhausted onto my bed.

"Would you like a cup of tea or coffee Luce?" Matt called out from the kitchen.

"No thanks," I replied wearily.

I heard him get out a cup from the cupboard and

move around in the kitchen.

"Hey Luce?" he called out again, just as I was closing my eyes. "What do you think I feel like - tea or coffee?"

I giggled, pulling the pillow over my head. He really was impossible!

Chapter Eleven

While I was waiting for the kettle to boil in the office kitchen, Yann walked in to grab a cuppa too. We were exchanging our usual daily morning banter, when suddenly he exclaimed, "Oh! I forgot to tell you - Sarah had her baby!"

"Oh Wow!" I exclaimed. I had completely forgotten that her due date was last Friday. "What is it?"

Yann gave me a puzzled look, then shrugged and answered, "You know - a little pink thing with no hair, no teeth, cries a lot, pees a lot and drinks milk from a tit."

As he poured the boiling water into his cup, I stared at him wondering if he was serious, which could certainly be the case. Seeming oblivious to my surprise, he added sugar into his coffee and looked up to see whether I wanted some. He stopped in mid action as he noticed my expression.

"What?" he exclaimed, cocking his eyebrow at me.

As I stared at him trying to figure out if he was having me on, his lips twitched into a grin and he burst out laughing. I playfully punched him on the arm and laughed too. I just never knew with Yann, he was a bit like Phoebe - anything was possible.

"Tell me, please!" I begged as he grinned.

"It's a boy," he finally said, as he picked up his cup and turned to leave.

"Wait! What's his name?" I asked, thinking of a hundred and one more things I wanted to know.

"Whoa! Stop right there!" He put his hand out like a policeman stopping traffic. "No more questions. I'm a guy remember? I don't care about baby details."

I rolled my eyes at him as he walked out of the kitchen, crossing Olivia on her way in.

Olivia screeched joyfully at the news and we raced into the artwork department to find someone who could tell us what we wanted to know. When? Where? How long? Did it hurt? How much? Léa, the receptionist, told us that the little boy's name was Leo.

"That's such a cute name," I said, and we *oohed* and *aahed* as we thought of Sarah and her little baby.

After work we set off in my car and headed for the hospital, all really impatient to meet Leo. I pulled into the hospital car park and felt my stomach tighten - I hated hospitals. Not that I went there very often, but I just hated the smell of disinfectant and that 'sick' feeling, the long corridors, the silence - and knowing that everyone behind the closed doors is sick - the only happy place being the maternity ward of course.

"*Oooh*, I love hospitals," cried Phoebe enthusiastically.

Typical! I thought amused.

"I just love seeing so many men in white all in the same place," she added, dreamily.

We made our way up to the Maternity ward and stopped in front of the nursery which stood right in the centre of the ward. We gazed gooingly at the babies, seven in all, lying in their little cots, trying to guess which was Leo.

"Oh look! look! look!" cried Phoebe excitedly. "There he is!" she pointed towards a little baby boy, all round with huge little legs layered with rolls of fat.

"Just look at those thighs!" cried Phoebe, still pointing. "It just has to be him!"

"Don't let Sarah hear you," Olivia said as we laughed.

We carried on looking at the babies one by one and Olivia suddenly stopped and called out to us.

"Come look! It's him! It's definitively him!" she said pointing to a little baby sleeping peacefully. "He has Sarah's nose, there's just no doubt it's him!"

Phoebe and I stood and stared at the little baby's nose, turning our heads in all directions to see it from all angles and wondered how on earth Olivia could see a resemblance to Sarah's nose when he was so tiny.

Phoebe suddenly grinned.

"Umm, I doubt that's Leo," she said as she pointed towards the little pink sticker on the cot indicating that it was a girl.

"Oops!" Olivia giggled. "We headed to Sarah's room, knocking quietly before going in, and were met by the mother sitting on her bed, all smiles, with little Leo quietly lying in her arms. We looked at each other and burst out laughing. We kissed Sarah telling her about the 'Spot Leo' session.

She laughed and gazed adoringly down at him. He was so tiny and so precious, with his little face, his little hands, his little feet... I envied Sarah.

"Could I?" I asked, dying to hold him. Sarah nodded

and smiled as she delicately passed Leo over to me. After a few awkward manoeuvers on my part, trying to figure out how to hold such a tiny thing without dropping it or breaking it, I finally managed to find a reasonably safe position. It was heavenly holding him and seeing those tiny little hands and feet, and smelling that gorgeous baby smell. I was mesmerized by the little creature in my arms. How could such a tiny thing make me feel so small and vulnerable?

We spent half an hour getting Sarah to tell us all the gory details of the birth. She didn't remember much of it except that it had hurt like hell and that she'd thought she'd burst having had to push so hard and for so long. She had discovered a whole new vocabulary of swear words she didn't even realise she knew! Her husband was pretty impressed and the doctors were just laughing saying that it was often that way.

We all took turns holding Leo, fighting over the time we could keep him. He was back in my arms again and I was gazing down at him, as he lay there half asleep. Suddenly I noticed his face scrunch up like a sponge, and he let out an ear-piercing wail. How could such a tiny body make so much noise? I stared at him in disbelief.

Sarah laughed at my expression. "Pretty impressive huh?"

I grinned and handed Leo back to her as she popped open the front of her nightgown and then her bra and Leo began sucking away happily. We left them to it as we heard the bell signaling the end of visiting hours.

As we walked out of the hospital I couldn't help sighing. Just imagine how wonderful it would be to have a little baby of my own…

Chapter Twelve

With all the hype over Sarah and baby Leo, I realised that I had forgotten to ask Olivia about the internet guy Pierre, so I headed straight to her office the next morning to find out if he'd written again.

He had; and he was definitely French and lived in Paris.

"*Oooh*, how romantic."

She laughed. "We've just exchanged basic banter so far about work, lifestyle, interests and so on, but we've written three to four mails to each other since I answered his first one," she said.

Just then I heard John calling me and raced back to my desk.

To my great frustration Olivia was working on a huge campaign and was hardly ever at the office over the next ten days and if she was in, she was stressed out to the max and had no time to gossip. So I didn't get more out of her than a quick smile when I asked about Pierre and a vague, "He's fine. We're still writing to each other regularly."

As for Vic and Sam, it seemed that there wasn't anything much going on. I had spoken to Vic who assured me things were the same as usual, Sam still working a lot, busy with Reps and not very often around. She didn't seem too phased by it, but I still felt uneasy. She often preferred to pretend that everything was rosy instead of admitting something was wrong. It was just how she was. Matt also hadn't seen Sam lately as Sam was always working. I just hoped that working was really what he was doing…

By the time the campaign had been launched ten days later, my curiosity was insatiable.

"Welcome back you," I grinned, as I plonked myself down opposite her. "So go on, don't keep me waiting, I don't have all day you know!"

Olivia laughed and told me that they were now writing to each other three or four times a day. She said that they had amazing conversations, sometimes about life in general or sometimes just about their day at work, a film they might have just seen, or him telling her his weekend. She explained that it could be as superficial as it was deep. I looked at her, slightly stunned. I hadn't realised the relationship had developed that much over the last few weeks, and told her so. She admitted that she was a bit surprised herself but that they just had so much in common and so much to say to each other that they'd started on one email, then two, then three and so on.

"But did you ask him why he was on Match.com? I mean, you have a good reason, but what about him? If he's as normal as he makes himself out to be why does he need Match.com to find a woman?" I asked, still rather skeptical about the situation.

Olivia turned to her computer and told me to come and read an email he had written;

Dear Olivia,

I can understand that you wonder why with my profile I have subscribed to Match.com. I don't have any problems meeting women here in Paris, and I didn't plan on signing up, but came upon it by error while searching for something on the net. As they say you have seven days free access, I thought why not - it might be fun. It's so hard to find THE woman that why not give myself all the possible chances… and now I am glad I did.

Je t'embrasse,
Pierre

"I love the stilted English," I said grinning. "But he does write pretty well for a Frenchman."

"Yeah, he studied in England for a year. Keep reading," Olivia said, as she opened another mail.

Olivia,

I also do not believe that chances of meeting THE ONE *on Match.com is extremely or at all likely, but still I find it rather poetic to see all those people who try their luck despite this... I don't believe that it's any different than buying lottery tickets in a way. But even just finding a new friend on the net shows good things sometimes do come of it... I tried scanning a photo of me to send to you but the scanner is not working, I will try to organize that for you soon.*

Bisou,
Pierre

"*Oooh, Bisou,*" I said teasing Olivia who playfully punched me. "Has he sent you a photo yet?"

"No, he's still getting organised but should be sending it sometime next week. To tell you the truth, I don't really want to see what he looks like."

"But why?" I asked incredulously.

"Well... I've got an image of him in my head, you know like when you read a book, you develop the character in your head? Well, it's the same. I've created him as I think he is and I'm scared of being disappointed when I see what he really looks like. Does that sound really shallow?"

"No, not at all. Do you think you'll like him less if he doesn't meet up to your image of him though?"

"I might be a bit disappointed but it's been such a non-physical thing so far that I hope it won't influence the way I feel. That's what's pretty amazing about it, not knowing someone physically or seeing them, but getting to know the real them. I feel like I've got a new friend and it's so much easier opening your heart to someone you can't see. I guess I don't feel vulnerable like I do when I'm going out with someone, so that gives me more space to open up and really be me. It's amazing the things we've shared over the last few weeks," She explained as I gaped at her. This had taken on another dimension!

"Actually, I can't remember if I told you that he rang me the other day!" she said, eyes sparkling.

"*He rang - and you didn't tell me!*" I cried in exasperation.

"Well, it was at night and the next day I didn't see you. Anyway, he has a really deep voice and his English is so cute with his gorgeous French accent and his 'zis', 'zat' and 'zeres' as they can't say the 'th' sound.

"*Love is in the air…*" I sang as her phone rang.

I looked at my watch. I mouthed a 'got to go' and she nodded and waved as she carried on her conversation.

I headed out to the Port Louis Waterfront to meet up with Matt at the Two and Sixpence pub. He had come earlier to meet Sam for a drink after work to catch up a bit as they hadn't seen each other since the brunette incident.

As I walked into the hotel, I spotted them talking in a far end corner of the bar. They seemed very deep in conversation. I hesitated, feeling that I'd be interrupting something. They didn't even notice me coming and as I got closer I heard Sam saying, "I really don't know what to do. I feel so trapped."

I hid behind the crowd and did a U-turn back outside. I didn't want to hear anymore as I'd feel like I was betraying Vic. I phoned Matt on his cell phone and told him that I was making my way into the hotel and to look out for me. When I made my second entrance they were already looking more relaxed and by the time I reached them, they had changed the conversation and were now discussing their favourite subject; football!

"Always football isn't it?" I said innocently as I kissed

Matt and smiled at Sam, not showing any signs that I had heard a bit of their conversation. I couldn't wait for Sam to go so that I could find out what they had been talking about. I was worried about Vic. Maybe there really was something going on.

We chatted a few minutes before Sam said he had to leave. We waved him off and as soon as he was out of earshot I blurted out, "What's up with Sam? Why does he feel trapped?"

Matt stared at me, startled.

"Matt?" I said impatiently waiting for an answer.

"I won't even ask how you know what we were talking about," he said, shaking his head in bewilderment.

"When I arrived, you were both so engrossed in your conversation that you didn't notice me approaching. Then I overheard what Sam was saying so I turned around and left. I didn't want to hear any more. But now I want to know."

"I can't tell you Luce," he replied. "He trusts me and needed to talk. Don't make me betray his trust please."

"Matt, I'm your girlfriend, you *have* to tell me!" I exclaimed in exasperation.

"You're also his wife's best friend and he's my friend, not yours, and he trusts me with his problems and made me promise not to tell you."

"He can't do that!" I wailed.

"Of course he can!" he replied grinning.

"I can't believe you hide things from me!" I pressed on, actually hurt by that thought.

"Oh come on Luce! You don't tell me everything Vic and Olivia tell you about their private lives. You know how I love hearing details and gossip but I don't press you with it because I respect the fact that they are your friends and not mine. The things they share with you are for your ears not mine - I'm your boyfriend, not theirs," he finished calmly.

I grumbled, not knowing how to fight back as I knew he was right, but still exasperated that he wouldn't tell me what Sam had said. I mean, it was different for the things Vic and Olivia told me, I'm not sure how, but I just knew it was! Men shouldn't keep secrets from their girlfriends; it's just not the done thing. Girls have so much they share with their girlfriends that it's normal that some things remain between 'the girls'. But men... no, it just didn't make sense.

"But I'm your girlfriend!" I moaned again, not able to

control myself.

"Lucy! I can't tell you and that's that!" Matt said sternly. "All I can say is that, as Vic already told you, Sam's not feeling like himself lately."

"Why does he feel trapped?" I persisted, wanting to understand.

"I think he's just feeling a bit frustrated at having got married so young," Matt explained, choosing his words carefully.

"Well it takes two you know!" I snapped back, fiercely protective of Vic.

"Of course, and I'm not saying it's Vic's fault. All I'm saying is what he feels right now."

"What else?" I pressed on, taking a sip of my diet coke.

"That's all you need to know - honest, it's all I can tell you and it pretty much sums up the general picture. So let's leave it at that, Ok?"

"No, it's not Ok!" I shouted obviously a bit too loudly, seeing a few heads turn to look our way. "Vic's my best friend Matt, and if Sam's cheating on her, I have to tell her!"

"Lucy! Of course he's not - well not that he's told me anyway. Where do you get that idea from?"

"Vic said he's never up for sex these days and thinks he might have someone else. It makes sense doesn't it? I mean, what guy doesn't think about, and want, sex 24 hours a day, 7 days a week?"

Matt burst out laughing as he drained the last of his beer then stood up.

"Let's go Miss Doctorate in Sex and Men!" he said grinning and taking my hand. "Besides I'm dying to have..." he paused, then grinned at me suggestively.

"Matt!" I exclaimed, nudging him hard in the chest as he laughed.

"What? I only wanted to say 'dinner'! Now who's the one who's obsessed about sex around here huh?" he grinned, nudging me back.

"Oh shut up!" I grinned back.

We walked along the Harbour Front in a companionable silence, just admiring the reflection of the lights on the water and the huge cruise ship that was docked in the port.

"It must be quite hard keeping sex alive after ten or twenty years of marriage though," I suddenly said.

"I think that's why it's important that wives make the effort to keep fit, buy sexy lingerie, prepare little candlelit dinners…" he said grinning wickedly and clearly repressing his laughter.

"That is such a pathetically macho thing to say!" I cried out in indignation, failing to see the mischievous gleam in his eyes. "Why do men assume that we don't need to be turned on? I mean, do you think that after ten years of marriage, when your willies will have become all old and wrinkly, that just looking at you will still turn us on?"

He chuckled, his eyes twinkling. "You sure have a way of putting things into perspective - but just know that this big man here will never become too old and wrinkly to turn you on baby!"

I burst out laughing as he took my hand and pulled me into Pasta Delice, an Italian restaurant we both loved.

"Come on, let's eat woman!" he said as I hit him on the arm.

As we sat down and ordered lasagne and salad, I decided to let it rest and we chatted about the days.

When Matt got up to go to the toilet, I sat back, thinking about Sam.

Damn him for making Vic miserable! And, to top it off, the last thing Matt needed was to hear a married man telling him that he felt trapped in his marriage... He was ruining all my chances to finally get that ring on my finger.

Chapter Thirteen

The next day my grandmother popped in for her usual three minute bum-on-the-edge-of-the-seat visit.

"Hi love," she said, grasping her handbag tightly under her armpit as if she was worried someone would suddenly grab it from her.

We exchanged our usual "Come in" - "No, no, I'm not staying love" - "You can still sit down for a minute" - "Oh, Ok then, but just for a minute" banter, as I led her to the sofa where she deposited her bum on its very edge, all the while telling me she was just about to go.

We talked for a few minutes before she suddenly mentioned that she had played Scrabble with Matt's grandmother who'd asked her whether she knew what was going on between us and if we'd ever get married. I smiled, knowing that my grandmother was probably even more curious to know the answer to that question, but would never dare to ask me straight out, and she had finally found a way to do so.

"Of course I told her that I didn't have a clue and that it really wasn't my business," she added quickly before I could say anything.

"It's all right Gran, but I don't really have much to say except that things are really going great between us but there is still no talk of anything more permanent," I said honestly.

"Well, she's completely exasperated by the situation and says she's going to give him a good talking to the next time he drops by to see her."

"Oh Gran, that's the last thing she should do. He hates feeling pressurised, if anything it'll have the reverse effect on him," I said despairingly.

"That young man, and he's not even particularly young, really needs, uh..., how do you young people so elegantly put it? Oh yes, a good 'kick in the butt'!"

I laughed, but I couldn't have agreed with her more.

"I know, but there's nothing I can do about it," I said, bleakly.

It was up to Matt... and if he didn't get his act together then it would be up to me to decide how long I wanted to keep living in a no-end relationship...

I already knew that I wanted to marry Matt but if he didn't want to get married – well to me anyway – was this relationship really worth hanging on to? Would it ever bring me happiness? And a husband... and kids and the white picket fence....

Chapter Fourteen

Hi Sis!

Me again and another postcard from yet another train station! This time I'm on my way to civilization - Vienna (but just for 2 days unfortunately). So this is my town Zilina. Not super modern as you can see ☺ but the people are really nice. I was actually planning to escape last night but it looks like I'll be sticking around... for the time being anyway!

Lotsaluv
Natalie

P.S. I definitively think I was mad in ever accepting this traineeship!!! (Something everyone knew all along!)

P.P.S. So have you dumped him yet?

I couldn't help laughing, although I knew I should feel somewhat annoyed at her pessimism with regards to Matt's intentions, but I didn't. I knew she only wanted the best for me anyway. I put the postcard on my fridge next to the other one, got myself a drink and headed to the phone to call Vic. The phone rang endlessly before it was finally picked up by an out of breath Vic.

"Hi! Sorry I took so long to answer but that little monster of mine stuck Superglue on the kitchen stools and Jessie's skirt got stuck on it so it caused a major drama which I was trying to sort out when the phone rang," she ended breathlessly before I even had time to say hi.

How she knew it was me, was beyond me - then again, she probably would have answered like that whoever it was!

"What a brat!" I said unimpressed.

"He's quite a little devil I must say, but so funny," she said lovingly.

I decided not to comment on the fact that he was a nightmare.

"I don't know how you keep your cool; I'd be going up the wall by now if I had three kids to handle." Especially such undisciplined ones, I almost added but decided against.

"Of course you wouldn't, not when they're your own. Besides the maternal instinct kicks in as soon as you see your little baby for the first time and from then on it's pure joy. You'll have no trouble and besides, Matt will be a great help as he's amazing with kids. My kids love him, he has such a way with them. Hey! Maybe you should try to put him in a situation which makes him yearn even more for kids and next thing you know he may pop the question!"

"I doubt it could work Vic," I said.

"Why not? I mean if you don't want to fall pregnant before he proposes, try to make him want to get you pregnant!"

"You think everything is so simple!" I sighed.

"Well of course it is!" she said laughing.

"Of course it isn't! Besides, how am I supposed to find babies to put around him? As far as I know 'rent-a-baby' doesn't exist!"

"It doesn't have to be a baby - hey! I could lend you my kids for a day if you like? That would actually be a brilliant idea!" she said enthusiastically as my eyes popped out in horror. "He'd love it and they're a wonderful example of how great kids can be."

Surely she couldn't mean that! But judging by the look on her face, she clearly did! I grinned as I realised that one day I would probably be saying the same thing about my monsters (if I had any that is)!

"Um…thanks for the offer – it's tempting… but no thanks" I said, trying to keep a straight face. "Besides, I don't think I'd survive a whole day babysitting your kids Vic."

"I really should hang up on you, you know. I can't believe you have absolutely no shame in trashing my kids like that to my face!"

"I'm not trashing your kids but it's just that I don't have the energy level to cope with them, that's all," I said, feeling guilty for not making an effort to hide my horror at the thought of being faced with her kids for a day.

She chuckled like a proud mother hen. "They are quite a handful at times, but it's worth it. But then again, it's true that it might be best that you start with babies, and one at a time!"

"That sounds more like it," I said, warming to the idea. "And I actually have a great idea! My friend from work just had a baby boy, he's the cutest thing, and I'm sure she'd love me to babysit him!"

We chatted on as she gave me tips and told me anecdotes about her kids when they were babies, and then finally she began talking about Sam. I was relieved, as I hadn't wanted to be the one to initiate the conversation in case she became suspicious.

"Sam's so strange these days… I hardly see him and when he's around he's so distracted that I have trouble communicating with him. And you know me and conversation, it's never an issue! He's forever working late; but then again how much work can someone do in one day? I mean, why this sudden all-work-no play attitude? He was never like that before. I guess he's under a lot of pressure to live up to their expectations. It's a huge challenge for him." She paused. "Oh, then again, maybe he's just sick of me…" she said, sounding unusually dispirited.

"Vic! How can you say that?" I exclaimed, feeling guilty as the sight of the brunette flashed before my eyes.

"Well, it's possible. I mean, we've already been married for 12 years. It's a long time…"

"Have you discussed your feelings with him?"

"No, not really," she sighed. "I just asked him if everything was Ok and he answered vaguely that he was a bit stressed out with his work load. I guess I've been nagging him a bit about his long hours though. But hey!" she added, as I could imagine her flicking her long blond mane over her shoulder, "I'm sick of going to bed alone every night; I'll end up having to buy a sex toy or something!"

"VIC!" I exclaimed both amused and slightly shocked.

"What? Doesn't everyone need sex now and again?"

"Yeah, I guess, but it sounds like you're hanging out for the stuff, more something a guy would be saying than a woman!"

"Well, I'm a hot blooded woman and right now I'm feeling pretty sex crazed!" she said and I burst out laughing before changing the subject. She clearly didn't know that Sam was taking gorgeous brunette representatives out till all hours and I wasn't going to be the one to tell her. Not for the moment anyway. I'd just have to wait and see what Sam would get up to next...

After hanging up, I lay on my bed thinking; maybe it was a pretty good idea having Leo over for a few hours with Matt and I. It might give him a taste of what it could be like for us and how wonderful it would be to have our own family. I decided I'd call Sarah and see whether she was game enough to let me look after him one day.

I hadn't had much practise with babies, well none really, but then again it was supposed to come naturally wasn't it?

Besides, Matt had had plenty of experience with his nephew and nieces, so as long as he was around I'd be fine and, more importantly, so would the baby! I have no idea whether I'm mother material; I think I could be... but then again, who knows?!

Chapter Fifteen

I reached up to take a file off the top of the cabinet, and looked across through my outstretched arms to see Mr Delano leering at me from the doorway.

"Well hello there, you sexy lady," he squeaked, his eyes running up and down my body.

"Good morning Mr Delano. Can I do something for you?" I said, trying to act business like, pretending that I hadn't heard the sexy lady bit.

"*Oooh*, that sounds naughty," he winked. I cringed. There was seriously something off here. This guy was becoming sleazier and sleazier every time he came over.

"I had no intention of making it sound naughty; I was just wondering what you were doing here as I haven't ordered anything from you and have already told you that I didn't need anything at the moment," I snapped as I turned my back on him and sat down, reaching for a file behind me.

Before I knew what he was up to, he had leaned in close across my desk and his hot breath fanned my face as he whispered, "Let me just get that for you, sweetcakes."

I watched dumbstruck as he stretched over me to take down the file, not even attempting to be discreet about staring down my cleavage.

"I'm not your sweetcake and I really think you should leave now, Mr Delano," I said clenching my fists, trying to stop myself from slapping his slimy face.

"You do now, do you? Well, I don't want to leave you yet baby," he replied, looking coyly at me. Maybe he thought he was sexy when he did that!

"DON'T call me baby!" I snapped, infuriated by his brazenness. "I am going to call my boss."

"Relax sugar. I'll leave now. But don't worry - I'll see you again real soon," he chuckled throatily as he winked at me again.

It seemed clear that his intentions weren't purely business related. But what exactly was he hoping for? I just didn't know what I should do about him.

When Matt came over later that evening, I was still feeling rather uneasy about my encounter with Mr Delano.

"I'm sure you're just getting too worked up over this guy," Matt said, reassuringly after I related the story.

"I can't help it, he gives me the creeps," I answered scowling.

"Don't worry Luce, you have ol' Mr Muscles here, ready to fight all who dare mess with his woman!" he said fletching his muscles and wiggling his eyebrows at me comically.

"You're not taking me seriously Matt!" I cried.

"I'm just trying to make you relax and stop panicking. I'm sure he'll soon get tired of playing that game and stop. Let's just wait and see what he does next."

"I don't like this, I really don't…" I said my voice quivering.

I hated the fact that nothing I said or did seemed to faze Mr. Delano. If I was friendly then he milked it for all it was worth. Then when I was cold and borderline mean, he seemed to think that that was even better! He never seemed to actually believe that I was angry with him. I didn't know how to react anymore, but I just didn't like it at all…

But right now I had more important things to worry about than Mr. Delano and his wandering eyes; Sarah would be dropping Leo off later for our babysitting session! I knew Matt was a natural and would be fine, but I wanted to try to impress him with my maternal ways... I just hoped that the maternal feelings they talk about don't only happen when it's your own baby? That it's just one of those things that comes naturally to all women? Otherwise I'm in deep trouble and my plan will be completely ruined. My plan was that by the time this night was over, Matt needed to be desperate to have a baby with me. Hardly too much to ask surely?!

I tidied up my apartment not wanting Sarah to think that she was leaving her son in a dumpster. I wish somcone would invent a huge vacuum cleaner that sucked up everything that was in its way and then spat the items back out where they were meant to be - DVD's on the DVD rack, magazines in the magazine rack, shoes in the cupboard, dirty plates in the dishwasher and so on and so forth. But as the magic vacuum cleaner didn't yet exist, I had to run around trying to make it look half tidy again. Just as I was putting the last plate in the dishwasher, the phone rang.

"Hi Luce, it's Matt. I'm sorry but looks like this will take me a bit longer than expected, but don't worry I shouldn't be more than an hour late."

"Matttt! You can't do this to me!" I wailed in panic.

"What am I going to do alone with a baby all by myself for an hour? What if I let it fall or something?"

Matt laughed. "Stop dramatizing. You'll be fine. You're great with kids."

"This isn't a kid, it's a tiny baby and I'm just not used to looking after small little creatures. I'm so clumsy I'll end up breaking it or something!" I said on the verge of tears.

"I'm really sorry but I can't be there any earlier. I know you'll be fine. Just trust yourself. I have to go. See you later. And Luce... just RELAX!" he said reassuringly.

"Matt! No! Wait! Don't leave me like this!" I exclaimed, but he had already hung up.

How was I going to cope with Leo on my own for a whole hour? I didn't know the first thing about tiny little babies. I had helped Matt look after his nephews and nieces but they were little kids, not tiny fragile and easily breakable little creatures!

I had really been counting on him to help me out here; to look after the baby entirely while I admired them both adoringly from a distance, all the while seeming to be helping out a lot too - for example, fetching clean water and nappies, getting the bottle ready for his feed, choosing a nice place to put his little bouncing chair and toys… all very essential parts of looking after a baby too!

I didn't have much time to fret about it though because the doorbell rang. Oh my god! Sarah and Leo had arrived! I felt my heartbeat accelerate wildly. I opened the door and smiled nervously at Sarah standing there with Leo in her arms. I could feel butterflies fluttering in my stomach. How could I possibly handle this on my own?

"Well, aren't you going to invite me in?" she asked amused, clearly having seen the fear in my eyes.

My feet felt glued to the floor as I continued to gaze dumbly at Leo wondering what on earth I was going to do alone with a two month old baby for a whole hour.

"Lucy? Hello-o?" Sarah said again, grinning, before adding. "You know, I won't take it the wrong way if you've changed your mind…"

If I'd changed my mind? Well of course I'd changed my mind. I was in a state of complete panic. Oh my God! What was I going to do? I couldn't send Sarah home with Leo - what would Matt think of me?!

"Change my mind? How can you even think such a thing?" I suddenly exclaimed with false sincerity.

She raised her eyebrow at me and laughed.

"Oh Ok, fine, you win," I sighed, resigned to admitting the truth. "I was thinking of doing exactly that, but I wouldn't be able to face Matt afterwards if I did."

"You'll be fine," she said smiling, as she handed me the sleeping Leo. My heart melted with longing at the sight of him cradled peacefully in my arms. There was something so magic about the feel of a baby. All my panic evaporated for a minute and Sarah looked on happily.

"See, I knew it would take you just a few seconds to fall for him!" she said, clearly very pleased with herself.

He was absolutely adorable, and for a second I did forget all my panic and fears. "Please dear Lord, let this little baby sleep for another hour," I said in silent prayer. As I snapped out of my daze, I realised that Sarah had reached the door and was waiting for me to show her out.

"You'll be fine. Look at the size of him and look at the size of you. How can he scare you so much?"

When you looked at it that way, it really seemed ridiculous, but just knowing that he was completely and utterly dependent on me was terrifying.

"He should sleep for another half hour at least. I've prepared a bottle for his next feed - it ought to be in about two hours but don't worry, he'll let you know when he wants it!' she added laughing. "I've also put a few nappies, a change of clothes and everything you need to change him in his bag."

My face must have reflected the horror I felt at changing a nappy because Sarah suddenly went off in a wave of hysterical laughter and said reassuringly, "It's not that bad honestly!!"

I closed the door behind Sarah and decided to put the sleeping Leo down in his carry cot. I leaned down intending to put him on his side. The only problem was that I didn't know how I would remove my arm from under him after putting him down. Hang on… this can't be too difficult, I told myself as I attempted to lay him peacefully down for the second time. Where do I put my hand? Oh! Oh! There goes his head. Ok, let's try this side, maybe I'll have a better grip… There that's better. Oh no! Is his arm Ok there or is his body weighing down too hard on it? I tried to yank his arm out as gently as possible and jumped in surprise as he groaned in response, half opening his eyes. I held my breath, praying he wouldn't wake up.

Oh thank you dear Lord, I whispered as I saw him close his eyes and fall into a peaceful slumber once more. I settled down next to him half watching TV and half gazing at him with a mixture of awe and fear. Fear that the moment for him to wake up would arrive before Matt did…

Chapter Sixteen

My prayers were soon answered as I heard the door open and saw Matt's smiling face before me.

"You wouldn't believe how relieved I am to see you!" I said, getting up to greet him with a quick peck on the lips.

"Has he been here long?" he asked looking down into the carry cot, smiling. "He's cute isn't he?"

"Sarah arrived about three quarters of an hour ago. I almost fainted with fear when I saw her on my doorstep, knowing you wouldn't be here for another hour."

Matt laughed and I followed him into the kitchen and filled him in on the details as he got himself a coke.

"You see, you managed just fine," he said smiling. "You actually, truly, really managed to handle a *sleeping* baby for over forty five minutes Luce!"

I elbowed him playfully as he laughed, clearly finding his joke extremely funny.

Half an hour later, Leo had woken up, been fed and was now lying contentedly on my knees while Matt and I 'goo-gooed and ga-gaad' over him.

"Oh my God! What was THAT?" I screeched, jumping up in surprise and sending Leo flying five feet up in the air. I had just heard a huge explosion coming from somewhere around my knee area where Leo just happened to be lying. Matt chuckled as he took Leo from me, turned him around, lifted the side of his nappy and grinned.

"Little Leo just left you a little present there, a smelly one too!" he said, screwing up his nose.

"You're joking! That huge noise emanated from that little bottom? His nappy must be bursting!" I stood up taking Leo back from Matt. As I started walking away, Matt burst out laughing.

"What?" I said turning towards him questioningly.

"You don't have to hold him so far away from you Luce. It's in his nappy and won't smudge all over you. It's not contagious either you know!'

"Oh shut up, smart arse!" I said feeling stupid as I realised that I had been holding Leo at an arm's length like you would a dirty bin bag or something. I groaned. I had no idea how to change a nappy. I stopped and looked at Matt who was reading the paper. I hesitated then decided I had no choice but to swallow my pride. It was an emergency here.

"Matt? Will you come and help me please?" I said, eyes pleading.

He looked up, grinned and jumped up. "Sure!"

I smiled gratefully and headed towards my room where I awkwardly placed Leo down on his little changing mat. His big blue eyes gazed at me inquisitively as if asking me if I knew what I was about to do and what I had got myself into just to impress Matt.

"Ok, here goes," I said mostly to myself. I carefully undid the side straps slowly delaying as most I could the actual seeing-the-business time. Matt watched, a permanent grin set on his face.

"You're loving this aren't you?" I said looking towards him.

"Every minute of it," he said chuckling. "I just love seeing you squirm."

"Gee thanks," I said, as I finally undid the nappy and burst into a fit of laughter I saw a tiny patch of brown muck, not even enough to dirty a little ball of cotton wool.

"Is that *it*?" I exclaimed.

"Well, what did you expect, it's only a baby - it's all relative isn't it?"

"All that noise for *this*!" I said laughing again as I wiped his little bottom clean.

I grinned as I looked at his tiny little willy. "It's so cute!" I exclaimed as I pointed it out to Matt. "Do you think he realises that that little thing is going to control most of his life one day?!"

Matt chuckled and I continued cleaning him when I suddenly noticed his little willy rise up and before I could move or do anything, I was sprayed by a huge ray of pee squirting out of it.

"*Aaargh!*" I screeched as I jumped back. Too late. I had pee all over my t-shirt and even on my face.

Matt was bent double, laughing. "That'll teach you to stare at little penises Luce!"

I took a Kleenex and wiped myself clean. I couldn't help giggling as I looked down at him, lying there calmly, having no idea what all the fuss had been about.

"You little devil!" I said affectionately and began cleaning him up again.

I had just done up the last of the little buttons on his Babygro and put on his cologne when he looked at me and let out another huge explosion!

"Oh *noooooo*!" I wailed despondently as Matt rolled on the bed laughing once again.

"It's NOT funny!" I said pissed off that all my hard work had been for nothing.

"Here, let me do it this time," Matt said, getting up and taking Leo from my arms. I heaved a sigh of relief and watched him as he did everything I had just done again, but with so much ease. It was as if he did it every day.

Leo was sleeping peacefully when Sarah finally picked him up a few hours later.

"So, you actually survived, Lucy?" she said teasingly.

"She was great!" Matt replied, putting his arm around my shoulders. "Bit tense at times, but overall handled it really well."

I punched him playfully and replied, "Who made you the great master of baby care?"

As we relaxed in front of the TV, I wondered if my little plan had worked and if it had made Matt yearn for his own baby… I looked at him as he stared blankly at the TV, clearly miles away.

"What are you thinking about? You look miles away," I said fishing for information.

"Oh, I was just thinking of Arsenal's defeat last night. I can't believe they let themselves get beaten in the last few seconds of the match!"

Oh well… so much for him yearning for babies!

Chapter Seventeen

"It's a wonder any work actually ever gets done in this office!" John said tetchily, as he entered my office, causing us to jump up guiltily from our slouched positions to a more professional sitting stance. "What with the endless tea breaks, coffee breaks, lets-add-a-bit-of-hot-water-to-our cold tea breaks, toilet breaks, fag breaks, getting some air breaks, not to forget the famous the-boss-is-out breaks!"

Where had he suddenly appeared from? He wasn't supposed to be back for another hour! Who did he think he was just showing up unannounced like that? What did he expect? Did he really think we'd all be sitting at our desks working studiously?!

"Umm… I was just getting some info about the new… uh… Pongo campaign from Lucy actually," Olivia said lamely, making us smirk like school kids.

John glared at us. He was in one of his moods again. "Sure you were Olivia," he said coldly, as he turned and headed towards his office. He stopped halfway and turned back to me.

"Lucy, I really *hate* to put you out of your way," he said with mock civility. "But I'd like to see you in my office, notebook in hand, in let's say... five minutes. Wouldn't want to interrupt your work session with Olivia now, would I?!"

"Wouldn't want to interrupt your work session with Olivia now would I?" I mimicked in a whisper, pulling my tongue out at him as he turned around to leave.

"I saw that Lucy! Very mature," he called out over his shoulder as he closed his door. Olivia giggled, hiding her mouth behind her hand. As usual his bad moods and comments had no effect on me whatsoever and I grinned maliciously back at Olivia.

"Ok, I'd better get back to work," she said, getting up and heading towards the door.

"Let's have lunch. I haven't even told you about my babysitting exploit and you haven't told me about Pierre."

"Ok, but I have to go shopping - there's a half-price sale at Women's Haven and I really need new work clothes."

"Ok great, sounds good. See you later then."

At lunch time, as we strolled through the shopping centre heading towards Woman's Haven, I filled her in the babysitting session. Needless to say that the peeing incident had her in stitches!

"I can't believe you actually let Vic convince you to do such a thing!"

"Well, at first I thought 'no way', but then I imagined Matt and I playing house and I kind of liked the thought." I said slightly embarrassed.

"You sound desperate there girl!" she said making a face at me.

"Of course I'm desperate! Wouldn't you be after spending four years with someone?" I retorted, slightly pissed off.

"I know - I'm sorry. It just seems desperate in a kind of senile way! You know, a kind of movie type of thing?"

"Well it was Vic's idea after all so it pretty much explains it!"

"So, what do you think Matt thought of it all?" she asked.

"I have no idea. He seemed to have enjoyed it but I

don't think it made him think on a wider scale."

"So, what now?" she asked.

"I don't know Olivia. I have to shake myself up but I get a knot in my stomach every time I start going through what I should say to Matt and the ultimatum I should be giving him. I'm so scared of losing him, and everything's been going so well..."

"Yes, but will this relationship ever give you what you want? I mean, you want a husband and kids and if Matt can't give you that, then you should leave him once and for all. You're both not getting any younger you know, and you must keep reminding yourself of that, no matter how great the two of you are getting along."

I sighed irritably, not wanting to hear what I knew was the truth.

"Enough about that! How's your mysterious French cyber lover?" I asked, wagging my eyebrows at her making her laugh.

"He's off in Bordeaux somewhere on business this week, so I've only been receiving SMS messages. It's terrible because I really miss him."

We walked into the shop and browsed silently through the rows of clothing, lost in our respective thoughts. I was happy for Olivia but scared that she was getting too involved in something which was not yet concrete and which could blow up in her face at any moment.

Granted, my relationship with Matt could also blow up in my face at any moment if he decided he didn't want to marry me, but it wasn't the same somehow. She was giving herself entirely, well not physically, but certainly her heart, to this guy she had never met; who could be stringing her along and making up everything he shared with her. There was no way she could know. It made me uneasy for her because she was really falling for him.

"Here, you try this while I try these on," she said in her usual bossy way, breaking through my thoughts. I took the white, lacy top she had handed me and admired its finesse. I had to agree that she had great taste in clothes. She had three suits in her arms and we headed towards the changing rooms.

I was just pulling the top on over my head when the sound of a high pitched male voice made me freeze. It sounded exactly like Mr. Delano!

But what on earth would he be doing in a woman's clothes shop and on the other side of the island from where he lived?

I yanked the top down, my heart racing, and peeked over the top of the changing room door.

My blood froze. It was him!

Chapter Eighteen

"Olivia!" I hissed through the partition between the changing rooms, as I watched him feigning interest in the stand of sunglasses on the counter, clearly the only thing remotely male in the shop.

"Olivia!" I said again, pounding against the partition.

"What's up?" she said as I saw the tip of her face emerge over the panel.

"Look over there!" I said through gritted teeth. "It's him again - Mr Delano!"

"What the hell is he doing here?"

"Good question! And I'm going to find out!" I said determinedly as I tore through the changing room door and headed towards him.

"What are you doing here?" I snapped angrily as he gave me a look of feigned surprise.

"And may I say you look ravishing," he said ignoring my angry greeting as his sleazy gaze leisurely swept over my body, pausing on my lacy top. He then looked up and leered at me.

"You haven't answered my question!" I insisted, ignoring his comment.

"Aren't I allowed to go shopping?"

"And what is it that you're after in this shop? A pretty pink dress with a little bow on the back maybe?" I said sarcastically, hands on hips for effect, doing everything in my power to stop him from realising how upset I was.

"It's a free world isn't it? And who says I haven't got a present to buy for a woman?"

I cocked my eyebrow at him knowingly. Had he followed me into the shop? Where had he followed me from? Was he behind us all the way from the office? Was he waiting in his car just outside the gates of the office waiting for me to leave? Or did he just happen to be in the shopping centre and see us go into this shop? I hoped that the last option was the real one as all the others made me shudder. I would of course prefer to believe his story about buying a present, but somehow I just didn't.

I turned to the sales girl who had followed our conversation with growing interest and said, "How about you show this nice man your collection of clothing for that woman friend of his. Be sure to show him every last item now would you?" I said as I saw his face change.

Not in his plan clearly. I whispered in the girl's ear that I would give her a generous tip for her time. Olivia had come out of the changing room by now and was observing us too.

"We're leaving!" I said, grabbing her arm, not wanting to be in the same room as him for another second.

"But I have to pay for these!" she cried showing me the two shirts she had chosen.

"You'll come back later! The lady will keep them aside for you," I said through clenched teeth, as the shop assistant nodded. "And Mr. Delano, the next time you decide to follow me, try being a bit more discreet because showing up in a woman's clothes shop is really blowing your cover!" I said coldly. "Then again, the next time you decide to follow me, I'll call the police!"

I stormed out of the shop, both furious and shaking with fright, not bothering to listen to his reply but catching something which sounded like "see you soon". He didn't seem in the least bit troubled by my threats.

"I swear I'll call the police the next time he does something like that!" I exclaimed almost in tears. "He freaks me out that guy!"

"I must say that it seems a bit weird that he just happens to have found himself in the same shop as us," Olivia said.

"I told you and Matt that I didn't have a good feeling about him didn't I?"

"Calm down Lucy. Maybe this is just a coincidence. He was strolling through the shopping centre and saw us and decided he wanted to talk to you. You know like when you have a crush on someone you want to see them. I mean it doesn't have to be the actions of a sick man, just a love struck one."

"No! This is not healthy!" I replied my voice shaking. My heart was still racing and the hairs on my back were still standing on end.

I told Matt about it later and how scared I had been. This time he was furious and made me promise that if anything like that happened again, that I would to ring him up right away so that he could come give Mr. Delano a piece of his mind – or his fist for that matter!

Maybe Olivia was right and that it was true that he was lusting after me and just wanted to see me, but I just had a strange feeling about it all… I just hoped that I was wrong…

Chapter Nineteen

As things between Olivia and Pierre turned into a 'romance', I began to feel really frustrated as despite all my attempts to open Matt's eyes, I still had no sparkling diamond on my finger and I couldn't see any sign of it coming up in the near future. I really felt that I'd waited long enough, but I also knew that giving him an ultimatum would definitely mean that I might lose him...

Finally, after watching the movie *P.S. I Love You* and crying my heart out, I decided that I wanted a man to love me like Gerry had loved Holly. I deserved to be loved like that, and I would go out there and find that kind of love if Matt couldn't give it to me.

The time had come. I was going to do this. My heart was racing, I felt sick with fear, but really determined to go through with it. I was shaking all over as I walked towards Matt who was sitting at the table reading the newspaper.

"Matt, we have to talk," I said nervously.

He looked up from his newspaper, one eye on me and the other still on the article he was reading, and lifted his eyebrow quizzically.

When he saw the look on my face, his eyes grew serious and he put his newspaper down. Was that a trace of worry I saw in there too? I suddenly wasn't so sure I was doing the right thing and remained quiet.

"Go on," he said gently, "I'm listening."

I tried to psyche myself up. Still, I couldn't seem to form any words, my mouth had suddenly become dry and my heart was bongo drumming away. He was looking at me expectantly.

"It's been over a year now since our last break up and since you promised me that we wouldn't just drift along again… but you're still petrified of getting married and refuse to talk about getting engaged and basically we aren't getting any younger… and I really want a family Matt. I can't wait for you forever, no matter how much I love you. I want more."

He looked at me, not saying a word. His eyes were full of anguish and clouded with indecision. I wanted to reach out to him and hug him, but I knew that for once I wouldn't. Not this time.

Finally he spoke, "I just don't think we should be too hasty in deciding something so important Luce..."

"*Too hasty*!" I repeated, not believing what I was hearing. "For crying out loud Matt, it's been FOUR years! How hasty is that? How much more time do you consider 'not hasty' to be?"

Matt didn't answer and just stared into space, looking despondent.

"You know Matt, if I honestly thought that you'd be able to make up your mind in six months' time, or even in a year's time, I'd stick around... but the truth is - if you can't do it now, then you'll never be able to say "Lucy, I love you, will you marry me?". Not in a month, not in six months and not in a year. I know that now and that's why I can't carry on like this anymore..." My voice was shaking and I didn't trust myself to say anymore without crying. My heart was breaking.

He looked up at me, pleadingly. "Luce, don't do this - you know I love you. I just don't know why I'm so scared of getting married. It's just so final. What if we're not good for each other? What if we mess it up and end up hating each other? What if our kids end up miserable because of us...?"

"But what if it works out? What if it's meant to be? What if we have a wonderful life together? It's a decision we have to make. Once we go for it, we are in it together and we do everything in our power to stay together. Love may be a feeling, but it's also a *decision* Matt. And I'm so sorry, but I just can't stick around waiting and hoping for you to decide you love me enough to at least take the risk."

He looked completely shattered as he ran his hands through his hair and stared at his feet. My heart went out to him as he looked so crestfallen.

"I can't tell you what you want to hear Luce… I just can't. It's something too important to be said lightly and I'm just not ready. I wish I were, but I'm not... I know I love you and that I can't imagine life without you, but…" He shook his head sorrowfully, not saying any more.

My eyes filled with the tears I could no longer control and I let them have free reign down my face. He got up and put his arms around me. We hugged, four years of affection, love, friendship and companionship between us. I couldn't imagine life without him, yet I knew that I'd never be happy staying with him this way, no matter how much I loved him. I pulled away from him gently and, shoulders drooping, went to get my bag.

As I walked past him again, I stopped and looked up at him.

"Take care of yourself Matt…" I said my voice breaking.

Tears rolled down our faces and he lifted his hand to wipe away a tear. Feeling my resolve weakening by the millisecond, I turned around and walked out the door.

I didn't look back. I knew if I did that I would go running back into his arms and that we'd both have a good cry and tell each other that things would be Ok - and they probably would, but we'd just end up back in our rut again.

I got into my car, switched it on and drove off. Blinded by tears, I switched on the window wipers only to be met by the screeching sound of the wipers on the dry window. I switched them off and took a Kleenex out of my glove box and wiped my eyes instead. I felt so lost and empty. But I also felt relieved. I'd done it, I'd finally done it. It was so hard, but I knew it was the right thing to do.

I drove on, sniffling and blowing my nose almost having to resolve myself to using my sleeve as I had finished the last few Kleenexes in the box.

I rummaged through my glove box and found an old, but clean, KFC paper serviette and gratefully blew my nose in it, 'With all due respect Colonel,' I mumbled, laughing nervously at my own stupid joke.

Suddenly I looked around me and realised that I had no idea where I was heading. As realisation dawned, I stopped, did a U-Turn and went back on my tracks. I walked wearily up the stairs again and let myself in.

Matt was still sitting at the table, head in his hands. He lifted his head as he heard me come in, clearly confused by my return and I saw a flicker of hope in his eyes.

"I'm sorry Matt, but I'm not coming back to tell you I regret my decision," I said quietly. "I'm still leaving you, but I can't be the one to go…"

"Wh-What do you mean?" he said looking completed puzzled.

"We're in my apartment Matt," I said gently as he looked around in a daze.

He smiled sadly at me, kissed my cheek tenderly and walked towards the door.

"I sure will miss you Luce," he said looking back towards me.

"I'll miss you too Matt," I said, as tears resurfaced and the door closed behind him.

It was over.

Chapter Twenty

I spent three days in bed, watching soppy videos like *'Casablanca', 'Love Story', 'P.S. I love you', 'When Harry met Sally'* and cried my heart out.

I used up all my stock of Kleenexes (two boxes), all my stock of paper serviettes (even the lovely ones with little fish on them – well, we can certainly say that they were swimming after I'd used them!!) and I got to the last roll of toilet paper when the anger took over and my tears dried up.

In fact, I'd gone from being sad, to angry, to desperate, to angry, to lonely, to angry, to confused, to angry, to depressed, to angry, to angry, to ANGRY!! And that's when I stopped crying. I swear I could hear my poor red-blotched nose singing praises to the Lord that the nose blowing was over!

As I still wasn't in the mood to get out of bed - my third day off work - I started watching videos with the sole purpose of accentuating my anger.

So out came the *First Wives Club'* (well I almost felt like I'd been one!) and *'War of the Roses'*.

By the end of the day I was seething with anger and determined to get revenge. I fell asleep that night with thoughts of Matt begging me for mercy and me just laughing in his face.

The next morning I forced myself out of bed and made myself a cup of coffee. Saturday today... At least I didn't have to ring work again! Unfortunately my anger and determination of the previous night had vanished and I just felt completely deflated. I really should get up and get dressed, I thought. Even just to go for a walk or something. But then again, I just wasn't ready to face the world yet. I grabbed a magazine and hopped back into bed, tomorrow I'd force myself to get moving...

Yes, tomorrow...

Having abandoned my magazine and opted for a nap instead, I bolted in surprise as I heard the doorbell ring. Well ring isn't quite the word to describe it, 'drilled' would be more appropriate, and there was no doubt in the world who was doing the drilling! It could only be my grandmother as she hasn't quite grasped the concept of a doorbell yet. She hasn't realised that you can just press the doorbell once, and then wait. She thinks that she has to leave her finger on the buzzer until someone comes to the door!

I straightened myself up as best I could as I made my way to the door.

"Coming Gran!" I called out.

"Hi love," she said smiling warmly as I opened the door. She stood there, handbag set firmly under her armpit, freshly applied bright red lipstick, and her hair had obviously just been brushed again on the way up the stairs.

"I'm just dropping by for a minute to see how you are as I noticed that your car hasn't moved for a few days. Is it broken or are you ill?" she said looking concerned.

"No I'm fine. Come and sit down," I said leading her towards the lounge.

"No, no, I'm just about to go," she said, declining my offer to sit down as anticipated.

"Go on, sit down just for a minute," I insisted as she knew I would.

She finally gave in and sat on the very edge of the sofa as usual. I had no idea how she didn't slip off the edge actually!

We chatted for a while before she suddenly asked me how Matt was. I didn't quite know what to answer but ended up telling her the truth.

"Well done my girl!" she said gleefully, to my utter surprise. "Let him come crawling back to you, and don't you worry, he will!"

I laughed, and changed the subject feeling better at the thought of him coming crawling back to me...

I decided to phone my parents that evening. I needed a dose of TLC and no better place to get it from than from my parents. I got the impression that they were both relieved to hear that I had finally broken up with Matt.

"He doesn't deserve you," my Dad said gently. "If he loves you, he'll come back to you, love. I'm sure he will - but for now you have to be strong my pet."

My parents had been completely exasperated by Matt's commitment phobia and I think they had really begun worrying about me.

I finally headed back to work, but was in a daze and looked awful. Even John went easy on me. Olivia had probably told everyone what had happened. No one spoke to me about it, except Phoebe who told me how sorry she was.

It was better that way, otherwise I don't think I could have kept it together. I would have crumbled. I felt so empty and my heart physically hurt I missed him so much.

Every day, as soon as I got back from work, I dove into bed and stayed there until I was too hungry and had to get up. Olivia had taken me to the supermarket during the weekend after she had realised that I wouldn't bother if left to my own devices. She had helped me pick out plenty of microwave dinners for one, which had tears pouring down my face.

"Microwave dinners for *one* Olivia - it makes me so sad..." I had whispered fighting the huge sob that had been threatening to come out.

She had comforted me and helped me to fill up the caddy with everything I would need. She forced me to buy plenty of comfort food too, which meant that I found myself eating a huge mars bar at 3am, or a box of Pringles at 11pm, or a box of my favourite Oreos biscuits for dinner. I just floated through the days, in a daze, feeling numb and missing Matt like crazy. I had picked up the phone to call him so many times on reflex before realising that I couldn't do that anymore... then sitting down and bawling my eyes out.

Two weeks had already passed and I had a whole Saturday to drag myself through. I went to visit my grandmother, who very diplomatically told me that maybe I should try her new shampoo as it smelt wonderful and left her hair shiny and soft. I spent the rest of the day just lying in front of the TV watching whatever was on. At six o'clock that evening the phone rang. I decided not to answer it. I just wasn't in the mood. But then thinking it might be Matt, I dived for it at the last minute.

"Hi Lucy, it's Olivia," she said cheerfully.

"Oh... It's you," I said, unable to hide the disappointment in my voice, and in fact not even trying to.

"Gee, thanks for your enthusiasm," she said sourly.

"It's just that…" I started weakly and she interrupted, saying gently, "I know, you thought it might be Matt – don't worry, I understand".

"Well, yeah, I guess I hoped it might be him. Stupid of me really…" I said, almost in tears again.

"It's more than understandable, but really, you've been moping around for two weeks now and I've had enough of you feeling sorry for yourself. You're getting dressed and we're going out tonight!" she said with a 'don't mess with me' attitude.

"No, I don't want to," I grumbled, thinking that facing people and life in general was just too much of an effort.

"Go on! There's nothing quite like alcohol to make you forget your heart troubles. Remember the old days when it was a regular occurrence?" she said enthusiastically, as though it had been a great achievement.

"No… umm… well, actually, maybe you have a point there," I said, with a small grin. "But where would we go?"

"There's a great new pub that everyone's going on about lately and it's only about ten minutes from here. I'll pick you up at 8pm Ok?"

"Ok," I said, twisting the phone cord around my finger, not totally convinced that it was a good idea. Suddenly, realising that I'd actually have to get dressed up, I cried out, "Oh, noooooooo! I caaan't!"

"What now?" she said, exasperated. I could tell she'd had more than enough of my foul mood.

"I have nothing to wear! I'm fat and ugly! I can't go out looking like this!" I whimpered looking down at myself in despair.

"Don't be stupid, you're far from being fat and even further from being ugly, so just put on you Levis and a sexy top showing your huge cleavage…" she said, as I could imagine her chuckling on the other end of the line.

"Ha! Ha! NOT funny!" I interrupted. "You're meant to be making me feel better here, not making me feel worse by commenting on my non-existent breasts!" I wailed.

"Sorry! Just trying to make you laugh!" she said, obviously still grinning. "Seriously, just wear your Levis and that white top you just bought at Fashion House recently. It looks great on you and you'll look just perfect."

"Oh, alright." I said, giving in as I decided that it might actually do me a world of good to get out of the house, and of my bed for that matter!

I looked at my watch; six o'clock. I had two hours… how was I going to clean myself up in just two hours? I might just have a little lie down and think about it. I really didn't have the energy right now… just half an hour then I'll get up, I decided as I stretched out lazily on my bed, enjoying the softness of my pillows under my head…

Suddenly, I bolted up and looked at my watch. It was

already 7.45pm! I'd fallen asleep! Oh no, I mumbled as I raced into the shower. Believe it or not, my Levis *and* my top were *both* clean! I guess that's one of the advantages of spending so much time in bed. No need for clothes so they stay clean!

Olivia came to pick me up at 8 o'clock sharp and after having to wait at least 10 minutes for me to finish getting ready, we finally headed off. I couldn't believe I was actually on my way to a pub. It was the last thing I wanted to do, but I guess I needed to stop moping around feeling sorry for myself. Life had to go on. I wasn't in the mood to talk so we drove along in silence, listening to music. Olivia respected my lack of conversation and just quietly sang along to the music. Suddenly, I noticed that we had stopped. Olivia turned towards me, and smiled widely.

"Here goes my dear! Prepare to have fun - if you still remember the meaning of the word of course!" she added mischievously.

Did I?

Chapter Twenty-One

As Olivia led me through the huge saloon swinging doors with big haystacks curled up on both sides of the entrance, country music rocking away inside, I had to admit that I had begun to reconcile myself to the idea of being here. Maybe this wouldn't be so bad after all…. Just being out and seeing people all around me enjoying themselves already made me feel better. I was going to try to forget Matt for the evening and just enjoy myself. I really needed to get my life back on track.

We headed towards a group of friends to say hi. Josh, Alex, Rachel and Paul greeted us warmly. They all knew that Matt and I had broken up, but no one mentioned it thankfully. I was surprised that Matt wasn't with them, but was hugely relieved. In fact, if he'd been planning to come I know Olivia wouldn't have brought me along.

Olivia and I headed to the bar, and then began our non-stop Tequila shooters and Gin and Tonic night.

I don't think there ever was a moment when I didn't have a drink in my hand, something to do with everyone wanting me to forget my troubles, if you ask me!

The Country Western band played until midnight and was then replaced by karaoke. I was getting 'happier' by the drink, and even found myself checking out the male potential – well, it took me a whole 30 seconds to reach the conclusion that there was none, but hey! At least I looked!

As the night wore on, people became 'braver' and there were numerous appalling interpretations of songs which were hilarious to watch. A few were quite good, but most people got totally soaked in beer. Luckily there was a net between the stage and the crowd so the singers only got the beer on them and not the cans!

Josh and Rachel did a great interpretation of "Row, Row, Row Your Boat", medley style, which had us all in stitches. I couldn't believe they actually had that song on the karaoke! As we were watching them, a guy with a big cowboy hat started chatting to me. He tried to convince me that his name was Rex and that he came from Texas. I kept telling him he couldn't be a cowboy because he wasn't wearing big pointy boots and a gun. I then noticed that standing on his other side was a dishy looking dark haired guy, much younger than him, whose eyes twinkled with mirth as he watched us. I hadn't noticed him earlier.

"Hey you!" I found my mouth saying before my head could get in there and stop it. "You're pretty disshy aren't you?" I grinned drunkenly as he burst out laughing.

"Why thank you! And who do I have the pleasure of talking to?"

"I'm Luchy," I replied, relieved that I had an easy name to pronounce.

"It's nice to meet you Luchy. I'm Greg."

"Not Luchy! Lu-chy!" I tried to enunciate, not realising that he was pulling my leg.

"Oh, Ok, got it. Lucy right?" he chuckled and winked.

"Yesh! Are you from Texchas too?" I asked.

"No, can't say I am," he replied, smiling.

"Yesh, it's obvious, you aren't wearing the big pointy cowboy bootsh!"

He grinned as Olivia grabbed my hand, excused us and dragged me away and back to the others.

I wanted to resist her but somehow couldn't find the strength.

"Ni'sh to have met you both," I said over my shoulder and threw a wobbly wave.

"Wow! He'sh pretty hot that one ishn't he?" I said to Olivia, looking back towards Greg.

"I don't think it's a very good idea, you're not in a state to come on to anyone right now," she said laughing.

"Ya know Olivia, I n'ver rea'lish'd that I wash sho funny!" I said, as she burst out laughing.

"Ease off the alcohol a bit Luce!"

"Tut-tut," I said shaking my head and my drink at her, before walking off to find my next drinking partner.

I strolled past the stage laughing at the poor guy being soaked in beer, and suddenly felt myself being pushed towards the stage. I looked back and Josh and Rachel pushed me harder, telling me to go and sing something. I struggled, but in my state, it was a waste of time as I could barely stand up, let alone find the strength to resist being pushed. So I found myself on the stage being applauded and encouraged by the crowd. I had no idea what to sing but I felt quite motivated all of a sudden. The fleeting realisation that I was a really awful singer shot through my head, but disappeared just as quickly, drowned out by the alcohol level in my blood. I put my drink down and looked blearily through the songs trying to find something I liked, but before I knew it, the music to *"Single Ladies"* had come on and I had no choice but to go along with it. I shrugged and started singing, or shrieking would be a better adjective to use in my case! I sounded like a cat being strangled.

But the crowd cheered me on and I still hadn't been soaked in beer, so I started really getting into it and did a bit of a dance. Whoa! Not that step, I told myself, as I almost crashed to the floor. I was having trouble reading the lines on the screen. I couldn't understand why they had to write every line twice! It made it bloody confusing and I kept thinking I needed to sing them twice! As the song wore on, I felt braver and began feeling sexy too, swaying my hips and rubbing my hands up and down myself, God's gift to sexiness. I could see Olivia, Rachel, Josh, Alex, and Paul in the front row and leaned down to sing for them, feeling like Michael Jackson in front of his audience. My Texan cowboy and his sexy friend were also there cheering me on. I felt so cool! Eat your heart out Matt!

When the song ended, I proudly curtsied, almost falling over as I leaned too far forward. Olivia rushed up to me and couldn't talk as she was laughing so hard. I felt a bit pissed off but couldn't be bothered getting angry as she handed me another drink. I took a sip and noticed that it was water. I was about to complain when I realised that I really needed to sit down. My head fell onto my hands on the bar. I felt my eyelids starting to grow really heavy.

I suddenly heard someone ask me if I was feeling Ok. I looked up with a bit of trouble and thought I recognised the sexy guy I had talked to earlier, Greg or someone, although at this stage everything seemed very blurry and I couldn't quite get my eyes to focus. Was there smoke in here or something?

"Would you like to go get some fresh air?" he asked, smiling kindly.

I really needed fresh air. I just hoped that I wouldn't throw up all over him. Actually, I didn't feel like throwing up, I just felt like sleeping.

"Yesh, that w'uld be ni'sh," I slurred gratefully.

"Grab onto my arm and I'll lead the way," he said gently and I did just that, stumbling and trying hard to stay up.

The fresh air felt wonderful. We sat down on a bench and just sat there quietly, me not having the energy to talk and him obviously knowing that I wasn't in a state to carry out a conversation.

"Am really shorry about thish," I suddenly blurted out, my eyelids growing heavier. "I don't norm'ly drink sho much but my boyfriend jusht dumped me," I explained as clearly as I could. My tongue seemed to weigh a ton!

He told me not to worry and that he didn't mind staying with me.

"You're rh'eally shexy you know? But rh'eally ni'sh too," I mumbled, trying to look up at him. He chuckled as I rested my head against his shoulder. It was so comfy. I might as well just close my eyes for a minute…

Chapter Twenty-Two

AHHHHH! My head was throbbing. I couldn't move it hurt so much. I tried to open my eyes, but they refused to cooperate. I hadn't had a real hangover for so long and now I remembered why I had avoided them! I rolled over onto my stomach, groaning at the pain in my skull, and then jumped in surprise as I felt my hand land on something warm and fleshly. I moved my hand and tried to pinch the flesh to be sure that I wasn't dreaming.

"OUCH!" I definitely heard someone shout out this time. I quickly snapped my arm away and tried to remember what had happened last night, but couldn't for the life of me fathom how I had actually got home from the pub. Oh no, this wasn't good, this wasn't good at all. Surely I hadn't had a one night stand with a stranger from the pub? I vaguely remembered talking to quite a few men last night, one who had a cowboy hat on and one who was really handsome, but it was all a big blur. Oh my god! How could I have slept with a total stranger! It's so not me!

Or even worse, what if I've gone and slept with Josh or Alex!! My heart was pounding as hard as my head but I was keeping my eyes firmly shut. As long as I didn't see who was next to me, I could pretend it hadn't happened! I just wanted to keep reality at bay for a little while longer...

Then I heard the person next to me clearing their throat – the person who was next to me, IN MY BED! *OH MY GOD!*

"Hi there!" I heard a friendly, and if I was not mistaken, amused male voice say. His voice sounded kind of familiar but I couldn't remember who it was associated to, so that definitively ruled out Alex and Josh as I knew I would have recognised their voices! This voice was kind of deep and sexy with what sounded like an American accent...

I could feel him staring at me, willing me to open my eyes.

"You might actually like what you see you know," he said, reassuringly, although I could tell he was smiling. I cringed and my eyes stayed tightly shut.

"Oh, come on, I swear that I'm not that ugly," he said obviously finding my blatant refusal to open my eyes extremely entertaining.

I groaned loudly. I couldn't believe this was happening to me.

"I've never slept with a complete stranger before," I grumbled, disgusted with myself.

"Oh well, you have nothing to worry about there honey," he replied, sounding cocky. Just as I was breathing a sigh of relief, he added, "Because we sure didn't get any sleep last night!" he added, laughing heartily.

My eyes popped open as a burst of pain shot through my head again. I quickly closed them again without looking at him.

"*Please* tell me you're joking…" I begged plaintively.

"Now why would I do that?" he asked, annoyingly chirpy when I felt like death warmed up.

Finally, my curiosity got the better of me and I slowly opened my eyes and glanced towards the stranger who had found his way into my bed. He was sitting there, leaning against the pillows, with a huge grin on his face. He was gorgeous. I vaguely remembered him from last night but couldn't quite place him. He had dark brown hair that kept falling into his light hazel eyes. My eyes fell to his bare chest – oh my! He was heavenly. Suddenly, my mind seemed to register what my eyes had been looking at and I shot up in bed. He looked *naked*!

"Oh my God! You're not naked under there are you?" I asked him in a whisper, wincing as I pointed towards his midriff and the sheet.

He raised his eyebrows and whispered sexily, "Come have a look and see…"

I scowled angrily at him and he laughed.

"It's not funny!" I wailed, and my head fell into my hands. What a mess! Never, ever, am I drinking again!

"Now, now, honey, no need to get your knickers in a twist," he reassured me, using a sort of strange Texan drawl. "Well, I guess that would apply if you were actually wearing any!" he added chuckling.

I gasped in shock and peeked under the sheets as he laughed. I did have knickers on under my t-shirt and glared up at him, not in the least impressed by his joke. As to how the t-shirt ended up on me is another story which I didn't think I wanted to find out just yet.

"Ha, bloody, ha! You sure think you're funny don't you!" I said, grumpily, looking away.

"My Lordy Lord, aren't we Miss Grumpy this morning," he drawled, teasingly. "You really were much more fun last night lady!"

"What's with all the 'Lordy Lord, lady and honey' – are you Texan or something?" I asked annoyed.

He laughed before speaking in a normal American accent. "No, I'm just teasing you actually and trying out the accent for size. Remember Rex from last night? Well he's from Texas and I spoke with him for a while and found his accent kind of cool."

I nodded, vaguely remembering the Texan with his boots and cowboy hat.

As he got out of bed, I realised with relief that he was actually wearing boxer shorts. My eyes were drawn to his super toned and muscular body. He was delectable.

"We didn't sleep together last night by the way," he said over his shoulder as he put last night's t-shirt back on. "Well, we did sleep together," he grinned. "But we didn't have sex - we just slept."

I let out of huge sigh of relief.

"To be honest, my ego and I are rather hurt that you are so relieved," he said, amused.

I grinned. He was actually really nice. "It's just that I have never taken a stranger home before or had sex on a first date - I guess I'm one of those old fashioned girls. And if it had happened and I couldn't even remember any of it…"

"Trust me, if we had really slept together, you would have remembered!" he chuckled.

"Pretty sure of yourself aren't you cowboy?" I laughed, starting to feel a little better although my head was still pounding.

"Listen, why don't you just relax? I'll just root around in the kitchen and make us some coffee while you take some panadol for that head of yours, then I'll tell you about last night and how I ended up in your bed."

"Thanks, that would be great," I smiled gratefully at him as I got out of bed and went hunting for some Panadol. I could now relax knowing that I hadn't actually had sex with him. Not that that would have been such an awful thing, I thought smiling. He had a body to die for. I shook my head, trying to change the direction of my thoughts, but groaned as I felt the remnants of my drinking binge rattle through my head again. I took two panadols, brushed my teeth, put on a pair of pyjama bottoms and headed straight back into bed.

"How do you like your coffee Lucy?" I heard him call out from the kitchen. I grinned realising that we hardly knew anything about each other. This was such a new experience for me.

"One sugar, with a touch of milk please."

"Ok, coming up!" he said, as the delicious smell of coffee wafted through from the kitchen.

He handed me my cup and I smiled gratefully up at him. I took a sip and sighed in contentment, "Umm… it's just perfect, thank you."

"It's a pleasure. So shall I finally tell you how I ended up in your bed then?"

"Do I really want to hear this?" I asked, grimacing.

As it turned out, I had fallen fast asleep on his shoulder and Greg didn't have the heart to move me, so just sat there for a while. Olivia had finally burst out the pub a few minutes later in a panic, having looked everywhere for me. Greg laughed as he told me that Olivia had fired a hundred and one questions his way and repeatedly warned him that he better not have done anything to hurt me. He had reassured her that I had just fallen asleep and that nothing had happened. Then they had tried to wake me up, but I was out cold. Finally Greg picked me up and took me to Olivia's car.

"You carried me?" I asked, embarrassed.

"Sure did! Over my shoulders like a sack of potatoes!" he said, winking.

Ooh! He was so sexy.

Anyway, as it turned out, apparently I woke up when he put me down and I refused to let him go. I insisted that he was my new best friend and that I would only go home with him.

"I'm so sorry," I groaned in embarrassment and I hid my face behind my hands.

"I didn't mind, honestly. It was actually quite a laugh. You were so drunk!" he chuckled.

Olivia hadn't been happy at all apparently, but Greg had reassured her and given her his phone number, I.D number, address, showed him his business card and finally she had agreed.

"Sure wasn't easy convincing her to trust me. She's one protective friend that one." He grinned. "But then again, I thought it was great that she looked after you like that."

"Yeah, she's a great friend. We look out for each other."

Olivia explained how to get to my place and made him promise to call her when we got here.

"You might want to send her a text to tell her that you are alive and well actually. I'm surprised she hasn't called you actually."

"Oh no! I had put my phone on mute last night!" I cried, and raced to my bag. There were 5 missed calls from her and 3 text messages asking me if I was Ok and to please call her. I quickly sent her a message to say that I was fine and that he was wonderful. I added a P.S. 'I'll tell you all tomorrow' so that she wouldn't call me now.

"Ok, so then what? Did I wake up when we got back?" I asked genuinely curious as I just couldn't remember anything.

"Yes, you were awake but really drunk. You got changed yourself though and said 'thanksh you sho much' about 100 times and 'you're sho ni'sh'. Then you fell on the bed and you were out for the count!"

"Umm, Ok, but that doesn't really explain why you ended up sleeping in my bed?" I said, teasingly. "Why didn't you sleep in the spare room?"

"Have you seen the state of your spare room, and the bed in particular?" he answered, eyebrow raised.

I blushed as I remember that it was in fact full of old clothes, books and boxes of things that I was meant to have given away ages ago.

"Fair point," I giggled. "But how about the sofa?"

"Ah, come on. Look at my size and look at the size of your sofa," he said plaintively. "You were out cold anyway so I knew I would have no choice but to behave myself."

I burst out laughing. "What a gentleman! But I understand, don't worry. No harm done anyway."

Suddenly he grinned and looked at me quizzically.

"What?" I asked confused.

"I was just wondering if you actually remember my name?"

"Of course I do! umm…" I said, pretending to be searching in the recesses of my memory. "Got it! It's Graham!"

He laughed not sure if I was joking or not.

"Just pulling your leg *Greg*!" I grinned, rather relieved to have remembered. I was slowly putting the pieces of the evening back together in my head and remembered Rex and Greg very well.

"Oh *noooo*! My singing!" I groaned despondently as I suddenly had a vision of me on stage. "Did I really sing *Single Ladies*?" I winced.

He hooted with laughter. "You sure did. You were really wild up there! It was hilarious."

"For you maybe!" I said morosely.

"You seemed to be having the time of your life anyway," he said in amusement. "But before we go on reminiscing, I don't know about you, but I'm starving. How about we keep talking while having some breakfast?"

"Good idea. I think I've got some eggs and tomatoes in the fridge and some bread to make some toast. How does that sound?"

"Fantastic!" he said jumping up. "I'll help you."

We headed to the kitchen and fell into an easy banter, teasing each other and laughing at each other's jokes.

We had a lot in common and the same sense of humour.

"So you live in America? How long are you here for?"

"Actually, I'm flying back tomorrow morning," he said, looking at me with what I sensed was disappointment.

"Tomorrow?" I said, as my heart plummeted.

We sat down to eat and he told me about his hometown, his family and friends and his work. He was funny and smart and gorgeous. I was falling under his charm. I found out by the way he spoke about the people in his life that he was also caring and kind and thought that he was definitely someone I could have become friends with - or more, much more, if you listened to my raging hormones.

After breakfast we went to lie on the sofa in front of the TV, really comfortable in each other's company. It felt like we'd known each other for ever. We watched Mr. Bean and were in stitches as we watched my favourite episode, Mr. Bean in church. We talked nonstop, him asking me all about Matt, Olivia, my job and my family. He seemed so interested in everything and asked endless questions. We ordered pizza for lunch and then my eyes started feeling really heavy again.

"Maybe I should go because you look like you could use a rest," he said, grinning as I yawned for the third time.

"Where are you staying?" I asked, sleepily.

"In an apartment not far from here actually, so I can just walk," he said.

"Do you want to leave?" I asked surprising even myself.

He smiled and almost shyly said, "Actually, to be really honest, I would actually love to spend the rest of the day with you."

"I'm definitively Ok with that."

We headed to my bedroom and both fell on the bed happily.

"Umm, pure heaven," he mumbled, snuggling into the pillow.

"Sure is…" I replied dreamily, as I looked at him sprawled on my bed.

Calm down girl! Behave yourself! I had never felt so turned on by an almost stranger before. He was just so flipping hot, funny and nice. Damn it! If he wasn't leaving tomorrow, I think I would definitively be over

Matt in no time!!

"Do you have a girlfriend back home?" I asked, pretty sure that he did. He turned and repositioned himself on his side, looking towards me.

"Not right now, no. I've also just got out of a long term relationship myself."

"Who did the dumping?" I asked, curious.

"It was actually a mutual decision. We no longer wanted the same things. She became too money minded and power driven for me. I'm more a family type of guy and I like the simple things in life."

"Good on you," I said, smiling. He smiled back and our eyes locked. My heart was doing cartwheels again. We stayed in silence for a few minutes, just enjoying each other's presence.

"Why didn't you try kissing me or anything last night," I suddenly asked sheepishly. "Am I not your type?" I added almost in a whisper as I blushed, feeling stupid.

"Are you serious?" he exclaimed, seeming genuinely surprised. "How could you not be my type? You're gorgeous, smart, funny and… so sweet," he said, looking deep into my eyes again. I tried to understand what I was seeing there but wasn't sure. It sort of looked like he wanted to kiss me and I could hardly breathe from wanting him so much to do just that.

"Why then?" I blurted out before I could stop myself.

"Because you're just not a one night stand kind of girl..." He said softly, as he reached out to put his hand over mine, his eyes never leaving mine.

I shivered from his touch and from wanting him so much to kiss me.

"For once, I really wish I was..." I whispered, my eyes not leaving his.

"Come here you," he said, tenderly, reaching out for me.

And then he kissed me...

Oh my...

Chapter Twenty-Three

I looked at myself in the mirror and saw that I was radiant after my day and night with Greg. He had left early as his flight was leaving at 11am I was sad to see him go but at the same time I was so grateful to him because he had given me hope again. He had made me believe that I could love again, that there wasn't just Matt out there and that I would find someone else to love me. It was definitely what I had needed.

I wasn't fooling myself that I no longer loved Matt. It still hurt just to think about him. I was also not kidding myself that I had fallen head over heels in love with Greg, although he was pretty wonderful, but I was just really grateful to him for having appeared in my life when he did. We will never know what would have happened if he had stayed on, but I doubt that I would have been ready to start another relationship so soon after losing Matt.

I reached my office, and not feeling overly motivated, the usual for a Monday morning, I sat at my desk staring at my reflection in my computer screen. Wow!

It all seemed so surreal, I couldn't believe I had actually met a gorgeous young American and had spent all day and night with him yesterday. Olivia popped her head in through the door, grinning like the cat that got the big, big mouse.

"Why are you grinning at me like that?" I asked laughing. "But first of all, thanks so much for letting me make a complete fool of myself on Saturday night and letting me get up there and sing!"

She laughed. "I didn't even know you were up there until I heard a familiar screeching sound coming from the direction of the stage!"

"I'm sooooo embarrassed," I groaned, as I put my head in my hands.

"Don't worry about it," she said, trying to comfort me. "It was hilarious and you sang so badly that no one actually believed it was your real voice."

I winced vaguely remembering the laughter and the cheers.

"Who cares about the singing? What about Greg? I was in such a panic when I couldn't find you anywhere! I knew you were extremely drunk and felt so guilty for not looking out for you. I looked everywhere before going outside and that's when I saw you snoring away on Greg's shoulder, dribbling onto his sexy chest."

"I *do not* snore, nor do I dribble thank you very much," I said, laughing.

"He seemed really nice and gave me so much personal information to prove that it was safe for him to take you home, that I couldn't refuse. He practically gave me his shoe size!" She laughed. "And to top it off, you were insisting he was your new 'besht friend'. It was so funny."

"He was so sweet Olivia. He's given me hope again. We spent the whole day together yesterday – and even last night…" I added grinning mischievously.

"You didn't?" she asked incredulously, her eyes popping out.

"It's not what you think. We didn't 'do the deed' so to speak, but it was really special. He was a real sweetheart. Exactly what I needed - a big dose of TLC."

"I'm so jealous!"

I felt so much better and my gloom and doom mood had finally lifted. It felt good. Ok, so as soon as I thought of Matt, my heart ached, but I just felt more positive about life and now had to just concentrate on not thinking about Matt! I asked her how Pierre was, making smoochy signs with my mouth to annoy her. She rolled her eyes at me and laughed but didn't reply, seeming completely engrossed in sharpening a pencil.

"Hello? Earth to Olivia," I said, trying to snap her out of her sudden reverie. She looked up at me and to my surprise, blushed.

"Olivia, you're blushing!" I exclaimed. "Are you having dirty thoughts?" I teased as she chuckled.

"*Hetoldmethathelovesme* yesterday."

"What?" I asked not understanding what she was on about.

"He told me *thathelovesme* yesterday," she said again.

"I get the 'he told you' and 'yesterday' bit but what's the rest?" I said, still not catching on.

She grinned and I realised she was doing it on purpose.

"TELL ME!" I pleaded.

"He said *Je T'aime* to me last night on the phone," she finally said sheepishly.

"No way!" I exclaimed utterly dumbstruck. Even though I knew very little French, *Je T'aime* is a pretty universal. This was so bloody weird and amazing and I couldn't quite believe it was really happening. How could you fall in love with someone you had never met for real?

"I know…" she said, laughing as she took in my shocked expression.

"So what did you say?" I asked intrigued.

"Moi aussi" she answered in French, hiding her face in her hands.

"Me too?" I asked understanding the 'moi' and guessing the rest. She nodded.

"NO! You didn't?!" I said in shock. "*Did you*?!"

"Well I do, Ok? It's so hard to explain or understand, but it's just the most amazing feeling. I have no idea what he looks like but I know so much about him and it feels like I've known him forever not just for a month and a half."

"Goodness gracious me!" I said in a theatrical English voice, as I shook my head and found that I could say nothing more. It just didn't seem real to me. She burst out laughing and suddenly grew serious.

"So now, I want to know how you're really holding up Luce?" she asked gently, changing the subject and catching me off guard.

I sighed deeply. "Well, much better after being with Greg all weekend I must admit, although I still feel like a piece of me is missing. I keep wanting to pick up the phone to tell Matt something or to ask him something, and then I realize that I can't do that anymore, and I just feel so sad... But the good thing is that I'm still feeling really angry towards him at the moment, so it does make things a bit easier."

"Good on you! He's such a fool!" she said heatedly. "Doesn't know what's good for him!" then suddenly grinned and added, "Actually, he would die of jealousy if he knew you'd been with Greg all weekend! Maybe I should make sure that he finds out!"

I blushed. "No, please don't tell anyone. It's so not me and I really just want to keep that to myself. It was so special in a way that I don't want to end up feeling guilty for being with him."

"My lips are sealed," she reassured me.

"Thanks, you're the best. And it's true, knowing Matt he would have been furious! Doesn't want me, but doesn't want anyone else to have me either! Well tough for him I say!"

She laughed and said, "Go girl!" before looking at her

watch and jumping up.

"Oh no, I've got to go soon, I've got a meeting. By the way, anything new on the Vic and Sam front?"

"No, I haven't heard anything about Sam since Matt and I broke up. I actually haven't spoken to Vic since our break up. She'll probably end up hearing about it through Sam I guess. She'll be upset that I didn't ring her, but I just couldn't talk about it, until now. I'll ring her later and see how things are on her side too. I've been too wrapped up in myself to care, I'm ashamed to admit," I finished, feeling guilty.

"Well, it's natural after what you've been through. Ok, must go. Chin up and remember I'm always here if you need me," she said as she stood up to leave.

After she'd gone I sat thinking about Olivia and Pierre. Where can these kinds of relationships lead to? I was worried about Olivia as she really seemed committed to him now and they hadn't even met!

Just then I heard my phone beep. I had received a text message.

"Am about to board the plane. Just wanted to say thank you for an amazing time. You are one special lady and don't you ever forget it. Take good care of yourself and don't let Matt ever hurt you or take you for granted again.

You deserve to be loved and cherished and if Matt can't do that, wait until you find a man who will. Hugs and kisses,

Greg

P.S. Every time I see Mr. Bean it will make me think of you – not that you look anything like him of course ☺

P.P.S Bit of friendly advice, don't ever quit your day job to try and become a singer – trust me on that one ☺

I burst out laughing but felt tears roll down my cheeks at the same time. I suddenly felt really tired and just wanted to curl up in bed and sleep. But I was at work and the day had only just started. I was in the middle of typing a presentation when my office phone rang. I absent-mindedly picked it up and almost dropped it again when I heard who it was.

"Hey sweetcakes! How are you? I'm down in Grand-Bay on the beach, the sun's shining and the only thing missing is you…" Mr Delano said flirtatiously.

"DON'T call me sweetcakes!" I yelled into the phone. "And what part of 'I'll call the police if you ever follow me again' made you think that I would want to join you anywhere?" I replied coldly.

He chuckled as I felt my blood boiling to bursting level.

"Yeah, yeah, play the tough cookie role but I know you think I'm sexy, so just stop fighting it!"

The cheek of the guy! I was so angry I couldn't think of anything to say which only made me angrier!

He laughed again. "You don't have to hide it anymore! I can't stop thinking about you and all the wonderful things we could do together – if you know what I mean..."

"STOP IT! Just STOP IT!" I screamed angrily into the phone.

"*Oooh*, I love it when she gets angry!" he said happily.

That's it! I was going to kill him; I'd spend my life in jail, but I wouldn't be able to control myself! He was just too much.

"You listen, and you listen hard. I'm hanging up now and don't you DARE call me again or come to the office again because I'll have you kicked out. I no longer want anything to do with you! Have you got that?"

"I know you don't mean that sweetcakes. I'll go now, but we will meet again soon."

I slammed the phone down shaking in annoyance and fear. This was definitely not a crush. He was sick.

My heart bongo-drummed into my chest and my palms began to sweat.

Oh my God! Would he show up again? When and where? What would he do? I was shaking all over as parts of *Fatal Attraction* flashed before me. Was the guy a nut? What exactly did he want from me?

Chapter Twenty-Four

As soon as I got home I ran myself a hot bath and poured most of the bottle of bubble bath into it. It was exactly what I needed, the whole bubble-bath-wine-and-candles therapy. I wanted to just bathe in the warmth of the memories of my day with Greg and forget about Mr. Delano and his phone call. I smiled as I thought of Greg... I wasn't in love or lust with him, I just felt a warm glow thinking back to our day together. We had been in a little bubble. Although I'd only known him a day, I felt like I'd known him forever. I definitely didn't want to think about Matt. So I poured myself a glass of wine, took a few candles into the bathroom and was about to light them when the doorbell rang.

Blast! I really didn't want to see anyone right now. I decided to ignore it. I could just say I'd been in my shower and hadn't heard it ring. But then it came again, more insistent this time. Still ignoring it, I began to light my candles.

But then the blaring *zzzzzzzzzing* became un-ignorable as the person, a very rude one at that, held their finger down on the buzzer, a bit like my grandmother but much worse, until I could stand it no longer and rushed to the door.

I opened it to see Vic standing there grinning. She was dressed in a long fuchsia skirt and tight purple top which gave her quite an impressive cleavage and looked really beautiful with her long, wavy blond hair cascading down her back. So I guess she had finally heard about Matt and I...

"I knew you were here and just didn't want to open the door," she chuckled, and she pushed her way past me and into the lounge. I saw with horror that she had bought her three monsters with her. They grinned up at me and rushed in, not one of them saying hello, and I saw their dirty hands and chocolate smeared faces and clothes and I knew that today wasn't one of their good days and that I was in for a hard time. I groaned and closed the door behind them.

Vic turned around dramatically, her waist length blond hair flying around her head like a halo following her movements. She could have been a Victorian heroine or played in one of those Shakespeare plays like Hamlet or Macbeth.

She looked at me with a look of concern and pity.

"You poor, *poor* thing... I *heard*,", she said, emphasizing the 'poor' and 'heard', as she put her hands to her mouth and shook her head in disbelief (she couldn't help being just a little over dramatic sometimes).

"You must be *devastated*." There went the intonation on devastated again. She was just one of those people who really should have been an actress but never was, so every time there is the slightest reason to, she rises to the occasion and puts on an amazing performance.

"Well a bit down of course, but life goes on," I mumbled. I had decided not to tell anyone else about Greg. It was my special secret that only Olivia would know about. I don't think I would even have told her if she hadn't known he'd come home with me.

Just then I heard a splash and ran to the bathroom where I'd completely forgotten about my running bath. I found the three amigos standing on the side of the bath, Christopher with the toilet brush in his hand, Jessie with a candle and Tim with a bottle of scented oil which I kept near the bath, and all about to throw their respective objects into the bath. There was already my beautiful multi-colored scented candle bobbing up and down in the water, thus explaining the splash.

"DON'T YOU DARE!" I said icily, as they all stopped with their objects in midair. The three pair of blue eyes and curly blond locks looked at me for a few seconds, mouths open, then Denis the Menace grinned at me, turned back to the bath, and threw the toilet brush in, which resulted in howls of laughter from the two others, before both the candle and the bottle of scented oil followed suit.

I looked back at Vic, waiting for her to react, as I felt the blood rush to my face in anger, but she just stood there laughing before saying nonchalantly, "Now kids, stop that, Auntie Lucy will get cross". None of them even bothered to turn around to acknowledge their mother but joyfully splashed their hands around in my bubble bath, soaking my bathroom and themselves in the process.

"Aren't they just adorable?" Vic said, turning towards me with a smile. I heaved a sigh of exasperation, stormed to the bath, switched off the taps and unclasped their grubby hands, one by one, off the side of the bath, and screamed angrily, "OUT, G-E-T O-U-T *NOW*!"

They looked rather taken aback as I doubted that Vic ever screamed at them like that. Even I was surprised as I was usually pretty patient with kids but I just wasn't in the mood today! Vic looked a bit stunned herself at first but quickly regained her composure and led her kids out of the bathroom.

"Next time you're staying at home! Mommy's nice and brings you with her to visit Auntie Lucy and that's how you thank me," she scolded them, but without much conviction.

"We didn't even want to come, you made us come because there was no one to look after us!" retorted Jessie.

I let out a snort of laughter as Vic looked at me shaking her head and laughing too. I'm not sure how I survived their visit without strangling all four of them.

They finally left, after Vic had got all the details about our break up and told me not to worry, that she would find me a man.

"Great" I mumbled sarcastically. "Just what I need…"

As I closed the door behind them, I heaved a huge sigh of relief and headed to the bathroom, where I looked at the mess, and decided I just couldn't cope with it right now and a shower would just have to do.

I stayed for hours under the hot water, feeling the tension drain away as the water flowed over me. I fell into bed after watching a bit of TV and dozed off as soon as my head hit the pillow. What a day...

Chapter Twenty-Five

I sat at the dining room table, papers spread out all over the surface as I tried to work out the state of my pitiful finances. I was coming to the sad conclusion that this month, like most months, I would end up being overdrawn. I really should look into getting myself an accountant – one that would take my salary and give me money I needed for groceries and bills and then refuse me any other income! I just didn't know how I could cut my expenses. Maybe I needed to get myself a better paid job – and why not, a more stimulating one while I was at it. I kept thinking how much I loved writing and really thought that I should look into a copywriting course. Even better, if I did do that, I could keep working in an ad agency which I absolutely loved.

My train of thought was interrupted by the sound of the phone ringing. As I picked it up I heard a low, husky American male voice saying, "Howdy darlin' how are ya?"

'Howdy darlin'?' I repeated to myself as my head buzzed trying to figure out who this man could possibly be. Must be someone playing a joke on me. It couldn't possibly be Mr. Delano, he'd never manage a real male voice like that!

"Josh, is that you?" I asked laughing. It had to be a joke.

"Whad'ya mean, Josh? I ain't Josh darlin'! It's me, Rex!" he drawled.

"Rex?" I repeated dumbly, "Ohhh, *Rex*!" I said again as realisation dawned. "Hi! How are you? I'm so sorry but I really didn't realise it was you."

How on earth did he get my number? Would Greg have given it to him? Surely not?

"Seein' as we got along so great an' all the other night, I was thinkin' that maybe I could pick you up and we could go grab a bite to eat. Hows' bout tomorrow night darlin'?"

I was completely lost for words. Didn't often happen but it was definitely happening here. Although I recalled having spoken to him and Greg for a while at the pub, I couldn't for the life of me remember our conversation, and how I had led him to believe that I would be interested in going out with him.

"Umm… how did you get my number Rex?" I asked confused.

"Well, you gave it to me sweetie pie! Took out your Revlon Colourstay-On lipstick, told me all about the wonders of the brand and how it stayed on for hours, then wrote ye' number on me hand you did!" he drawled.

Wrote ye number on me hand you did! I repeated to myself in shock. Oh my God! How many times had I done that during the night? How many phone calls would I be getting from strange men? How many *sweetie pies* and *darlin's* would I have to hear?

"Lucy? Are you there luv?" I heard, and snapped out of my reverie.

I mumbled a weak yes as he carried on, totally unfazed by my less than enthusiastic response so far.

"Soooo… whadda ya think darlin'?"

I had no intention of spending an evening with Rex. I just didn't have the energy. I was really bad at making up excuses and lying, so the truth it had to be.

"I'm sorry Rex, but I've just come out of a long relationship…"

"Yeah, with that Matt fella, I know honeybunch, you

told us about that, you did," he said as my mouth did a bit of yo-yoing to the floor and back. "But, don't you worry your pretty little head, because I'm exactly what you need to help you get over that silly little boyfriend of yours."

"You are?" I said dumbly, before I could stop myself.

"Trust me darlin', us cowboy's know how to treat our women. You know what they say about cowboys?" he asked.

"Uhh… they have big boots?" I answered weakly as he chuckled.

"No, we're *real MEN,* we are. Gggrrr…" he said, making a noise sounding like a dog growling. I shuddered. I realised he was waiting for me to say something. Yuck was the first thing that came to mind actually.

"I have no doubts about that" I replied, thinking it was good to flatter his ego before knocking him down "But really, I'm just not up to it and need some time to myself. I'm sorry."

"Oh well sweetie pie, what can I say? I'm disappointed but I understand," he said slightly downcast. "But take my number and call me if you change your mind you hear?"

As if! I thought inwardly and pretended to be taking down his number as he gave it to me and repeated it to him afterwards. Luckily my short-term memory was better than my long term one! As I hung up, shaking my head still not quite believing the conversation had actually happened, I groaned inwardly. Please God! Don't let me have given my number to anyone else. So much for the wonders of Revlon Colourstay-On lipstick! For once I wish I bought the cheap lipstick that came off on my wine glass!

I quickly typed a text message to Greg.

Never guess who called me up asking me out? REX, the cowboy!! My Lordy Lord! I got the shock of my life when I realised who it was. Apparently I wrote my number on his hand! Did you forget to mention that little detail to me the other day?! ☺

Lucyxxx

Then on second thought, I send a second one;

Do I run the risk of getting a lot more calls from unknown guys who I gave my number out to at the pub? (Note: I am mortified here – groaning really loudly, head in my hands with shame).

I was just starting to doze off when I heard a text come in.

Hey beautiful!

I was sitting in a lunch meeting with these really serious Japanese businessmen when I read your text and without realising it, I burst out laughing. Should have seen the looks they gave me!! Yes, you did go around writing your name and number on the hands of all the men you happened to see. But hey, you might meet someone nice, who knows ☺

Greg xx

Ps. Just joking – it was just Rex ☺

Chapter Twenty-Six

Olivia poked her head into my office looking towards John's office questioningly.

"Is he there?" she whispered.

"No, all clear," I grinned as she came in and sat down, coffee in hand.

"Did you have a good weekend?" she asked.

"Quiet. Went to my Aunt's beach cottage in Grand Bay and spent the weekend lounging around on the beach. And you?"

"Pretty quiet too. Except on Friday night – we went to the Banana Republic, a popular pub in Grand-Bay, with a group of girls from school – Jane, Lynn and Daisy."

"Oh yes, I vaguely remember them. So was it a good night?" I asked.

"Was Ok I guess…" she said looking away.

Something was up.

"What?" she said as I looked at her accusingly.

"You're not telling me something," I said, looking at her intently.

"What do you mean?" she asked, trying to sound nonchalant but failing dismally.

"I just know you're hiding something from me, I can tell."

She looked away again and sighed.

Bad news. It had to be bad news.

"Tell me," I pleaded.

"It's nothing really but you just probably won't like it too much."

"Just spit it out," I said impatiently.

"It's Matt," she said quietly.

"What about him?" I said trying to sound casual as my heart plummeted at break neck speed to the ground as I imagined him making love to a gorgeous long legged model.

"He was there," she said without looking at me.

"And?" I asked in trepidation.

"Well, he wasn't with anyone in particular…" she said as I felt myself relax, like a wave crashing onto the shore. "But he just looked like he was having a great time. He was being the life of the party, making everyone laugh – you know how he can be - and was pretty drunk I think."

Oh.

"See, it's nothing really, but I thought you might take it badly, that's why I didn't want to tell you."

He's having fun…

Without me…

"I knew I shouldn't have told you," she said, as she saw tears in my eyes.

"Don't worry, I'll be fine. It just hurts a bit that's all. If you must know, it's just my ego that's really pissed off – you know, just wanting him to drown in misery, preferably forever, because he's lost me."

"I know…" she said quietly.

"I think I'll just go to the ladies room, clean up my face a bit." I struggled to put a smile on my face, which seemed to have turned to clay.

"Are you going to be Ok?" she asked concerned.

"Of course," I said with a forced smile. "Life goes on. After all, it's rather hypocritical of me to be angry when I had a great time at the Lone Star and ended up with Greg to top it off!"

I turned and walked off towards the bathroom, trying to pick up the pieces of my shattered heart on the way.

He's having fun.

He's happy.

He doesn't love me.

I love him.

Bugger! Bugger! BUGGER!

Of course he has to get on with his life - but I wish he could have stayed miserable for a while longer. It's only been a few weeks after all! Ok, so I'd had a great night out only a few weeks after we broke up but it isn't the same. It just isn't!

It's funny how it's never the same if it's the other party doing the doing. It never feels wrong when we're the ones going out and having fun after the break up, but when it's the other - it's a huge blow to our ego... Another question to add to the 'human relationship' mystery, I thought glumly.

My day at work took forever to end - all I wanted to do was to go home and cry myself to sleep.

As I was taking the last pack of A4 papers out of the closet, I suddenly felt my heart begin to race. I hadn't heard from Mr. Delano since his phone call and I had tried really hard not to think about him, but I couldn't help looking over my shoulder everywhere I went. I was even scared of answering the office phone in case it was him on the other end. I hoped he had found someone else to harass, but deep down I just knew that I hadn't yet seen the last of him...

Chapter Twenty-Seven

The next day I marched into Olivia's office and plopped down on her chair.

"I'm leaving," I said determinedly.

"What, as in now? Did you get a half day leave?" she asked distracted, as she finished typing something.

"No, not as in leaving for the day, I'm leaving my job, and the country too for that matter!" I replied dramatically.

"You're what? But why?" she exclaimed baffled by my sudden outburst.

"I hate secretarial work and must be about the worse secretary ever. I'm messy, completely disorganized, can't remember a thing and hate filing!" I replied morosely.

"Fair enough. I've always known you didn't particularly enjoy the actual work side of your job, but what's that about you leaving the country?"

"The Pope has a more active sex life than I do since I broke up with Matt!" I wailed.

"The Pope never has sex Lucy – you do realise that don't you?" she asked grinning.

"And that's exactly my point – I can't see myself ever having sex again because I still live in the same country as Matt and I'll never get over him this way."

"Don't be ridiculous! Of course you will, it just takes time," she replied "And besides, you've already sort of been with Greg and asked out on a hot date by Mr. Cowboy himself - and that was just two weeks after breaking up with Matt – so of course there's hope."

"No, you don't understand," I wailed, shaking my head. "I won't want anyone else… in case Matt comes back."

"He won't come back Lucy, just face it."

"You're so horrible!" I cried. "How can you say that?"

I felt betrayed by her brutal honesty even though deep down I knew she was right and was only doing it for my good. But right then I felt hurt that she dare say such a thing.

"Because it's probably true…" she said gently. "And being your best friend, I have to tell you these things."

I dropped my head into my hands and mumbled, "I know, I know".

Then suddenly realising I was weakening on my new resolve, I stood up and said "But I'm still leaving!"

"O.K. fine - and where are you planning to go?"

"I have no idea!" I snapped. "Either back home to Australia or otherwise to an exotic location somewhere far, far away"

"If you really think that's the best option for you, then do it. But do me a favour; sleep on it for a few days. No impulsive moves until then," she gently urged me.

I thought about it for a moment and decided that I could do that despite being convinced that I wouldn't change my mind.

"Fine, one week," I said firmly, as I turned and walked out her office.

One week before I hand in my resignation and buy my ticket to Australia or some unknown destination... I felt happy and sad at the same time.

I'd be sad leaving my job (well the social side of it), my friends and my life in general. It would also be horrible to be so far from Matt... but it would do me a world of good too. Even if he does come back, I can't take him back as it's a hopeless situation. It's a no-win situation for me and I have to get away before it tears me apart.

Six days later I was still hesitating whether I should hand in my resignation the following day or not ... I sat in front of the TV not listening to a word that was being said, deep in thought on the pros and cons of staying or leaving. I still couldn't handle the thought of going thousands of miles away from Matt - I wanted to stay close by, just in case... I scolded myself for thinking that, but I just couldn't help it. I also thought of my job and realised that I loved working at Trends. It was an ideal, laid back, jeans and t-shirt sort of job which was exactly me as I hated wearing suits and getting all dressed up like Olivia did every day. Only problem was that secretarial work was really not my thing. Maybe a change would be an opportunity for me to figure out what I wanted to do with my life, to look into Copywriting courses or anything else related to advertising or writing.

I was snapped out of my reverie when the phone began to ring.

"Hi Lucy, its Vic, just ringing to see how you are?" she said, and listened patiently as I told her. Then, to my surprise, she suddenly interrupted to exclaim,

"I've found the perfect guy for you! He's a friend of ours from England who's been living here for a few months now. I've told him all about you and he'd love to ask you out to dinner one night. I said you'd be delighted, but thought I'd better check with you first."

"You did *WHAT*?" I screamed down the phone. "Do you mean you've set me up on a date without asking me if I was Ok about it?"

I was flabbergasted at her cheek – there's nothing I hate more than the idea of a blind date.

"Hold on to your horses! I told him I'd see if it was Ok with you first and that's what I'm doing! So… can I say yes?" she asked, barely able to contain her excitement.

"I don't know. Tell me more about him first," I replied, not at all convinced.

"He's really cute – brown hair, slightly curly with a little fringe falling into his eyes, very dark brown eyes, gorgeous angular cheekbones, huge biceps, oh, and to top it off, he has the cutest dimples when he smiles."

"Yeah… well, if he's so gorgeous why doesn't he have a girlfriend then?" I asked skeptically.

"He's in-between relationships at the moment and besides, he's only been here a few months."

"How old is he?" I queried.

"Umm… I'm not sure, but I'd say in his early thirties."

"Didn't you ask him?" I asked, doubtfully.

"Course not! It would have been a bit rude wouldn't it?" she answered tartly. I burst out laughing because when it comes to asking indiscreet questions, Vic was a pro.

"What does he do for a living?" I pursued my inquisition.

"He's a Marketing Manager in an Events company." Damn, he actually did sound normal enough. How was I going to get out of this?

"So???" she asked, clearly burning with impatience. "What do I tell him?"

I thought for a minute. This was really not me. What if we didn't have a thing in common and spent the whole dinner talking about the weather or our food?

I wasn't sure how much I wanted to risk putting myself in that situation and, with Vic and her exaggerations; I didn't trust her descriptions of him too much. Oh well, if Vic and Sam knew him at least it was safe. And what did I have to lose anyway? I thought back to Olivia telling me how Matt was having a great time. Well stuff him! If he didn't care, then I wouldn't either, I decided. I'd show him that I could find someone else.

"Ok, I'll do it," I said resolutely.

"YES!" she screamed in delight down the phone, making me hold the receiver away from my ear for fear of losing all auditory senses. "He'll pick you up at eight tomorrow night!" she said gleefully.

"B-But…" I stuttered, feeling panic rise to my throat, already regretting my decision. "You told me you hadn't confirmed it with him yet."

"Well I lied!" she said. "I've already given him your number!"

"I can't believe you!" I cried, annoyed. "And what if I had said no?"

"I just knew you'd end up agreeing – after all I'm just the greatest negotiator ever!" she said, completely unperturbed by my irritation.

I couldn't help grinning and then heard screams in the background, sounding like someone was trying to strangle a pig.

"What's going on there?" I asked amused but a bit worried at the same time.

"Oh, nothing much, just the kids," she replied casually. "I guess I should just go and check it out though. Knock him dead Lucy – don't forget to call me to tell me all!" she said shouting a barely audible goodbye into the phone. I walked back to my room in a daze.

I couldn't believe her. I couldn't believe myself! I was going on a blind date! I didn't even know what he sounded like... Oh shit! I didn't even know the guy's name!

I raced to the phone just as it started ringing.

"Hello?" I answered.

"JAKE!" I managed to make out over a lot of howling and screaming. "His name's JAKE," Vic screamed into the phone.

Ok, so I now knew his name and kind of what he looked like. Oh my goodness, what the hell had I got myself into this time? It was always like that with Vic – when we were teenagers she always made me agree to do stupid things, like running away from school at lunch time, sneaking away to go meet our friends when we were meant to be studying and so on and so forth. I always ended up getting into trouble while she conned her way out of every situation. It was so annoying, and here we were at twenty-six years old and she could still wrap me around her little finger in no time.

Suddenly I bolted up and ran to the phone again. There was no way I was going to let a stranger come to my door. I had to stop Vic before she gave him my address. The phone rang and rang. I knew she was there and that she only answered the phone if or when she could be bothered, otherwise she let it ring. It wasn't worth trying her mobile either as it was always off. I was determined to talk to her so I waited and waited, filing my nails, the little I had managed to let grow. I was down to my second to last toenail and jumped in surprise as I heard Vic's voice.

"Where the hell have you been? I've been waiting for ages you to pick up the damn phone!" I barked down the line.

"Oh really?" she answered, unfazed as usual. "Must say the kids were making quite a noise playing cowboy and Indians around the house, so I didn't hear it till now."

"Have you rung him yet?" I blurted out.

"Why? Are you planning to chicken out? I won't let you, you know," she said in a no-nonsense voice.

"I just wanted to know if you've rung him or not because I don't want you to tell him where I live. After all, I don't even know the guy. I prefer to go and meet him somewhere."

"Fair enough. So where do you want to meet him? Oh I know! How about the Lover's Nest?"

"Ha-ha! Aren't you hilarious!" I said sarcastically.

"But why? It's so romantic there, with candles on each table, dimly lit rooms, love songs played on the piano, a big open fireplace…"

"Hold it right there! I don't want to go there for exactly all the reasons you've just stated! This is a blind date I'm going on, not a romantic date. If we go there I might as well just stick a big "I'm desperate for love" sticker on my forehead!"

"Ok fine," she said resignedly. "I don't happen to agree with you, but I know you won't change your mind. So where then?"

We tried finding suitable restaurants, Vic coming up with more ridiculous suggestions in the likes of the

Lover's Nest whereas I on the other hand was suggesting the most casual places, such as Mc Donald's, Pizza Hut or Burger King!! I finally remembered a little Italian Restaurant, Il Ciao, ten minutes away from my house, which served delicious food and was always packed. At least there was no way it would be romantic and if we didn't have anything to say to each other, at least we'd have lots of people around to stare at or eavesdrop on their conversations! Vic was not impressed by my choice.

"Il Ciao!" she wailed. "But it's so loud and always packed there!"

"Exactly!" I grinned wickedly, feeling better. "It's perfect! Tell him to meet me there at 8pm!"

"Fine! But I think it's a terrible choice – you'll put him off before he even gets to see you."

"Well tough! Il Ciao or ciao Jake and the whole blind date thing, Ok?" I said refusing to give in this time.

"Ok, you win – Il Ciao 8 o'clock it is."

Well I guess that settled my decision to leave just yet! I couldn't possibly go now, I had to at least stick around some more to see what Jake was like, I thought. I realised that I felt relieved. I hadn't really wanted to leave. Maybe it would have been a good thing in a way, but then again, I didn't want to leave my whole life, just to get over Matt.

I felt butterflies fluttering in my stomach. I was so nervous. I'd never been on a blind date before. Wouldn't it be a nightmare if he was really boring or worse still, what if he was a real sleaze bag? I slipped into bed and picked up my book to try and take my mind off the whole thing. But it was no use, I re-read the same lines and pages over and over again as I worried about what I would wear, how I would do my hair, what I could talk about, how I would get out if things were too bad.

I finally fell into a fitful sleep dreaming that I had walked into Il Ciao as naked as an earthworm, except for a pair of white socks and white sports shoes.

Chapter Twenty-Eight

Friday night arrived before I knew it and the butterflies hadn't left my stomach since Vic's phone call. I felt sick with nerves as I stood in front of my cupboard staring blankly at the mess inside.

I decided to wear something casual which would make me look good but not like I was trying too hard. I finally settled on a pair of navy pants, which hugged my legs flatteringly, and a white V-necked blouse which V-d down quite low towards my cleavage - or my lack of cleavage would be more appropriate, I sadly reminded myself, as I looked in the mirror – but then again, nothing a push-up bra couldn't fix! It would just have to do. After carefully applying my dark blue eyeliner, I tried to put on the same colour mascara I had bought at a 'two for the price of one' sale. The only problem was that I was not a mascara user and was hopeless at applying it to my lashes. I managed to stick the tube into my eye, leaving a huge blob just below my right eye, and making my eyes water and my eyeliner run!

Oh no! I looked a sight. Now I'd show up with red eyes, just great, he'd take me for a drug addict or something. Hang on a minute! I stopped myself in surprise. Did I actually want to impress the guy? Did I really care what he thought of me? Of course not, I scolded myself, as I removed the whole lot off my eyes and left just a touch of lipstick. It was now five to eight and I was late!

I arrived at the restaurant entrance at five past eight and found that the parking was full. I smiled, pleased to see that the restaurant was packed. I reversed back out onto the street and lost another five minutes trying to find a spot to leave my car.

I burst through the restaurant door and was met by the delicious smell of pizza. My stomach rumbled loudly. *Please* don't do that to me in front of him, I silently begged it. I looked around the crowded room trying to spot a man sitting alone and fitting Jake's description. It sure was a loud place, I realised, as I took in the hum of voices and laughter in the restaurant and the hustle and bustle of waiters flying past with trays laid with lasagnas, pizzas and pastas. They smelt divine and my mouth began to water. As a waiter moved away from my line of vision, I spotted a tall, dark haired man sitting on his own slightly to my right. I looked around some more and not seeing any other man sitting on his own, decided that it had to be him.

My heart somersaulting wildly, butterflies still going strong, I walked up to him, chin up, attempting not to show how nervous I was. I quickly sat down opposite him as I didn't want people to stare at me. As he looked up from his menu, I flashed him my friendliest smile, trying hard to stop myself from blushing.

"Hi!" I said cheerfully, "So we finally meet!" and I held out my hand for him to shake. I was surprised to see that instead of looking happy to see me, he was in fact frowning and looking very confused.

"Hello?" he asked questioningly, as he limply shook my hand.

"Lucy - I'm Lucy," I replied, helping him out and still smiling brightly - although I felt that he could act a bit more enthusiastic about meeting me!

"Lucy?" he looked at me, still frowning. "I'm sorry, but do I know you?"

What a stupid question to ask, of course he didn't know me, that's what blind dates were about surely?!

"Well only by name of course," I said, my sense of unease increasing by the second.

"Oh, I'm sorry, I'm not very good with names," he answered, his brow creasing.

"Don't worry, I'm pretty bad myself," I said, wondering why he still looked confused.

"You're probably waiting for Louise," he replied, his brow suddenly clearing. "She's just gone to the ladies room, she won't be long."

"Louise?" I said bewildered. I was the confused one now. Was that why he looked a bit uncomfortable? He'd brought another girl on our blind date and didn't know how I'd react?

"Louise - my girlfriend," he added helpfully, looking at me as if to check my reaction. Oh my goodness, this was so weird! Asking someone out on a blind date when you already have a girlfriend and then actually bringing your girlfriend with you on the blind date!! What type of person had Vic set me up with?!

"Your girlfriend?" I repeated dumbly. I gazed into his aqua blue eyes, and thought 'the dirty bugger'. Then suddenly I felt something tugging at the back of my mind. What was it? I looked at him as he glanced towards the ladies room, obviously impatient for Louise to return. As he turned back towards me, it hit me. He had aqua blue eyes - and Vic had definitely told me that Jake's eyes were very dark! And I now remembered she'd mentioned something about sexy dimples. This man in front of me had no dimples whatsoever, apart from on his forehead.

OH MY GOD! My hand flew in front of my mouth. It wasn't Jake I was coming on to!

I felt myself burning up in embarrassment as I stared at him. "You're not Jake are you?" I finally managed to summon up the courage to ask.

"Jake? Who's Jake? No, I'm David Mc Ines," he replied impatiently.

I stood up slowly as he looked at me baffled.

"This is so embarrassing," I said, dying of shame. "I'm so sorry, but I thought you were someone else – please forgive me for bothering you," and I turned and ran out the restaurant, tail between my legs.

Oh my goodness! It was so bloody typical of me to get myself into messes like these! I just wanted to curl up and die. But then I looked back towards the crowded room and realised that there was a Jake somewhere in there, and that I couldn't stand him up in front of all those people. With a bravado I didn't know I possessed, I headed back inside, but this time I stopped a waiter and asked if there was a tall, dark haired man, with dimples, sitting alone somewhere.

He grinned at me. "Yep sure is. Well the tall, dark haired bit I'm sure about, but I must admit I didn't quite notice whether he had dimples when he smiled."

I grinned back in relief.

"If he's the gentleman you're looking for, he sure will be glad to see you, Miss. He's been looking at his watch every few minutes for the last fifteen minutes."

He directed me to a table on the far end corner of the room. I made my way to a man I hoped was Jake, and was relieved to see a pair of gorgeous dimples stand up to greet me.

Of course! I muttered under my breath. I now remembered Vic telling me that she'd showed him a photograph of me. I should have known it wasn't that David guy when he didn't recognize me! You're such an idiot Lucy! I scolded myself.

I still felt hot with humiliation as I thought of the David incident and I glanced back nervously towards his table, which, to my relief, was obscured by a big pillar. Thank you God, I said in a silent prayer. At least I knew Jake hadn't witnessed my 'faux pas'.

And just then, my foot knocked into one of the chairs

and I felt myself starting to fly through the air. Jake's dimpled smile quickly turned into a very distinct "O" as he leapt forward to catch me before I ended up swat on the floor. Not wanting to appear to be the swooning type, I found some hidden strength and righted myself just an inch before Jake's open arms.

"You must be Lucy," he said, smiling warmly at me as I tried to pull myself together and stop myself from running out the door.

"Here," he said, pulling my chair out for me. "Have a seat."

His amused gaze didn't leave my face as I sat down. "Do you always make such spectacular entrances?"

I felt my face burn again, but took courage when I saw how genuine his smile was and those dimples… and smiled awkwardly back.

"Yes…" I answered, nodding. "Spectacular entrances are definitively one of my specialties. You know, tripping over chairs, slipping on wet floors, slamming head on into glass doors… well just your average sort of thing!" I grinned up at him as he laughed, making me relax.

We ordered some wine and immediately fell into a comfortable chatter.

I really need not have worried about conversation as he put me at ease and talked non-stop. Usually I liked doing some of the talking, but tonight I was just relieved that one of us was talking and that we were actually having a good time.

"Vic tells me you're from England?" I asked.

"Sure am. An Englishman through and through."

He told me about his family and friends and how he'd travelled a lot and been all over Europe, to Asia and Australia. He shared amusing anecdotes of people he'd met and places he'd been to. I loved travelling, and his stories kept me enthralled. Then he began asking me all about myself, where I worked, about my family. He was a great listener and I found myself easily opening up to him. Suddenly we realised the restaurant was closing and that it was time for us to leave.

"Thanks for a great evening, Lucy. I really enjoyed it and would love to see you again if you agree."

"I'd like that Jake," I replied shyly.

"I'll call you soon," Jake said smiling. "Don't forget to work on your spectacular entrance for our next date!" he added, chuckling as I butted him playfully with my elbow.

We walked out towards my car in companionable silence, enjoying the fresh air and calm night after the stuffiness and noise of the restaurant. He was really relaxing to be with.

He left me with a peck on the cheek.

I was surprised to realise that I hadn't thought much about Matt tonight, just a few things Jake had said which I compared to Matt or thought 'if Matt had told that story it would have been much funnier' or 'Matt would definitely have had dessert and probably shared half of mine too'. But all in all, it had been a great evening and once again it gave me hope that I would eventually be able to get over Matt. It's true that I found it hard to imagine kissing him because he wasn't Matt, but I knew time would heal all that. It was just so nice to have spent a fun evening with a nice guy.

As I started to fall asleep that night, I wondered if he would actually call me…

Chapter Twenty-Nine

I spent the rest of the weekend with a grin superglued to my face, and there was just no way to make it go away. I hummed and whistled and even found myself skipping around my apartment! I was in total Jake-cloud land. I had a permanent image of his gorgeous dimples in front of me whether my eyes were open or closed. I even found myself cleaning up my apartment, scrubbing the bathroom floor and doing the dishes. Nothing fazed me. I was on a high and it felt wonderful.

I couldn't remember how long it had been since I'd felt this way. I'd been with Matt for more than four years so it had sure been a long time… and it felt bloody marvelous. Unfortunately as soon as the word Matt came into my mind, my bubble would burst, but I determinedly pushed those thoughts away and went back to my Jake bubble.

After lunch, Vic rang to see how the date had gone. I told her all about it, leaving out all the embarrassing bits as I knew the whole town would learn about it if I told her. She squealed in delight.

"See, I told you I'd find you someone! I just knew he was perfect for you. I just *feel* these things..." she said theatrically.

I laughed, not bothering to contradict her and if she wanted to believe she was a match-maker sent from heaven, I didn't want to spoil her fun. I was too grateful to her for that.

I spent the weekend contentedly lying around, watching TV and day dreaming. Rachel rang up to invite me to the movies but I just didn't feel like seeing anyone else. I was also scared of bumping into Matt and feeling miserable all over again. Tash was away at a training seminar and I decided to wait until Monday to tell her about Jake.

On Monday, I was up at the crack of dawn, excited to be up and I was rearing to go to work. An early rise was a once in a blue moon situation; it happened about as often as Haley's Comet or cow's jumping over the moon! At half past seven I was dressed and ready to go except that it was way too early to go to work as the office would still be closed. My grin was still glued on and I sat down on my verandah happily gazing out at the grey rooftops and thinking how wonderful life was.

It had been a very long time since I had driven to work completely relaxed and on time. It felt like it was the first time I was driving along these roads, I thought, as I admired the never ending sugar cane fields stretching far inland and the Moka mountain ranges in the background, majestic and glorious. Usually, it was all one big blur at the speed I drove at!

I arrived at the office at eight o'clock on the dot and was met by three pair of tonsils belonging to the very shocked faces of Yann, Andrew and Léa, who were always there at eight and knew that I never, ever arrived on time and never, ever arrived *before* the regulated time of eight thirty.

"Hi!" I said cheerfully. "Isn't it the most beautiful day?" and was met by three frowns joining the tonsils. In fact the sky was very grey and looked as if it would rain at any minute! I hopped along to my office, leaving the three of them still standing there trying to work out if they were actually awake or whether they had just been dreaming. I switched on my computer, whistling quietly. Olivia arrived at 8.20am and the look on her face when she saw me there sitting at my desk, computer switched on, was priceless.

"What the…" she said laughing and shaking her head in utter disbelief.

"I'm in lust…" I said batting my eyelids as I laughed.

"Lust?" she repeated puzzled, and just as I was about to explain, a flash of recollection came across her face and she grinned.

"*Ooh*! Of course - the blind date. Tell me about him!" she said as she grabbed a chair and sat down opposite me.

"Well… he's gorgeous, sweet, smart, gorgeous, gorgeous and oh, did I mention that he's gorgeous?" I grinned. "Seriously, he's tall, dark haired with very dark brown eyes, looks like he goes to the gym every day and he has gorgeous dimples.

He's from England, has 2 sisters and is over in Mauritius on a 1 year contract for an Events Management company."

"That's great Lucy!"

I went on to tell her all about the date, the David incident and all. The latter had her doubled over in laughter and even I couldn't help laughing although just thinking about it made me blush bright red.

"So are you seeing him again?" she asked.

"Who, David or Jake?" I asked chuckling. "I hope so. He's got my number and said he would ring, so I'll give him till Wednesday before I start to worry."

I went about whistling and smiling, happily typing away, answering the phone with joviality and being utterly charming. John was left speechless by my unusual behavior and I caught him staring at me a few times, frowning or shaking his head.

The next day, I was still feeling as buoyant as ever and working happily at my desk when the phone rang. I jumped and nervously picked it up, thinking it might be him. It was Olivia. She had been at a training seminar all morning.

"Can you come and meet me at Trianon Shopping Centre for lunch?" she asked.

"Yes sure, at what time? And can I ask why?"

"In fifteen minutes at the entrance of the food mall, Ok?" she answered, ignoring my question.

I was about to say goodbye when she blurted out excitedly, "He sent me his photo!"

A photo? Who sent her a photo and of what? I wondered. Then suddenly it dawned on me; Pierre!

Of course! Oh wow! Finally a photo to quell our curiosity. I wondered if Olivia had been disappointed after having had her own mental picture of him for the last few months... I finished off the letter I was typing, took my bag and left. Ten minutes later I pulled into the shopping centre, parked my car and headed to the little snack bar. Olivia was already there drinking a diet coke, gazing at what looked like a piece of paper but was probably Pierre's photo.

"So?" I said as I sat down opposite her. She jumped up in surprise then squealed excitedly; "Look! Look! Look!" and she passed me the photo.

I gazed at a friendly looking face, big brown eyes, blond hair, long angular features and a lovely warm smile. He looked older than I had expected but was definitely good looking.

"Wow!" I said grinning at her and handing her back the photo.

"I know..." she said gazing at it dreamily. "I'm pretty impressed myself. He doesn't look like I imagined him to look, but he's pretty cute."

"So you're not disappointed then?" I asked, curious.

"No..." she said pensively. "It's like dreaming of a Mars bar but ending up with a Snickers bar instead."

I nodded and smiled at her analogy. Being an ardent chocoholic, I knew exactly what she meant.

"So now what?" I asked, intrigued.

"Good question," she replied. "He wants me to come over to Paris to meet him."

I stared at her in disbelief. I really hadn't realised how far this thing had gone. She smiled sheepishly at my shocked face, but said nothing, waiting for me to comment.

"And?" I asked once I'd recovered.

She put her head in her hands, then looked up at me. "One minute I'm so excited I could scream it over the rooftops, the next minute I'm so terrified I could pee in my pants!"

"Just keep telling yourself that there are no strings attached," I said trying to comfort her. "No one is going to force you to stay in Paris if you want to leave. Really, you have nothing to lose – at least you'll finally know if this thing is worth getting involved in or not."

"I know, I know," she said wearily, obviously having thought about it from all angles.

"But it's still so bloody scary. What if he's a real nutter? What if we don't have anything to say to each other? What if we're sexually incompatible?"

"Only way to find out – go to Paris and meet him!"

Chapter Thirty

Tuesday night arrived with no word from Jake. I was now worried. Ok, so I had decided that I wouldn't worry until Wednesday, but it was already Tuesday night for goodness sake! Why wasn't he calling me damn it?! We'd had a great time at dinner, hadn't we? I had been charming company, if I do say so myself, and I felt sure that he had enjoyed the evening as much as I had. Had I gotten the wrong vibes then? Maybe it was too long ago that I was last in this situation. I decided to ask Greg, and he texted back straight away.

Lucy,
Of course it's not a bad sign!
He probably just doesn't want appear too keen and scare you off.
Relax woman! And remember, you're smart, beautiful and funny – why wouldn't he want to ring you ☺
Greg xxx

Despite Greg's reassurance, I didn't manage to get to sleep, thinking alternatively of Matt and Jake and basically just feeling really restless. So I was not in a good mood as I made my way to the office the next morning. I felt ridiculous about my stupid reaction towards the fact that he hadn't yet rung. I thought my behavior was childish and pathetic and I hated myself for it. I was so uncool! It wasn't as though I was in love with the guy anyway - I realised that it had more to do with my ego needing to be reassured after Matt not wanting me.

I spent all morning snapping at anyone who dared come my way, like a scary Doberman guard dog, making even Olivia give up and leave me to my bad mood. Just before lunch my phone rang and I answered rudely "Yeah".

"Lucy? Is that you?" I heard a familiar and cheerful voice say, and my heart boomeranged around my chest before settling back in its place.

Damn! I couldn't let him think I was that rude.

I put my hand on the phone and using a gravelly voice said; "No, I'll just get her for you."

I waited two seconds before saying a cheerful, "Hi! Lucy here."

"Hi, it's me Jake," he said warmly.

"Jake! Hi, what a surprise! I didn't expect to hear from you so soon." Liar, liar pants on fire! I blushed at my blatant lie.

"Who was that girl who took your phone? Not very polite is she?"

"Oh, that's umm… Mildred," I improvised lamely. "She's, umm... a temp helping out for a week. Yeah she's not very professional; I keep having to tell her off. I'll have another word with her when I hang up." I blushed some more as I continued to lie. What was happening to me?

"So, how are you?" I said, desperate to change the subject.

"Good. I've been wanting to call you since Monday, but didn't want to appear over keen."

I grinned and almost burst out laughing, thinking of Greg's text message. "You should have called - I would have liked that…" I said using a flirty voice. I just hoped John wouldn't choose now to walk in.

"So, do you want to come to the movies with me tonight?" he asked tentatively.

"I'd love to," I said, smiling into the phone.

He sounded relieved. "Wow, that's great. Do you want me to pick you up or would you rather meet me there?"

"If you'd like to pick me up that would be great."

My bad mood had evaporated and I now had a cat that ate the mouse grin. I raced to Olivia's office to fill her in. She shook her head at the huge smile on my face. "You're a deeply hormonally unbalanced woman," she laughed.

By the time we arrived at the movies it had already started – yes, I had been late again - and we rushed to buy some popcorn and cokes before heading into the movie.

As we made our way up the stairs behind the usher, I saw a few familiar faces, but preferred to concentrate on the little round light indicating the stairs. I could just see myself sprawled out on the steps, popcorn and coke gone flying and everyone looking at me laughing at my fate.

Being Mauritius, everyone around the island would know about it by eight o'clock tomorrow morning, and the story would probably end up being that I had fallen and broken my arm and both my legs as well as my nose. Mauritians love to gossip and exaggerate everything they heard.

We finally reached a row half way from the top on the right hand aisle and Jake gallantly let me go in first. I muttered several 'excuse me's' and stepped on numerous toes before reaching our seats, where I gratefully flopped down like a big Labrador, settling my size 12 butt comfortably into the seat.

I organised my popcorn and coke and was just about to turn my attention to the film when I heard a very familiar voice whispering hello into my ear. I felt goose bumps rising from the very tips of my toes to the very top of my head, as I turned abruptly to my left. I had to be dreaming. My heart did a triple somersault in the air, flew into a row of cartwheels then spluttered to the floor.

Matt was sitting next to me!

Chapter Thirty-One

OH-MY-GOD!

Here I was at the movies on my first real date with Jake and my ex-boyfriend was sitting next to me!! I really should buy a lottery ticket tonight, I thought! I mean what were the chances of this happening? I picked my eyes up from around the floor somewhere and just stared at Matt, dumbstruck.

As I snapped out of my daze I realised that he looked as surprised as I was. I muttered a quick greeting before turning my eyes back to the screen.

How was I going to survive one and a half hours sitting with Matt by my side! There was no way I would be able to concentrate on the movie. My mind was racing. Had he come with a girl? Damn, can't see, I muttered to myself as I tried glancing past him. I couldn't look without it being obvious, so after two failed attempts while picking up and putting down my coke and popcorn – three times in two minutes, hardly suspicious of course – I gave up. I stole another glance his way and saw him staring at me. I settled back, trying my best to follow the film, but bolted when I felt his breath in my ear again, "Are you going out with him?"

"It's none of your business!" I replied curtly, before turning back to the screen not allowing myself the time to see the expression on his face. My heart was on a roll, heavy metal concert style and there seemed to be no way of stopping it. I gave up trying.

I forced myself to concentrate on the film and watched with pleasure as Brad Pitt started undressing and we got a full view of his sexy butt. I unconsciously leant to the side. "Have you ever seen such a cute butt? I mean EVER?" I whispered.

"Not really into male butt's myself, but I'll take your word for it," Matt's amused voice replied in my ear.

Oh my God! I had leant over towards him instead of Jake. I gave him an evil glare, which broadened his smile some more as he turned back to the screen.

Oh no! This was really a nightmare.

I glanced the other way at Jake wondering whether he had witnessed all this, and saw him looking at me curiously.

"Is he a friend of yours?" he asked curiously.

"Um, I guess you could say that…" I mumbled feeling embarrassed. "It's Matt."

His eyes widened in surprise. "Matt? As in your Matt?"

I nodded, not wanting him to see the turmoil of emotions in my eyes at the mention of hearing '*your* Matt'. Before I realised what was going in, Jake had leaned over me and had extended his hand to shake Matt's.

"Hi, I'm Jake. It's nice to meet you."

If I wasn't so shocked I would have burst out laughing at the surprise on Matt's face. He quickly regained his composure, shook Jake's hand and smiled.

"Nice to meet you too, Jake."

Jake smiled before settling back down to watch the movie as if nothing had just happened. I discreetly glanced sideways at Matt to see what he was doing but he seemed engrossed in the movie too.

I still couldn't concentrate, and just wanted to scream with frustration. I needed to get out of here. I nudged Jake and told him I was going to the ladies room and not looking towards Matt, I hopped over the other people, not caring that everyone was probably staring at me. I went outside and dialed Olivia's number on my mobile phone. She'd better answer, I muttered to myself. She just had to.

"Lucy? Hi!" I finally heard her answer. "Aren't you meant to be out with Jake tonight?"

"I am. We're at the movies."

"So what the hell are you doing calling me?"

"Matt's here," I whispered.

"What do you mean 'Matt's here'? As in, here with you right now?"

"Matt is watching the same movie as us…"

"So? Lucy, it's a free country and Mauritius is tiny, you know that."

"He's sitting *next to me*!!" I screeched.

"Next to you?! What the hell do you mean?" she exclaimed in surprise.

"Yes, he's sitting on my left side and Jake on my right!" I exclaimed in total despair.

"*What?*"

"You heard me!" I cried impatiently.

"How? Why? What the…" she asked, confused.

"We arrived late and were ushered into a row. I couldn't see anything and it was only after we sat down that Matt said hi. I thought I'd die right then!"

"And Jake?"

"Well at first he didn't know, but then when I spoke to Matt by mistake he noticed and asked me who it was, so I told him."

"Oh my god! What did he do?"

"He leaned over me and introduced himself to Matt then calmly went back to watching the movie!!"

"You're joking! What about Matt?" she exclaimed.

"Well he just looked kind of amused by the situation. Just smiled and said hi back."

She burst out laughing as I fumed at her.

"Thanks for nothing Olivia! It's not funny at all. I'm going crazy here!" I wailed.

"I'm sorry, but you have to admit that it's a pretty amazing situation you're in."

"It's awful…" I groaned in despair.

"I have to go, but honestly, don't worry about it. Just ignore Matt and the movie's almost finished anyway."

I glanced at my watch and there was in fact only 45 minutes left! Almost finished - yeah right. I said goodbye and heaved a huge sigh as I walked back into the movie. My mouth fell open in shock as I saw that Jake and Matt were leaning over my empty seat whispering away and laughing at something Matt had just said. They looked up at me and smiled, settling back into their seats as I sat back down. I returned Jake's smile and ignored Matt's.

"You look angry?" Matt whispered into my ear two seconds later.

"Leave me alone!" I whispered angrily, not wanting Jake to hear.

He chuckled but turned back to the film. I glanced at Jake but he just looked at me and smiled. A few minutes later I felt shivers all through my body as Matt's breath once again caressed my neck as he whispered in my ear, "Why aren't you holding his hand?"

"Because I don't want to!" I shot back, not even bothering to look at him.

"Hold mine then," he said smiling, as he discreetly moved his hand across the armrest towards mine, which was firmly in my lap.

"STOP THAT!" I hissed through clenched teeth.

Jake turned towards me, looking first at me then at Matt.

"Is everything Ok?" he whispered in my ear.

"Sure, don't worry about it. Matt just gets on my nerves," I answered, forcing a smile.

"Do you want to swap seats with me?" he asked kindly.

I didn't want to give Matt the satisfaction of knowing he had made me change seats.

"Don't worry, it's fine. But thanks," I smiled back trying to reassure him.

He smiled down at me and squeezed my hand.

"Ok, if you're sure. Will you excuse me for a minute, I just need to use the gents' room," he said smiling and getting up.

I had no idea what the film was about and couldn't concentrate on anything except Matt's presence next to me.

"Will you come to a movie with me one day?" he asked, looking at me.

"Well, aren't we already watching a movie together right now?" I replied sarcastically.

"No, I mean if I officially invite you," he said seriously.

I stared at him in disbelief, not even able to answer. He rolled his eyes upwards and raised his hand in surrender, but I don't know if I imagined that he looked a bit sad before he once again focused on the screen. I was so confused. I felt like screaming. Feeling as if I was on the verge of a nervous breakdown, I decided to stop acting like I didn't care even if it made him see how much I really still did. I looked towards him. He obviously felt my eyes on him as he turned his eyes towards me, questioningly.

"Matt, please stop playing games with me…" I whispered, in a plea.

He looked up at me, and our eyes met for a few seconds. He didn't say anything and turned back to the movie. Five more unending minutes passed before I felt him lean towards me again.

"I'm sorry Luce... It's just… I wasn't expecting to see you here tonight, let alone be sitting next to you," he started, and then stopped, looking anguished. "… let's just say that you have no idea how much I'd love to be able to take you to a movie and hold your hand. And I guess teasing you and trying to make a joke of it is the only way I knew how to deal with it."

My eyes opened wide in disbelief as he looked at me for a second. Suddenly he grasped my hand for a second, squeezed it gently and stood up.

"Bye Luce," he said quietly, as he turned and walked out the cinema, leaving me in complete turmoil.

"I just saw Matt leaving. Is everything Ok?" Jake asked when he returned.

"Yes, fine," I answered, and forced a smile, not knowing what else to do or say.

As we headed out of the movie theatre, Jake said with a grin, "Well, that was a bit awkward for a first date, huh?"

"Sure was!" I replied, once again forcing myself to smile.

"He seems like a nice guy though."

"He is. You would probably get along great with him actually," I said, really smiling this time, knowing that it was true.

There was no sign of Matt anywhere, but I spotted Josh and Alex who asked me if I'd seen him as they had organised to meet him here but had arrived late and so hadn't ended up catching up with him. I guess that explained why Matt was sitting alone!

I told them that I had in fact seen him but that he had left the movie early. They were a bit surprised but I didn't give them time to press me with more questions and turned back and went looking for Jake who was talking to a colleague of his.

Jake and I went to the steak house next to the cinema and ordered wine. Boy did I need a drink! The evening was a bit of a blur for me after that, and I couldn't really seem to concentrate on anything. Jake sensed that I was troubled and was kind enough to ignore it and let me be. He did most of the talking, trying to change my mood, and I tried really hard, but I wasn't being me and he could tell. I was sad that our first date had not gone as well as it could and should have done. I really hoped he'd give me a chance to make it up to him…

Chapter Thirty-Two

I woke up thinking that it had all been a bad dream and groaned into my pillow when reality set in. My heart ached for Matt. Seeing him again had turned me inside out once more. It was so hard to let go. He was so much a part of me. But then I thought of Jake and how kind and thoughtful he was. He had hugged me before leaving the previous night, reassuring me that he understood how hard it must have been for me at the movies and that he would have felt the same way if he had been in my shoes. He had told me not to be too hard on myself.

"Next time we go out, things will be definitely be better," he had said. I was really glad that there would be a next time. I felt so relaxed in his company and knew that if I gave myself the chance, he was someone I could end up falling for.

I was so tired of all these feelings wreaking havoc inside my heart. And it was not helped when my aunt called me at work to tell me that my grandmother was in hospital. My heart thumped as all the worst case scenarios raced through my mind. I was on the verge of tears but she reassured me that she had simply been admitted for some tests relating to a kidney problem. She had a small infection and they wanted to be sure that things wouldn't deteriorate so were keeping her there for the night. I was so relieved. My grandmother was my only close relative here and she was so much a part of my life that I couldn't imagine it without her.

I stopped at the hospital after work to see her. I took the lift up and began looking for room 103. I didn't have to look too long as before even reaching the corridor leading to the room, I heard my grandmother's voice angrily saying, *"No...WHAT are you DOING? DON'T do that! Get away from me!"*

Then two seconds of silence and another screech, *"Panadol? No! I will NOT take Panadol! It's been seventy six years that I haven't taken Panadol; don't think you'll make me start now!"*

A silence followed where the doctor or nurse was obviously trying to explain the use to her and then her angry voice said, *"Fever schfever, I'm perfectly well! Wait! What are you doing now?"* I walked in to see the poor nurse trying to take my Grandmother's blood pressure.

"Hi Gran!" I said grinning.

The poor hospital staff must have been going crazy with her. She hated to be fussed over and was a stubborn old coot.

"Lucy! See what they're doing to me? It's ridiculous - I'm absolutely furious! Can you believe he tried to make me take a Panadol! I'm perfectly well and they're bossing me around taking my blood and force feeding me all sorts of medicines. It's infuriating! I will write to the hospital board as soon as I get out!"

I tried to calm her down and make her see reason, but she would have none of it. The nurse who walked in a while later with the dinner tray was met by a bellow from my Grandmother.

"GET OUT! I will not swallow one more pill so don't even try!"

"Gran, shush!" I said smiling apologetically at the nurse. "She's only bringing your dinner."

"Oh!" she said. "But I'm perfectly well and shouldn't be here," she said somewhat apologetically. The nurse nodded and smiled weakly, leaving as quickly as she could.

I stayed with her for an hour, talking and watching the daily soap with her. Every five minutes she'd heave a huge sigh and mumble away about it all being ridiculous and that she was perfectly fine. Poor thing, she hated to be sick and dependent on others. She was miserable here, and I hoped with all my heart that she'd be able to go home the following day.

The next day, I'd just settled down to start typing a report when Olivia burst into my office telling me excitedly that she'd just talked to John about the eventuality of her obtaining work experience in our affiliated Agency in Paris. He had thought it was a brilliant idea and would be willing to let her go for two months and would finance both her ticket and accommodation there.

"I'm going to go! I'm finally going to meet Pierre!" she screeched, bouncing up and down in the chair and clapping her hands with excitement.

Chapter Thirty-Three

My grandmother was thankfully back home the next day, although hyped up and enraged at having had to stay the night at the hospital. She couldn't stop going on about it. I asked her if she had met any nice old men in the corridors and she just laughed, tut-tutting at me. I told her I would drop by to see her after work.

Jake rang me up asking me if we could start our first date over again from scratch. "I would love that," I replied happily.

"Pick you up on Friday night for dinner."

I was thrilled.

On my way home from work I headed to the supermarket to pick up a few things. I was waiting at the red lights not far from the supermarket when I noticed a familiar car, also stopped at the red lights, but on the opposite side of the road. My heart beat faster as the hairs on my neck stood on end. It was Mr. Delano. What was he doing in Curepipe?

He lived in the North. But then again, maybe he had clients here, I chivvied myself. It was a free country after all. I tried to reason with myself, as the lights turned green and we drove off in opposite directions.

Thank goodness he was going the other way, I breathed in relief.

Ten minutes later, I was emptying my basket at the supermarket till when his familiar voice squeaked cheesily into my ear; "Well hello there! Fancy meeting you here."

My head spun towards him. "What are you doing here?" I exclaimed, incredulous.

"Well what do you think? I'm just shopping like everyone else."

I looked down at his basket and saw that it was empty. "Which explains your empty supermarket basket at the till does it?"

He laughed, unfazed by my revelation and grabbed a pack of gum and threw it into it. "There - better now?"

"You were driving in the other direction," I said, still

shocked that he was standing there next to me.

"So, you saw me at the lights too. I knew you noticed me just as much as I notice you!" he said triumphantly.

"I only notice you because you're always FOLLOWING ME!" I shouted as the teller looked up surprised.

"Calm down sugar! You're scaring the lady there," he smirked, smiling at her.

"Don't you DARE call me sugar!" I said through gritted teeth as I started packing everything into my shopping bag, ignoring him. He just stood there, a sleazy grin on his face as he stared at me. I was trying to control my nerves. Why didn't he just go away?

"Don't you have a life?" I asked cuttingly.

He just laughed and put his gum on the counter to pay. I walked off quickly, hoping I could get to my car and lose him before he caught up with me. I was shaking all over by the time I got to my driveway, and suddenly realised he could be following me! So I drove on, and drove aimlessly through the streets of Curepipe for over half an hour before heading home once again.

I looked nervously over my shoulder as I crossed the parking lot heading back to my apartment. It was eerie - I couldn't help feeling that he would jump out from behind a car at any minute...

Chapter Thirty-Four

Jake picked me up on Friday evening, looking devilishly handsome in dark grey jeans which hugged his body sexily and a white t-shirt showing off his toned chest. Wow! He really had a great body. I hadn't noticed how much until now. He took me to dinner in a lovely restaurant on the Waterfront. It was quiet and cosy. I was so shocked when the waiter gave him the menu and after glancing at it for 20 seconds he said decisively; "I'll have a steak with mushroom sauce, a salad and fries please. What about you Lucy?"

Oh my! I was completely at a loss here. Matt usually took hours to decide what he was having and debated every option with me, trying to get me to tell him what he wanted.

"Umm, I'll have what you're having thanks," I said, smiling, trying to shake thoughts of Matt out of my head.

"What would you like to drink? I thought I'd order a bottle of red Mouton Cadet if that's Ok with you?"

Once again, completely out of my depth at his take control attitude, I mumbled, "Um, yeah, sure… sounds great", I mumbled. As though I knew what kind of wine Mouton Cadet was and if I liked it!

I realised I enjoyed the feeling of someone taking control, but I was just not used to it. Matt isn't the most assertive person around and his indecision was both annoying and endearing. I kind of liked having to take care of him too and the fact that he always needed my reassurance and opinion was cute, but sometimes it drove me crazy. I would have to get used to this – it could be nice to be with someone who knew exactly what he wanted…

Dinner was delicious and the wine perfect. We talked easily all evening, telling each other about our lives before now. His last serious relationship had ended over 2 years ago as a result of him having to move too often because of his job. "I'm hoping that will change now," he said, winking at me and sending my heart into a flutter.

He was fun to be with although he didn't make me laugh like Matt did. Stop it! I scolded myself. You're with Jake now, not with Matt! Stop comparing them!

As he guided me out of the restaurant, he took my hand and kept hold of it until we reached the car. He dropped me at my door with a gentle kiss on my lips and said that he would call me tomorrow to do something. Yoopee! He wanted to see me again!

I felt light headed as I got ready for bed. It had been a fun evening and I had enjoyed getting to know him better. He was very English but it was charming, besides, I loved Hugh Grant and hearing him talk was so sexy. I was really looking forward to seeing him again...

The following evening, I was greeted by the delicious scent of tomatoes, garlic and spices. He told me to follow him into the kitchen as he hadn't yet finished cooking.

His apartment was small but tidy. He had a large living room which led into a dining room with a round table for six. His sofas were light grey with a few colourful striped pillows thrown onto them. It looked stylish and much more sophisticated than my apartment. You could tell that he was tidy, organized and very much unlike me!! Opposites were said to attract so it should be a good thing. Matt and I were maybe too alike...

"I'm impressed to see you cooking a meal. I'm not

used to seeing men in the kitchen, just in front of barbecues," I chuckled.

"I'm actually leading you on with this whole cooking thing because I actually don't know how to cook that many things. When I was at University, I used to go and spend a week at my grandparent's place in the country during the holidays and my grandmother insisted that I learn how to cook a few dishes. She said that it was something that they didn't teach us at University and that it was just as important as education, according to her!" He laughed, as he turned and stirred the sauce, tasting it before adding a touch more salt. "She only taught me a few dishes she thought were essential and easy, such as spaghetti bolognaise, a good roast chicken with vegetables, rice and curry, lasagna and an omelette."

I grinned. "Well, that's not bad at all. I'm impressed."

Dinner was delicious and the conversation was light. When we sat down on his sofa and he put his arm around me, I snuggled into him. The more I got to know him the more I realised that he was a very confident man, humble, but sure of himself. It made me feel safe to be with him.

I started telling him about Mr. Delano and how freaky it all was. He sounded very concerned and told me that I must tell him if he ever followed me again. He seemed to find the situation rather alarming and felt that I should have already gotten a restraining order against him or at least contacted the police, to scare him off if anything. He didn't really buy into Olivia's theory that the guy was just acting like a dumbstruck teenager. I shivered thinking about him. Jake tightened his hold on me, and looked at me tenderly.

"Don't worry sweetheart. I'll look after you."

I smiled dumbly at him my heart skipping a beat. Our eyes locked and I knew he was going to kiss me.

Finally…

Our lips met, tentatively at first, gently, tenderly and then parted as the kiss just exploded… It was exquisite… exciting. And my heart was beating wildly. But he wasn't Matt. Damn! Where did that thought come from? Jake seemed to sense my sudden withdrawal and pulled away, looking into my eyes questioningly. I pulled him back to me and we snogged like over-excited adolescents on his sofa until it was time for me to go. He asked me if I wanted to stay over, but it was too soon. I didn't want to do anything I would regret. He didn't seem to mind and kissed me again before waving me off.

Oh my! Looks like I've found myself quite a man, I grinned. Then I heard another little voice fighting its way in.

"But you don't love him like you love Matt." Oh will you just shut up! I snapped at whoever that little voice belonged to. Let me enjoy my after-snog glow and forget about Matt. He doesn't want me, remember? Jake does!

Yeah, but do you want Jake? the irritating little voice replied. Who wouldn't? I mean, have you seen the guy? I snapped back. Tell your heart that! it said, as I put my hand over its mouth and refused to allow it to utter another word!

To get into the spirit of the new boyfriend thing, something which hadn't happened to me for years, I decided I needed to stock up on some sexy lingerie. I had become rather lazy with Matt and wore whatever old, big, small, pretty, ugly knickers and bras that I could get my hands on. I don't think I actually had a matching pair of knickers and bra anymore.

Sometimes, Matt would say, "Hi Grandma" and I would look down at my undies and realise that I had worn that huge pair of granny looking undies again. Every time I wore them I told myself determinedly that I would throw them out. But they would somehow find themselves back into my knickers drawer! Matt thought it was hilarious.

So at lunchtime, I raced to the nearby shopping centre and went straight into the gorgeous lingerie shop 'Love Story'. I strolled through it looking through rows and rows of gorgeous silky underwear and bras, all sizes, shapes, colors and fabrics. My pulse accelerated as I took it all in, thinking where such accessories usually led to… This shop had the sure-bet things, the to-die-for, must-have ranges.

I pulled out a matching pair of silky cream knickers and bra, with a really fine lace lining the sides of both the top and bottom. The bra, obviously made to conceal the least amount of breast, went up to just above the nipple area, ending with the beautiful lacy frill. I could just imagine myself in them, the soft silky cream contrasting beautifully against my tanned skin (of course in my imagination I had bigger boobs and a much firmer and flatter stomach!). I decided to try them on. The effect was stunning, if I do say so myself. The bra was a push up bra so ideal for my little breasts, and the cream in fact looked great against my olive skin. I gasped at the price tag but decided I just had to have them and deserved to spoil myself a bit after all the hardships I'd been through recently!

I raced back to the office, extremely excited by my purchase and so disappointed that none of the girls were back from lunch yet, that I almost burst into the artwork where John was working with Yann and Andrew to show them. But then thought it might not be a highly professional move.

Olivia came back ten minutes later and I was waiting by the door. She loved it and said there was no way Jake could resist me in that.

"Not that he would be able to resist you anyway of course," she added teasingly and laughed.

Jake and I talked to each other regularly on the phone during the week and planned to see each other after work on Friday.

Drat! As I was getting ready to head home to 'prepare' myself for Jake, he called me to say that he was unfortunately still stuck with a client and wouldn't be able to make it to my place before at least nine.

Hearing this, Olivia begged me to go down to the Caudan Waterfront for the Hotels' TGIF (Thank God it's Friday) session - drinks half price till eight - with her. I agreed as at least it would make the time pass more quickly until Jake arrived.

As we made our way towards the terrace, I stopped dead in my tracks. My heart left my body and I could barely breathe.

Matt was here…

Chapter Thirty-Five

My hands went clammy and my feet were superglued to the ground. I'd seen that done by a Hypnotist at a show before, but believed that the people were in on it and were only pretending not to be able to move. Well I am one converted believer, let me tell you! I honestly could not move my legs, hypnotised by Matt's presence only a few meters away from us. Olivia carried on walking, oblivious to my slight technical problem.

Suddenly she turned around frowning, looked around her and finally spotted me, standing statue like, eyes expressionless. She came back towards me looking puzzled.

"I was talking away until I realised you were no longer answering and turned around to see that you had disappeared. I must have looked like a right idiot talking to myself!" she said half laughing, half serious.

I said nothing. I was watching Matt get up from the table he was sitting at on the terrace with a few of his work colleagues, and to my immense relief saw him wave and head off in the other direction.

"Lucy!" cried Olivia worried. "Earth to Lucy!"

I shook my head trying to shake myself back to normal and tentatively tried to move my legs. They moved. Realising that Olivia was still staring at me worriedly, I pointed towards Matt's back fading into the distance. She looked to where I was pointing and turned back, blankly.

"It's Matt…" I said feeling teary all of a sudden. I know that I had seen him at the movies but it had been dark and all a bit surreal, but here, in the pub, I don't know, it just hurt.

"Matt! Where?" She looked again but he had gone.

"Olivia, it's so weird, I just felt paralysed when I saw him …" I said.

If I'd been hoping for sympathy from Olivia, tonight obviously was not the night I would be getting it.

"Snap out of it Lucy! It's O. V. E. R. and you've got a wonderful man who cares about you, so forget about Matt! That's an order!" she barked impatiently. "And besides, you'd better get used to it because you'll often bump into him when you go out. You know that."

I knew she was right but it sure had blown me to see him there, smiling and laughing with his colleagues. It was so strange thinking that it was really over between us, forever… It was just so hard to accept. It was fine when I didn't see him, and having Jake helped a lot, but every time I saw him it just brought everything back.

Olivia grabbed my arm and pulled me towards the bar as I was still in a semi zombie state. She ordered two glasses of white wine and pulled me outside, where we saw Josh, Rachel and Alex sitting at a table. As we sat down Rachel whispered in my ear, "Luckily you didn't come sooner, Matt just left."

"I know - I saw him leave actually," I said forlornly.

She patted my arm sympathetically and changed the subject. I downed my glass of wine as if it was water and felt the heat of the alcohol bringing me back to my senses. Josh went in to get me another glass and I started chatting away to everyone, telling Rachel about Jake.

Suddenly Olivia grabbed my arm again.

"Look over there!" she said pointing towards the bar. "That's that sexy guy I was telling you about a few weeks ago - the one I met at the exhibition."

"Where?" I said needing specifications as after all there were over thirty men in suits in the general direction she had pointed to.

"The one in the dark blue suit with a yellow and blue tie."

"What, the old guy with the white hair?" I said spotting a man who suited the description.

"He's not *that* old!" she snapped. "Just because his hair's slightly graying doesn't mean he's ancient you know."

"Sorry!" I said laughing. "Didn't realise you were so touchy about him."

In fact he was tall and had a great athletic body and as he threw his head back and laughed, I had to acknowledge that he was in fact handsome in a rugged kind of way.

"Not bad actually," I said to Olivia, whose eyes hadn't left him, although she was hiding behind me so that he wouldn't see her looking. "But he's still old," I insisted further.

"Well so is Matt," she snapped back.

"Matt's old'*ish*. He's OLD!" I said protecting Matt, but grinning, enjoying teasing her.

"He's not old, *OLD* - let's just say he's old'*er*!" she said after a few pensive moments.

"Ok, deal! As in he's-older-than-me-and-could-be-my-grandfather type of old'er!" I said, raising my eyebrows questioningly, trying not to laugh.

She suddenly burst out laughing.

Just then he left the bar and came towards the terrace. She jumped up saying that she was going to talk to him. I watched her greet him and as he smiled back at her, I could see what she meant about his smile. They chatted and laughed for a while, before heading back to the bar where they continued their conversation.

I looked at my watch and realised that it was already eight and I had to go home. I was cooking (with the compliments of "La Dolce Vita" restaurant take away menu) for Jake tonight. A nice quiet, romantic candlelit dinner at home... I had to have a shower and put on my new accessories before he arrived at around nine. I was determined to forget Matt and enjoy being with Jake.

I said goodbye to everyone, and not wanting to bother Olivia, who seemed really fascinated by whatever the guy was going on about, told Rachel to tell her I'd call her tomorrow. Wonder where Pierre fits into the scheme of things tonight? I muttered to myself, as I made my way back to my car.

I raced around my apartment, tidying up as best I could and setting the table, with a candle lit in the centre, putting on a Midnight Blues CD to set the mood, dimming the lights before heading for the shower. I had fifteen minutes to get ready.

I stood in front of the mirror staring at my bra and knickers, admiring my reflection. I wasn't a vain person, but I just had to admit that I looked really good. I was actually quite tempted not to bother with any other clothes and open the door in my gear. Didn't Bridget Jones run out in her underwear after Sam Darcy in the film? Well I could just pretend he'd surprised me or that I hadn't realised that I was actually only wearing my underwear!

But on second thought I didn't know him enough to know whether it would please him or scare him off. So I put on my little black dress over it and was brushing my hair when the doorbell rang.

"I'm coming," I called out, as I quickly sprayed some 'Allure' perfume in all the important spots and raced to the door.

"Hey there! You look beautiful," he said, looking at me appreciatively with a smile.

He was looking pretty dashing himself in jeans and a blue polo shirt. He drew me into his arms and we kissed passionately on the doorstep before I pulled him in, worried that my grandmother would see us from her kitchen window.

All thoughts of Matt had thankfully disappeared, although earlier on at the pub had showed me that I still had a long way to go before completely getting him out of my system. But for now I was thrilled to be with Jake. I wasn't in love with him… yet! But he was just so easy to talk to, warm and kind, and called me beautiful all the time, that it could definitively happen.

We didn't quite make it to dessert…. that he liked my new lingerie is rather an understatement! Waking up the next morning I felt oddly pleased with myself for a reason I couldn't quite grasp in my semi-conscious state. As I turned over, throwing my arm out over the right side of the bed, spreading out happily, I heard a male voice cry out in pain and I bolted-up in surprise.

We stared at each other in a dazed silence, him rubbing his nose painfully and me blushing. But after the initial surprise we both fell back against our pillows and laughed as he pulled me towards him and kissed me tenderly, morning breath and all, neither of us noticing or caring for that matter.

We spent the day lazing around in the apartment, only leaving to walk into town to get something to eat. We strolled through the streets of Curepipe and Jake pointed out the Chinese shops all along the street. "They never cease to amaze me – I mean look at that," he said, stopping in front of one of the shop windows, pointing inside. "The shop is tiny yet you can find anything you need in there! Look, just in the window you can get anything from an alarm clock, to a watch, shoes, bras, t-shirts, handbags, schoolbags, cutlery, water and wine glasses, dishes, pans, cameras, bedside table lamps, perfumes, socks, CD players, make up… and the list goes on. It's just fascinating!"

I laughed and nodded in agreement. Those shops were like Pandora's boxes, you never knew what treasures you would find in them. We chatted on as we headed towards Pizza Hut, having planned on eating there. We passed the market square and the noise and smell of the stands floated around us. Just as we walked past the market the delicious aroma of samousas and chili balls rose up to meet us. "How about we forget about the pizza and have some typically Mauritian food instead Jake?" I offered. Jake smiled and agreed. We ordered samousas, chili balls and dholl pourris. What a feast. It was delicious. Stomachs full we walked leisurely back to my apartment.

He left at six, having to head to the west coast until Monday for a business meeting - one of those business Golf dos. In this case it was a big international company, the mother house being in New York, who were thinking of hosting an International Golf tournament in Mauritius and needed a good Events Management company to take over the organisation. Jake had to go to the Paradis Hotel Country Club to meet the big MD. He wanted me to join him there but I knew that he would be busy all day playing golf and he'd probably be having a business dinner that night, so I kissed him at the door and told him to hurry back. Wow, I thought, my boyfriend plays golf! Sounds so sophisticated! Matt was more a football and rugby kind of guy. To be honest, I also thought that golf was an old man's sport! But I knew that it was also a great way to do business these days.

I rang Olivia to ask her how her night had ended at the pub with the grey haired man. "Julian – his name's Julian," she said irritated.

"Ok! Ok! Don't be so touchy," I answered completely unfazed. "And in case you're wondering, my lingerie was a huge success!"

She laughed. "I didn't doubt that for a minute. So, is he everything you thought he would be in bed?"

"Even more…" I said dreamily, remembering the night before.

"That's great Luc - I'm so happy for you. Are you seeing him again tonight?"

"No, he's at a golf tournament," I said grinning, anticipating her reaction.

"Golf huh?" she said laughing.

"Yeah, I know. But it's just for work. Just you wait till you see his body and you'll realise there's nothing old and golfy about him," I said cheekily.

She giggled. "Let's go to the movies tonight then?" she asked, changing the subject, although I was too high on lust to notice. "Phoebe rang and she doesn't have anything on tonight either."

"Yep, I'm in. What are we watching?" I asked. "And at what time?"

"I'll pick you up at eight – no, make that ten to eight," she said, knowing that eight my time, was ten past eight! "As for the movie, not sure what's playing, we'll choose one when we get there."

"Ok, sounds good, see you then," I said hanging up before remembering that she hadn't told me about last night. Oh well, later, I thought.

We ended up watching a rerun of, *The Proposal* with Sandra Bullock which was excellent. I'm all for the soppy happy-ever-after endings and to top it off, Ryan Reynolds is just so gorgeous! Afterwards we headed to the Spur Steak House, the only restaurant found in the cinema complex. As Phoebe went off to the ladies room, I turned to Olivia. "So, how did it go with the grey haired…oops, I mean Julian, last night?"

She sighed and blushed.

"You're blushing!" I exclaimed delighted, pointing at her face.

"Oh shut up!" she answered, petulantly.

"Please tell me," I begged, intrigue by her reaction.

"I kissed him!" she blurted out then hid her head in her hands.

"You kissed him?" I asked, but not quite understanding her horrified expression, I added teasingly, "Did his false teeth fall out in your mouth or something?"

"You're so horrible!" she cried, obviously less amused by my joke than I was.

"So why the horror stricken look on your face?" I pushed on, not responding to her outburst.

"*I* kissed him! I'm so embarrassed..." she winced.

"I'm sorry but I don't get it," I said still confused.

"He was leaving, had left actually, when suddenly the wine in my blood let out a huge 'I want him' feeling in my head and I raced out after him..."

She stopped and I waited.

"He had almost reached the car park when I called out to him to stop. He looked surprised to see me and asked me what was up. It was then that I leaned up and kissed him, spank on the mouth!"

I burst out laughing as she hid her face behind her hands.

"He stayed still like a statue for a few seconds and then kissed me back, tongue and all. It went on for a few minutes, before he pulled away and smiled, telling me that he really had to go. It was so embarrassing - he looked at me with a fatherly expression Lucy! I felt like I was about six years old. I wish the earth had swallowed me up there and then! I turned around and ran back to the pub and downed three tequila shots one after the other before having to be dropped home by Alex."

"Oh, you poor thing," I said, not able to stop myself from laughing.

"The worst thing is that he was an amazing kisser – false teeth and all!" she added, giving me a mean glare.

"Umm… where does Pierre fit in here though? I thought you were in love with him?" I asked genuinely curious.

"*Oh noooo,*" she wailed in despair. "I feel so guilty. I don't know what got over me. I just miss physical closeness I guess. It's great and all talking and writing and telling each other that we love each other, but I guess I'm just craving the physical affection. It's awful though because I really feel as if I've been unfaithful to him. It's just so weird."

"Are you going to tell him?" I asked gently, realising that she was torn up about it.

"I don't know. Probably not, what's the use. But knowing me I won't be able to keep it in."

I smiled at the truth of her statement.

"No don't, not now anyway," I advised her. "Nothing much happened and besides you're not in love with the other guy, so it just isn't important. Put it in a corner of your mind with the other 'Olivia's mistakes' and leave it there to rest."

"But that's lying. I don't know if I can do it!" she cried, horrified.

"No, it's not a lie - it's just an omission of a detail which he doesn't need to know. It means so little to you and it'll probably really hurt him and make him doubt you, it's not worth it. You made an impulsive mistake, just forgive yourself and leave it at that. "

As we saw Phoebe head back to the table, Olivia signaled me to say nothing.

"Those toilets are so quaint," she said sitting down. "I don't really understand how they expect us to pee into those wall things though. It must be a modern version of a toilet for ladies. I swear I can't keep up with technology these days. Luckily they kept one old fashioned toilet for less up to date people like me!" she said happily as she picked up the menu, oblivious to our dumbstruck faces. Olivia and I looked at each other and burst out laughing.

"What?" cried Phoebe as she looked around wondering who we were laughing at and where the joke was.

"Nothing Phoebe, nothing," I said shaking my head in mirth. She would never cease to amaze me.

We ended up drinking two bottles of wine between the three of us before heading home, me talking about Jake and Matt, Olivia about Pierre and Phoebe about Jonah, her recent boyfriend.

I fell gratefully into bed, realising that I was in fact pretty tired as we hadn't actually slept much the previous night. I smiled contently thinking back to the previous night with Jake...

Chapter Thirty-Six

The next day, I decided to stay home and relax in front of the TV. I was surprised to hear the phone ring at 11 o'clock, as no one ever rang me on Sundays on my home phone.

"Hi Lucy, it's Nadia. I was just ringing to see how you are?"

Nadia is Matt's sister. She had rung me at work once just after we broke up to say that the whole family were devastated that we had broken up and that Matt was an idiot. But I hadn't heard from her since.

"Hi! I'm good thanks. Things are finally looking up. I've met someone and he's really nice."

"I'm so happy for you - but so sad for Matt... He's such a fool," she said sighing.

"Please don't. I'm just trying to get my life back on track again and it still hurts so much just hearing about Matt," I said pleadingly.

"I'm sorry. I just wanted to see how you were," she said. "The kids really miss you too. Just yesterday they asked Matt when you were coming back to see them. Chloe even told him, "I missth Lucy – besides you were much more fun when she was here. Now you're alwaysth grumpy!"

I burst out laughing, but tears stung my eyes. I loved those kids and really missed them.

"Nadia, I know you mean well, but I can't do this yet. I'm so sorry. I know one day I'll be able to come over and see you all, but it's too soon. Please tell the children that I send them my love and will come and see them soon."

"I understand Lucy. But Matt's miserable you know… he's lost without you."

"It's just not enough. He just doesn't love me enough…" I said wearily.

"He does. He's just too scared to acknowledge it," she answered sadly.

"Nadia please don't," I said, my voice breaking. "Thanks for calling. I know you mean well."

I hung up before she could shatter my heart into any more pieces. Why had she done that? I had told her I had met someone else and that I was better. Why tell me that Matt was miserable and loved me? Damn it! Get out of my head Matt! Leave me alone!

Needless to say that the phone call took me on a downward spiral and had me depressed and in bed all day. In the late afternoon, Jake rang telling me he would drop by. I had to snap out of this mood. I couldn't admit to why I was in this state – he would leave me and I needed him. I had a shower, got dressed and even put on a bit of eyeliner trying to make myself look bright and fresh, and bursting with happiness!

Jake arrived, looking divinely handsome in white golf attire. We had a drink and he told me about his event and filled him in on the movie and the Phoebe toilet incident. He laughed and said, "You sure have spun out friends Lucy."

"Phoebe's really something else I must admit," I said, giggling.

"Even Vic's quite something," he added, grinning.

"Yes, I know. Do you get on well with Sam?" I asked, as I finished off my yogurt, surprised that I hadn't actually thought of asking before now.

"I've never met him actually," he answered, and just as the words were out of his mouth, his hand flew to his mouth. "Oh-Oh… I wasn't meant to say that. I don't suppose you want to pretend you didn't hear that by any chance?"

"What do you mean?" I asked confused.

"I promised I wouldn't say anything," he continued, looking guilty.

"I still don't get it, please explain," I asked, completely lost.

"Well… I actually don't know Sam at all and I only met Vic once – at the supermarket…"

As he went on to tell me the story, I was in total shock. I was furious and told him that Vic would be hearing from me.

"Tell her I'm sorry, I didn't do it on purpose," he said, feeling bad. I told him he wasn't to blame but that he really should have been honest with me from the start. Although he didn't lie, it was lying by omission. He said he hadn't wanted to betray Vic as he was so grateful to her for having set us up, which is pretty sweet and made me forgive him straight away.

As soon as Jake left I grabbed the phone and dialed Vic's number.

After a few rings Christopher picked up the phone.

"Hi Christopher, can I speak to your mum please?" I asked.

"What for?" he answered rudely - obviously caught him on a bad day again!

"Please, it's important," I said trying to keep calm.

"Why, what did you do?" he asked.

"What do you mean 'what did I do'?" I asked surprised and annoyed.

"Well, adults always say things like 'it's important' when they have done something wrong and have some explaining to do," he answered. How old was he? Six or sixty!

"Please just get me your mum," I asked again, trying not to shout.

"She's not 'ere," he replied, just as I heard her voice in the background asking him who was on the phone.

"I just heard her voice!" I exclaimed.

"No, it wasn't her, it's the maid," he lied without a trace of remorse in his voice.

"I know it was her – *JUST GET HER FOR ME*

DAMN IT!" I screamed, not being able to stay calm for a second longer.

He said no more and two seconds later Vic was there cheerfully greeting me.

"Vic! Where did you say you'd met Jake?" I barked as soon as I heard her voice.

"So nice of you to ask me how I am," she replied sarcastically.

"Vic! Don't mess with me!" I warned menacingly.

"Ok, Ok, fine. *Relax*," she said resignedly. "Jake? Mm…" she mumbled, seeming to be thinking about it. "I'm not sure, it's been a while you know."

"Think!" I snapped.

"Well…probably at some friends place…" she said vaguely.

"Ok, let me try another question – exactly how long have you known him for?" but this also seemed like a difficult question as she remained quiet.

"VIC?" I shouted.

"Yeah, yeah! Don't spit a dummy at me, I'm trying to think, and at 9 p.m. on a Sunday night, it's not that easy!" she said, totally unfussed but clearly annoyed at having to answer my questions. "Well, actually, we hadn't known him for that long before I set you two up," she finally confessed lamely.

"*HOW LONG*?" I said through gritted teeth.

"Well… a week or so," she said almost in a whisper.

"And where did you meet him a week or so before I went out with him?" I asked again, waiting for her to finally tell me the truth.

"Umm… I told you, at a friend's place - I think," she mumbled again, unconvincingly.

"*THINK HARDER* and tell me exactly where it was!" I shouted again - I wouldn't let her get away with this.

"Ok, Ok…" she said with resignation. "I confess, the truth is that I saw him in the supermarket and thought he was pretty cute. So I started following him around the shop and then I noticed his basket, and I just knew…"

"Excuse me! His *basket*! You're such a pervert!" I exclaimed, "As if a guy can be judged by the size of his basket!"

"His *supermarket* basket you twat!" she said bursting out laughing. "Now, who's the pervert here??!"

Feeling pretty stupid, I muttered a little embarrassed "Oh" before getting a grip on myself again.

"And so what if it's his supermarket basket!" I suddenly blurted out. "Why does that make it any better?"

"Well, as I was saying before I was so rudely interrupted by your sexually obsessed imagination…" she answered, obviously loving every minute of it. "I followed him around the shop and watched the things he put in his *supermarket* basket."

"*And?*" I snapped impatiently, not understanding what she was getting at.

"Well, if he'd bought instant noodles, beer and baked beans, I would have known that he wasn't a very classy type of person – not to mention a very 'windy' one!" she added and chuckled, clearly amused by her joke. "You can tell a lot about a guy by what he has in his supermarket trolley you know?" she said with conviction. "Don't you ever read woman's magazines?" she added.

"I really can't believe you sometimes – I really think you should seriously consider seeing a psychologist, no actually, make that a psychiatrist!" I exclaimed.

As usual she completely ignored my outburst, and

carried on with her analysis of Jake's basket.

"Lucy, you should have seen the things he bought; steak, vegetables, yogurt, chocolate, muesli, fruit. I just knew that with that kind of stuff he couldn't be a bad guy and that he'd be perfect for you!"

"Perfect for me because he bought steak, vegetables, yogurt, and chocolate – every second guy buys those things Vic!" I burst out, exasperated.

She acted as if I hadn't spoken and talked on.

"Anyway, so I introduced myself and we got talking. He told me he'd arrived a month ago and that he was single. I asked him if he'd like me to introduce him to a few friends. He was really keen and that's when I thought about the blind date thing. And he was all for it. I showed him a photo of you I had on my phone and he could hardly contain his excitement. So we exchanged phone numbers and I phoned him again the next day to settle on a day and time and then I called you and that's that," she confessed. "What's the big deal anyway?"

"You give a total stranger your best friend's number and it's no big deal?" I shrieked angrily at her.

"Of course I wouldn't give it to just anyone! I just *knew* he was perfect for you. And he is, isn't he?" she asked, then muttered, "Oh blast! There goes my nail! Had some false nails stuck on yesterday," she informed me, "You know, to try and stop me biting my real ones, but they're crap and I've just lost my second one."

"Arrrrrg!" I screeched in frustration, but couldn't help wanting to laugh at her attitude nevertheless. "You really are something aren't you?

"What? What have I done now?" she wailed. "Don't tell me you're strongly against acrylic nails or something now!"

"No Vic, I'm not. But I just don't think that giving your best friend's number to a stranger in a supermarket is a very nice thing to do. He could have been a psycho for all you know…" I said in a reprimanding tone. "And DON'T tell me psychos don't buy steaks!"

"Ok, I admit I took a risk by doing that. But it's all worked out for the best hasn't it?"

I was still angry with her for doing such a stupid thing. But then again, I was really glad that she was a little on the crazy side as otherwise I wouldn't have met Jake. I also knew that she had only done it because she wanted me to be happy - and maybe, just maybe, she had been spot on about Jake and I…

Chapter Thirty-Seven

As I was making my way up the stairs to my apartment after work, I heard the phone ringing. Thinking it might be Vic calling to see if I was OK about the whole Jake thing, I raced to the door, dropping my keys in my haste, picked them up, this time dropping all the contents of my bag before finally making it inside. I threw my five shopping bags full of microwave food on the floor, and raced to pick it up.

"Lucy?" said a barely audible voice, but one which I'd recognise in a crowd of a thousand people all talking at the same time. My heart began to race.

Had I imagined it?

"Matt?" I asked tentatively.

Silence.

"Matt, are you alright?" I asked, worried that something had happened.

"I just wanted to hear your voice…" he said softly.

I felt my insides belly flop into my stomach and my heart fly off to the moon or thereabouts. Oh-Oh! Ping pong ball alert in the throat area!

"Don't do this to me Matt," I begged. "Please don't…". I was finally doing OK without him and just couldn't cope with this.

"I'm sorry…" he replied with remorse. "But I just really needed to hear your voice."

"I understand," I said, knowing how he felt as I felt it so often. "But please, don't call me again." I brushed a tear making its way down my cheek. I hadn't even realised that I was crying.

He stayed quiet for a bit then whispered, "I miss you so much… The other day the kids were asking me where you were and when you would be coming to see them. And I just didn't know what to say. I thought my heart would break. I'm so confused Luce."

I couldn't answer as fresh tears made their way like an avalanche down my face. I didn't want him to know that I was crying.

"I miss you too Matt…" I finally managed to say,

barely able to stop myself from bawling down the phone.

We stayed there for a few minutes, neither being able to say anything. It was so hard sitting there and knowing that it just couldn't be - that we'd never be together again.

I had to get off the phone. I couldn't bear it anymore.

"Bye Matt," I said quietly.

"Don't go…" he pleaded.

"You know I have to," I answered, no longer hiding the tears in my voice.

"I know… I'm sorry."

Despite it being hard it was also wonderful to hear his voice and to feel him so close, even for just a few minutes. It was also very comforting to know that he also had the need to hear my voice and that he missed me.

"Bye Matt," I said again, knowing we had to stop torturing ourselves like this.

"Bye Luce," he said sadly as I put down the phone and let my tears fall freely.

I cried for the good times and the bad times and for the frustration and hurt I felt at him for letting me go instead of holding me back and telling me that he couldn't bear to live without me. I had thought that I was doing a good job getting over him, and that Jake had practically made me forget him, but hearing his voice had turned me into a pile of mush and made me realize that although I really like Jake and think he's wonderful, I still loved Matt deeply.

Suddenly Vic and her Jake story and everything in general seemed so pointless. In the space of a few minutes, I had lost interest in everything…

Oh Matt…

Damn you Matt! I said throwing myself on my bed in frustration, feeling like Scarlet O'Hara in Gone with the Wind.

Chapter Thirty-Eight

I got out of bed feeling exhausted and shrieked in horror at the sight of my face. My eyes were red and in fact so puffy that they were barely visible, having almost completely receded into their sockets – the result of having cried myself to sleep. I think that there's probably a neuron somewhere in my head connected to my eyes, with the code word "Matt". As soon as it is said, heard or even just thought of, the neuron goes into action and down rolls the tears. Sort of like a knee-jerk reaction!

I splashed bucket loads of freezing cold water over my face wondering how I was ever going to get myself to look semi-presentable in the half hour I had to get to work. I fumbled through my make-up bag hoping to find some miraculous cure, but was faced with the cruel reality; one Cocoa Revlon lipstick, one Nude Revlon lipstick, one empty tube of Cocoa Revlon lipstick and a black eyeliner with a broken nib. I sighed and wished that for once I was more like Olivia with her endless beauty products for all occasions and any emergencies which may arise. This was definitively an emergency situation.

I gave up and settled for a long hot shower and thought to hell with it - I just wasn't in the mood to care! As I drove to work I thought back to my conversation with Matt and couldn't get over the effect that just hearing his voice still had on me. The Stupid Twat! I muttered to myself. I mean, how hard is it to say 'I love you – Will you marry me'!

I jumped in surprise as I was shaken out of my dreams by a car horn blaring behind me. I had stopped at a set of red lights and I hadn't realised that they had turned green. I waved my hand to excuse myself, and sped off, quickly lost in my thoughts again.

I knew deep down inside of me that Matt loved me. Maybe it wasn't the for-ever-after type of love though… Who knew for sure whether it was a 'for real' love anyway? Even I didn't know for sure whether Matt was THE one. All I knew was that I loved him and that I wanted to be with him and I'd do whatever it took to make things work.

Why was I reminding myself of all this – he was the one who hadn't caught on yet! Eternal passion was what he thought he needed - ha! flippin' ha! As if it existed!

I pulled into the driveway leading up to the office, and parked my car under the big old oak tree. I glanced at my face in the rearview mirror before getting out and was happy to see that my eyes had decided to meet the challenges of the new day head on, and were actually looking almost normal again. I put my bag down on my desk, glanced at the huge pile of work in my 'Things to Do' tray, and headed straight to the kitchen for a coffee fix. No way could I face the work right now and after last night, I knew a lot of caffeine was called for before I would be any use in the office. Luckily John was away at a training seminar until after lunch, which meant that I could ease myself into the work at my own pace - that is, a semi-comatose one.

Olivia wasn't in the office either. I sighed and sat down at my desk staring into space, my thoughts going from Matt to Jake.

I sent a quick text to Greg – I hadn't written in a while. He'd told me in an email that he had met a girl and that it was going really well. I thought I would be jealous but I actually wasn't at all. He had become a really great friend. I trusted him fully and felt that he understood me completely although we had only spent a day and a night together. He was a great sounding board for my doubts and dilemmas.

I was still lost in my thoughts, when suddenly I felt chills run down my spine. I looked up and saw Mr. Delano standing at the door, watching me with a creepy smile...

Chapter Thirty-Nine

My heartbeat accelerated as I watched him making his way towards my desk. I tried to say something, but nothing came out, so I just stared at him dumbly. He was once again wearing blue trousers with a striped shirt. Today the stripes were blue, red and white. His hair was styled in a John Travolta in Grease hairdo, full of gel. Yuck!

"Hello Miss Lucy. Just thought I would drop by to give you these," he said and, to my horror, produced a bouquet of yellow roses from behind his back. "Since you were so mad at me at the supermarket the other time, I thought these might help."

I stared at him in disbelief, lost for words. For once I wished John would barge into my office or tell me he needed to see me in his office straight away.

"You can't give me flowers!" I finally exclaimed in indignation.

My outburst was greeted by an incredulous gaze.

"Well I just did, didn't I?"

"I don't want them! I have a boyfriend, as you very well know, and I don't take flowers from my stationery suppliers - it's unethical," I exclaimed heatedly.

"I'm not just your stationery supplier surely?" he said, winking at me suggestively.

"Actually you're no longer even that anymore!" I snapped.

"Now, now, no need to get excited! Can't you just say 'Thank you' like any normal girl would?" he asked unfazed, as he stole a glance towards my breasts. What a dirty sleaze!

"Get out of my office *NOW*!" I shouted, adding threateningly through clenched teeth. "I swear I will call the cops if you don't leave *right now*! And take your stupid flowers with you!"

"Ok, Ok, don't get excited. I thought it would please you."

"OUT!" I screamed, not caring if the whole office heard me. I'd be happy for any one of my colleagues to come to my rescue right now anyway.

"I'm going, I'm going," he said raising his hands in surrender. "For now…" he added slyly, giving me another once-over before turning his back and finally leaving.

I fell back on my chair as I looked out the window to make sure that he was really going. I shivered. When was he going to stop chasing me like this? Should I report it as harassment? I just didn't know. I would have to discuss it with Jake. But all I knew was that it couldn't carry on like this. I was freaking out here.

I had started having nightmares about him chasing me around my apartment with a butcher knife, wanting to rape me. I felt myself break out in a sweat at the thought of it. Breathe Lucy, breathe, I said to myself, trying to get my heart rate to slow down. This was turning into a real horror movie. I was now seriously scared of the guy. He hadn't tried anything up to now, but who knew what he had up his sleeve?

Jake rang me in the evening and I went over to his place to have some Chinese take away with him. On the way I realised that the Mr. Delano episode had managed to make me forget about Matt's phone call, which I guessed was a good thing.

I told Jake about the sleaze ball and he thought that I should ask for legal advice. Matt's dad was a lawyer and I told Jake that I would call him to see what I should and could do about it. I wasn't in the best of moods following Matt's phone call and Mr. Delano's visit, so I didn't stay long after dinner, telling him that I'd had a long day. He hugged me reassuringly.

"Don't worry Luce; I won't let Mr. Delano hurt you."

I held on tight trying to reduce my uneasiness and calm my nerves. I was scared of going home alone, which was just ridiculous. I was furious with myself for letting that stupid idiot get me so freaked out. But he had, and I was completely freaked out.

Chapter Forty

The next evening, Jake was going to the pub with work colleagues and representatives from the States and I decided to stay in. I was tired and still on edge, and just not in the mood. Olivia was going to the pub with Rachel and Phoebe but I didn't want to risk bumping into Matt again. So I flopped on the couch and zapped my way through the channels trying to think of anything but Mr. Delano or Matt.

In the middle of a really tense bit in *24 Hours*, the phone rang. Damn! I moaned as I got up and picked it up.

"Hi, it's me, Vic," she said. "I just wanted to tell you how sorry I am about giving your number out to a stranger. I know you're right. It was a stupid thing to do. But I just want you to be happy."

"I know, I forgive you, although it was stupid!" I said sternly. "But I know you did it out of kindness."

"Is Jake with you now?" she asked.

"No, he had to go to a work thing. I was just watching *24 Hours*," I said. "How are things on your side?"

"Well…" she seemed to hesitate before quietly adding, "Actually - not so good."

I was really surprised as Vic never complained or ever admitted to anything being wrong. Things were always rosy if you listened to her talk. This was new.

"Oh!" I said, not finding anything else to say. I was worried as this really was out of character. I asked her what the matter was.

"I can't really talk now, the kids are here." I waited for her to go on. "Listen, do you think I could come over to your place tonight?" Once again, I was taken by surprise as we lived thirty minutes away from each other.

"Of course you can. I'll be here," I said, worried.

"Thanks. I'll just organise the kids and get someone to watch over them for me, then I'll come over," she said, sounding relieved.

What was up? She was going to drive thirty minutes to come and talk to me tonight. What had happened? Was it Sam? Had he finally done something stupid?

Vic and Sam had started going out when she was sixteen and he was nineteen. It was love at first sight. Before that Vic had always been a bit of a wild one, having her first French kiss at the ripe old age of ten - which had me, the innocent still-playing-with-dolls one, completely shocked when she told me, and exclaiming, "But Vic, you're mad! Don't you know that that's how you fall pregnant!" As I carried on brushing my dolls hair, she told me that I was ridiculous and that babies were not made that way - that there had to be a willy and a mummy getting stuck together for a baby to be born. I didn't believe her and told her that she was completely wrong. We were both ten then.

Anyway, after that she'd gone from one guy to the next falling into love as fast as she fell out of love. Until Sam.

He was tall, handsome with huge biceps and a sexy smile. He fell head over heels in love with the crazy, wild and completely eccentric Vic. He was the stability she needed and she was the spice he in turn needed. They were perfect together, although they tended to fought quite a bit. I reckon they just liked the making up bit afterwards!! Anyway, although it wasn't directly due to the French kissing, she fell pregnant at twenty-one and they had gotten married before the baby was born, and have been married since.

The doorbell rang two hours later and I opened it to find Vic standing there dressed in a sexy black outfit, with make-up piled high on her face and her long, blond hair falling in curls down her back. She looked stunning.

"I know I'm a classy chick and all, but you really shouldn't have gotten so dressed up just to see me," I said laughing.

"Ha! Ha!" she said, grinning. "Actually, Sam came back before I left so I decided to dress up like this and told him I was going out on the town – alone – and not to wait up for me!"

My eyes did a goldfish number on me as I laughed.

"So you can't throw me out until at least twelve o'clock ok?" she said laughing.

"Sure, no problem," I answered smiling and shaking my head at her scheme. "But are you going to tell me what's up or am I going to have to die of curiosity?"

"Yes, I'll tell you but pleeeeease, get me a drink first. Got any wine?"

"Wine? But you never drink wine?" I said surprised.

"I do now!" she said mischievously.

I walked to the fridge and took out a bottle of white wine and opened it.

"Is pizza OK for dinner 'cause I really don't have much in my fridge," I asked, as I gazed at the yogurt, the three bottles of diet coke, the butter and three eggs sitting in my fridge.

"Surprise, surprise," she said sarcastically. "Pizza's perfect. Hawaiian preferably."

She flopped down on the sofa and sipped her wine while I rang up and ordered.

I came back and sat down on the other sofa settling myself in comfortably.

"So, do you want to tell me what's up?" I asked gently.

"Well… I guess. I don't know where to start." She sighed and looked down into her glass.

I waited knowing she'd talk when she was ready.

"It's still the same problem - this stupid new job of Sam's! It's turning our lives upside down," she suddenly blurted out, fidgeting with the stem of her wine glass. "All the other Managers are single and so have no consideration for a married man and his wife and kids. They set up meetings that start at eight o'clock at night and go on till ten or eleven o'clock. Or they decide to go out to dinner, make it a dinner meeting so he has no choice but to attend. Or the worse yet is that they take him to pubs supposedly saying that they'd work there too. But needless to say that after two glasses of beer, no one wants to talk about work anymore! They are putting ideas into his head…"

"What do you mean, ideas?" I asked.

"Oh, I don't know," she replied evasively, as I felt her clam up all of a sudden.

I stayed quiet, willing her to carry on. She continued to sip her wine while fidgeting with the glass stem.

"Go on," I gently urged her. "You can tell me."

"Well, it's just that I don't see him much these days and knowing he's out with single guys makes me feel insecure. They seem to make him wish he was single and that he didn't have the baggage of a wife and kids…"

She stared ahead of her and I waited.

"The other day he rang up and told me he'd be working late again at the office. Three quarters of an hour later I rang there to ask him if he'd eat here or there - the guy who answered the phone told me the Managers had all gone out half an hour ago. It was the third time in a month that he'd disappeared without telling me, the last two times he'd ended up at the pub and came home drunk. I couldn't handle it, so I took my car and went to look for him at all the pubs I thought they might be at…"

"You did *what*?" I exclaimed.

"I know, I know - sounds pretty crazy, but I just had to find out if there was anything going on."

"So, then what?" I asked, curious and worried about the outcome.

"I found his car at the "Sports Café" and called him on his mobile. I could see him inside, saw him look at it, and when he saw my number he walked out to the terrace where it was quiet. I walked towards him as I asked him where he was and if he was almost done. I was standing in front of the terrace door, his back to me when he told me that he was at his office and had another hour or so to go. I felt myself go cold at his blatant lie."

"I then told him to turn around. He didn't understand why and wanted to know. I told him to humour me and just turn around and look at the door.

He swiveled around slowly and his hand went limp and his mobile phone and jaw both fell to the floor at the sight of me standing there behind the door."

She paused, taking a sip of wine and I could see the strain in her face and the pain in her eyes.

"I didn't wait for him to regain his senses and I ran all the way back to my car. I felt icily calm - numb actually. I heard him run after me but I just kept going, ignoring his pleas. He caught up with me near my car and begged me to let him explain. I told him I was leaving and that anything he had to say would be said when he came home - and I left."

"I'm so sorry Vic…" I said not knowing what else to say as an image of the gorgeous brunette flashed before me.

"He's turning into someone I don't recognise and quite frankly, someone I don't like very much," she said sadly.

We sat in silence both sipping our wine, her getting her emotions in control and me trying to find a way to comfort her without saying anything incriminating about Sam, because I didn't know what he was really up to.

"It's not too serious though is it?" I finally asked.

She looked up at me and stared at me for a long time, but her gaze was blank, her thoughts elsewhere.

"Honestly, I have no idea," she finally said, quietly. "When he got home he apologised and told me that he promised he wouldn't lie to me anymore. He had just known that I would be angry and hadn't wanted to hear it because he knew I was right and that I had every reason to be pissed off with him. Oh, Luce, I just don't know…"

"You have to work this out Vic. You have your 3 kids to think about."

"I know - but he needs to want it too."

"I'm sure he does. He's probably having a bit of trouble adjusting to the demands of the new job and the lifestyle that's expected to go with it," I said, desperately trying to sound convincing.

Just then the doorbell rang. It was the pizza.

We discussed it some more over dinner and we laughed as she checked her mobile and saw that he'd already called her nine times in the last hour and a half! She seemed more cheerful.

"I feel much better now that I've talked to you about it," she said smiling.

Poor thing... How humiliating. And when you have three children you can't just pack up and leave for a while to teach the other person a lesson - you have to stay and make things Ok, pretend that you're happy and that everything's fine, even if you then go and hide in the toilet to cry.

Would Sam come to his senses before it was too late?

Chapter Forty-One

I called Matt's dad the next morning to talk to him about Mr. Delano. He seemed thrilled to hear from me and we spent a while catching up. Like Nadia, he told me that Matt was a fool and miserable since we had broken up. I thanked him for his kind words and told him that I was sure Matt had his reasons. I then explained the situation with Mr. Delano and asked him what he thought I should do. He sounded concerned and said that if he carried on like this that I would definitely have to file a complaint with the police and if it continued I could then even file for a restraining order.

"Does Matt know about this?" he asked softly.

"Well, it had only just started when we broke up so he doesn't know that it has carried on. My boyfriend, Jake, is aware of the situation and is keeping an eye out for me."

"Well, I'm reassured that at least someone is there for you. But please don't hesitate to call me if he does show up again."

I knew it was not an 'if' but a 'when', but I didn't say anything. I thanked him and felt better after talking to him.

I'm ready for you Mr. Delano – next time it's off to the police station we go! I decided that I wouldn't let him ruin any more of my day and would go out and have a good time.

On our way to the pub that evening Olivia asked me when I was going to introduce her to Jake. I told her that he was also dying to meet all my friends but that he had been pretty full on with work lately and that when he had been free they hadn't been.

"We'll definitively try to organise something this weekend," I said, smiling.

"I'm leaving soon, so please hurry. Can't leave without meeting luscious Jake!"

Being a Thursday night, the pub was pretty quiet and we sat outside on the terrace. The sun was just setting and sky was beautiful.

"Let's get a drink," Olivia said.

As we were waiting for our drinks I heard a text message come in and saw that it was from Jake who wanted to know at what time I thought I would be home. I was engrossed in my response when Olivia suddenly said, "Matt!"

"No, of course it's not from Matt! It's from Jake", I said distractedly.

"As in, Matt has just walked into the pub with a tall, blond girl…" Olivia said quietly.

It took me a few seconds to register what she had just said but as it sank in my head flew up on its own volition and my eyes popped out. I looked towards the entrance.

"You forgot the adjectives 'flippin gorgeous' and 'legs up to her ears' Olivia," I said sourly as I gazed at the gorgeous blond who was looking up at Matt, laughing.

Olivia looked at me sympathetically obviously not knowing what to say.

"How do you say 'bollocks' in French?" she asked, grinning, obviously trying to lighten the atmosphere.

"Even in English no one uses that word, Olivia!" I snapped back impatiently. "Besides, only Hugh Grant gets away with saying it!"

My eyes were riveted on my new worst enemy. I gazed at her perfect figure, her blue eyes, long blond hair and legs, legs, legs... Why did he have to choose another Jessica lookalike, but one even more beautiful! What was wrong with brunettes, damn him! It would have comforted me to see him with a brunette who resembled me so that I could convince myself that he thought of me when he was with her.

"Maybe we should leave?" Olivia said gently.

"Are you mad? Leave Matt here with that...that... thing!" I said hysterically.

"What do you intend to do?" she asked as I looked dumbly at her. "There's nothing you can do about it except kick up a huge fuss and make a fool of yourself in front of Matt and the girl."

I knew she was right but I couldn't accept that it was the only solution. How could I stop Matt from being with that gorgeous girl and want to be with me instead! I couldn't handle the thought of him with another woman, I was burning with jealousy and I could feel my insides eaten up by it.

"I can't go..." I wailed.

"Luce..." Olivia said gently. "Be reasonable... You

and Matt are *over*. You don't want him back remember? You tried everything and he wouldn't commit to you. Do you want to be strung along again for a few more years while Matt continues being vague and indecisive?"

I listened to her words, knowing that she was right. That even if I yearned for Matt, I could never go back with him because he didn't want to get married and I did. But I just couldn't bear the thought of him loving someone else, it hurt too much.

"That's it, we're going!" Olivia said determinedly as she grabbed her bag and got up.

"No, we're not! I need to have a very strong drink first!" I said determinedly. "You want something?"

"A glass of wine thanks," she said in resignation, as she put her bag down and sat down again.

I stomped towards the ladies room, wanting to get myself together again, to see if everything was still in place as I felt in pieces, before getting the drinks. On my way back to the bar, I looked around and saw that Matt and the leggy blond had disappeared. Thank goodness, I thought, realising that I couldn't bear to spend the evening watching them cooing away at each other. I ordered the drinks and leaned against the bar lost in my thoughts.

"Hi Luce," a familiar voice catapulted me out of my reverie. I spun around towards him, too surprised to say anything and just glared.

"You're so beautiful when you're angry," Matt said quietly, smiling.

"I'm not angry!" I replied sharply, my heart racing and my whole body trembling. I wasn't sure if it was the fact that he'd called me beautiful that had gotten me into this state or just the fact of suddenly seeing him so close to me, without HER.

He smiled knowingly and said nothing, which only served to enrage me further.

"Stop staring at me with that pathetic smirk on your face!" I said angrily, wanting so badly to be able to act nonchalantly and show him how little I cared about the fact that he had come with someone else.

As I saw his blond walk back into the bar, my insides turned upside down.

"Your blondshell is looking for you!" I snapped at him, indicating the door and turning to leave.

He grabbed my arm, and I swung my head back towards him.

"Wait!" he said gently. "I'd really like you to meet her."

My mouth flew open like a hippopotamus yawning, not believing I was actually hearing that. I glared at him, so hurt and shocked, that I couldn't get any words out.

Then realising that he was signaling her to come our way, I snapped out of my daze and said coldly, "Don't you dare introduce her to me!"

He looked at me, surprised by my tone, but didn't answer. Once again, I turned to leave, but he held my arm firmly.

"Let me go!" I screeched, trying in vain to set my arm free.

He ignored me and I watched him wave towards the blond. She finally saw us, and, smiling, headed our way. I desperately tried to free myself from his grasp but his grin widened and he held on until it was too late for me to do a runner.

"Hi!" the blondshell said cheerfully. "You must be Lucy. I've heard so much about you. All good of course!" she grinned as she looked towards Matt.

Damn! I like her, I thought straight away. She seemed genuinely nice. Don't you hate that! She was meant to be a bitch. This was just not good.

"Lucy, this is Jenny," Matt said, still smiling as he added with emphasis. "My *cousin*."

"Jenny!" I exclaimed. "*You're* Jenny! I never knew you looked like this!" I blurted out before I could stop myself. She laughed warmly.

I had heard so much about her from Matt who kept in touch with her via emails. They'd been really close growing up and then she'd left at eighteen to go to University in South Africa and she had ended up staying there. She'd come back quite a few times since but I had been in Australia when she'd come the last few times. I'd seen photographs of the two of them together when they were 15 years old but she didn't look anything like this!

"It's so nice to finally meet you," I said happily. "Thank goodness you're his cousin as I nearly died of jealousy when I saw him walk in with you," I whispered in her ear as she laughed.

"I don't understand the pair of you," she whispered back. "Matt's obviously crazy about you and it seems that the feelings mutual, so what the hell is going on?"

I was about to answer when Matt cleared his throat.

"Ok, fine, I get it, I'll just get a conversation going here with my glass of beer," he said feigning to be hurt. "I know when I'm not wanted."

We laughed and our eyes met for a second, and we smiled. The three of us began chatting away when suddenly I saw Olivia walking towards us. I'd completely forgotten about her being here. I felt awful.

"Olivia! Come and meet Jenny," I exclaimed and added, "Matt's *cousin.*"

"Ohhh, *now* I understand," she mumbled as she greeted Matt and Jenny.

We spent the evening together and ended up having dinner at El Grecko's, a Greek restaurant not far from the pub. Matt and Jenny kept us entertained all night with anecdotes of the mischief they had gotten up to together when they were younger.

Before we knew it, it was time to go. I didn't want the evening to end. It had been so wonderful just being in Matt's company.

I arrived home at half past eleven and noticed a piece of paper and a chocolate wrapper under my door.

"Finished early so thought I'd drop by and bring you a Twix for dessert, but you're obviously still out partying ☺ and your mobile's off. Pity…

Guess I'll see you tomorrow then.

Jake xxx

Ps. Waited ten minutes in case you came back… sorry, couldn't resist eating the Twix ☺.

He really was so sweet. I opened the door and walked into my empty apartment, feeling lonely all of a sudden. I'd felt so happy this evening that my apartment felt really too quiet and empty. I wanted to see Matt so much it almost hurt.

I felt guilty as I looked down at Jake's note still in my hand. I shouldn't still feel this way about Matt when I had a wonderful man who cared about me and wanted to be with me. Matt didn't love me enough and never would, it was a fact I had to face. Jenny had told me tonight that she still believed that Matt was crazy about me, but that he was just too scared to take the plunge and then not be able to make me happy. It made me feel good to hear it, but then again it was frustrating, as I knew it wouldn't change a thing.

Matt didn't love me enough, that was the only thing

that I need know. I didn't often compare Jake to Matt anymore, but every time I saw Matt, I realised how different it was with Jake. Jake and I got along so well and he was caring and kind, but there were no real sparks for me. They had all fizzled out when Matt left. He was the only one who could ignite them again. I just hoped this would change with time.

I had to believe it would.

Chapter Forty-Two

I decided to call Vic up a few days later to see how things were going with Sam. I dialed her number and was surprised as it was picked up on the second ring and I heard Tim's voice saying hello.

"Hi Tim, it's Lucy, how are you?" I asked.

"Thfine," he answered.

"Can I speak to your mum please?"

"Yesth," he replied. I smiled, as despite him being a little menace, I melted when he spoke. He sounded like an angel!

I suddenly realised that he'd actually hung up. Typical! And there I was saying he sounded like an angel. I dialed their number again and once again he answered.

"It's Lucy again," I said, smiling into the phone.

"Yesth, mummy's in the thower," he answered.

"Oh Ok. I'll call back later," I said.

"Yesth. You know what? My mummy's got really big boobies. I thaw them in the thower."

I burst out laughing.

"Ith's true," he insisted. "And you know, I thaw my daddy and …"

"Ok Tim, just tell your mum I'll call her later Ok?" I said quickly, cutting him off before he gave me a detailed account of Sam's anatomy.

Vic called back fifteen minutes later just after I'd made myself a cup of coffee and was sprawled out in front of the TV. I told her about Tim and she was delighted that I could finally admit that he was a darling.

"So how are things with Sam?" I asked getting serious.

She sighed and I heard her lighting a cigarette.

"Well he's making an effort to come home a bit earlier since the other night. You should have seen him when I got home from your place! I thought he would be furious but he just took me into his arms and told me he really loved me and he was crazy with worry not knowing where I was and who I was with. Must say I felt pretty smug!" she added grinning.

I was relieved that Sam seemed to be coming to his senses. It was frustrating not to be able to have more inside info now that I was no longer with Matt. I just had to hope for the best. I knew Matt would do everything he could to convince Sam not to mess up and do anything stupid. But it was all up to Sam in the end.

Chapter Forty-Three

"I'm not going!" Olivia said with determination as she barged into my office and fell into the chair opposite my desk.

"Of course you're going!" I replied just as sternly, realising that her nerves were playing up again. She'd been a total wreck since she'd booked her ticket to Paris.

"I can't do it. I just can't!" she wailed, almost in tears.

"Olivia, Paris is a huge city – if you decide you can't stand the sight of him, you can just disappear without leaving a trace and you'll never see him again."

I knew how hard it was for her to grasp such a concept, as we were so used to living in a small community where everyone knew everyone else's business. She moaned as she put her head in her hands.

"I'm completely freaking out here," she said.

"I know you are and I'd probably be in the same state as you are now if I was in your shoes."

"It's just so scary. Up to now it's all seemed rather surreal somehow but now that it's actually becoming a reality, I'm not sure I can cope."

"You'll have a great time and besides, it's only for two months – it's not like you're leaving for ever and will be stranded there all alone if it doesn't work out."

"I know. But what if it doesn't work out?" she asked me anxiously.

"You'll cross that bridge when, and if, you get there. Don't go worrying about things that might never happen."

"It's easier said than done."

My phone started ringing. Olivia looked at her watch and sprung up.

"Damn! I'm late. I can't seem to concentrate on work at all," she said as she raced out of my office.

"You'd be really strange if you could!" I said laughing, but she was already out the door. She was such a workaholic and a perfectionist that she couldn't believe anything, even love, could get in the way of her work. And now that it had, she was completely out of her depth.

After lunch she called me to say that her Aunt had offered her the family beach cottage in the South of the island for the weekend and told her she could invite all her friends over as a farewell party.

"So of course you must come with Jake. I'll finally get to meet him before I leave."

"Sounds great! I'll call him right away to see if it's ok. But either way you can count on me coming for sure!"

Jake sounded really keen on the idea. "But not on Saturday as the Americans are here until late Saturday night. But I can come for the day on Sunday," he said. I was disappointed but then again, it was better than nothing.

I planned to drive down with Olivia on Saturday morning and the whole gang would be showing up for lunch. At least it would take Olivia's mind off her imminent departure. I couldn't wait to get down there. It was beautiful and still undeveloped in the South.

I was just finishing packing my bags when my phone rang.

"I'm picking you up in 10 minutes. Will you be ready?" Olivia said cheerfully.

"I think I should be," I said enthusiastically, knowing that I would probably realise at the last minute that there was something I had forgotten, thus making me late, but anyway she was used to me by now.

"You're ready? I'll believe it when I see it" she answered, chuckling. Then she cleared her throat as if she wanted to say something else but was suddenly nervous. "Listen Lucy, there's something I might have forgotten to mention..." and I just knew straight away what she was about to say.

"Matt's also coming..."

My heart plummeted and raced all at the same time. I guess I had known all along that there was a chance that he would be there too, but hadn't wanted to ask. I thought that Olivia might not have invited him because of me, but then again, I understood why she had. After all, I was with Jake now, so logically I shouldn't have any problems seeing Matt.

"I thought he might be," I finally answered. "I have to get used to seeing him around as we're all friends with the same people. I think the more I see him the easier it should become. It was fun with Jenny last time and went really well so there shouldn't be a problem."

"I'm so relieved to hear that. I've been hyperventilating here, not knowing how to tell you."

I laughed and told her I'd meet her downstairs in ten minutes.

I didn't know if I should tell Jake or just leave it. If I told him it might seem like it was a big deal for me to see Matt – which was the case but Jake didn't have to know that! On the other hand, if I didn't tell him, then maybe he would think I was hiding things from him…

In the end, I sent him a quick text saying that I was off soon with Olivia and that the whole gang, including Matt, would be there for the weekend. He replied "Great! C u tomorrow" - so I guessed all was fine with him.

We were already settled on the beach, when the boys arrived. Alex, Josh, Paul and Matt. They were talking and laughing as they made their way down to the beach. Rachel, Phoebe and Sandra had joined Olivia and I earlier.

"Hey girls!" Josh called out, as we all greeted each other and they sat down. I made sure not to make eye contact with Matt, who was wearing his sunglasses making it hard for me to see where he was looking. He seemed pretty relaxed as he teased Rachel about her teeny-weeny bikini and then told the boys they should go and get the tennis volley bats and ball to play on the beach.

"Don't forget the beers!" Josh called out.

Alex and Matt came back with the bats, ball and beers for everyone.

"Who's up for a game?" Matt asked and Josh and Olivia sprung up. Matt looked towards me, smiling mischievously. "So, are you up for it Lucy?"

I couldn't help grinning. I was pretty good and we used to love playing against each other to get the adrenalin pumping. We were like kids when we played, super competitive, each one always wanting to outdo the other!

"Sorry, not today. Don't want to break my nails!" I said dramatically, holding out my hands daintily.

Matt laughed, shaking his head, as he knew that my nails were the last thing I cared about and that if anything I tended to bite them! But he didn't insist and I was thankful for that. I didn't know how it would make me feel to play against or with Matt, so I preferred to watch from a distance. I suddenly caught him looking at me and as our eyes met, he smiled, making my heart skip a beat. Stop that Lucy! Stop looking at him! Jake is coming tomorrow! You are now going out with Jake who is gorgeous, kind, smart and assertive and who seems to really like you.

"Are you Ok?" Olivia asked me quietly, as she came back from fetching us some wine. "You look a bit put out."

Knowing she would tell me off for my reactions towards Matt, I just told her everything was fine and that I just had some sand in my eye. Ten minutes later, I decided to go for a swim to cool down and also to stop myself from looking at Matt. I could hear them laughing as they played.

I think Matt must have sensed my unease and probably felt the same way, as he kept his distance throughout the day and didn't attempt to sit next to me or talk to me alone. Once or twice our eyes locked for a moment and he smiled but nothing more than that. Relieved, I finally started to relax.

After we had all had quite a lot of beer and wine to drink, we decided to play a game of Pictionary - boys against girls. The boys were such cheats, but we still managed to stay in their wake and they were only one slot ahead of us on the board and there were just

4 slots left to the end. They threw the dice and it fell on 4. If they won this round, it was the end for us. But we had a chance as it was a dual draw. Olivia was drawing for the girls and Matt for the boys.

Matt picked up the card, looked at it and passed it to Olivia. She frowned and said to Matt, "I have no idea what this is."

"Come here and I'll explain," Matt said and whispered the explanation in her ear.

"Ok, got it, thanks!" Olivia said smiling, getting ready to draw.

"Ready, set, go!" Alex said as Matt and Olivia started drawing. We looked at Olivia's drawing and saw that it looked like the sea, then she drew what looked like a plane, so we said plane. She nodded then pointed to sea again and to plane. We tried plane landing on sea. She nodded but made us understand that it was another word. So we just kept trying to say words relating to the sea and planes but without success. Olivia was getting more and more frustrated by the second. Just then we heard the guys say, "It's over girls!" and burst out laughing.

We looked at Olivia and she looked back at us in sheer frustration. "AQUAPLANING girls!" Before we could react the boys howled with laughter again.

Realisation dawned on Olivia as she looked at the boys drawing – which was a car zigzagging and a puddle of water.

"MATT!! I'm going to kill you!" she screeched, realising that Matt had tricked her, before bursting out laughing too. I couldn't help looking at him and grinning widely. He looked mightily pleased with himself and all evening as soon as someone would say "What does aquaplaning mean Olivia?" we would all be in fits of laughter.

After dinner, I strolled outside to get some air and admire the waves crashing onto the reef not far from the beach. It was so relaxing. The beach was completely deserted, golden under the rays of the almost full moon.

I heard footsteps behind me, and didn't have to turn around to know that they belonged to Matt.

"Do you mind if I join you?" he asked hesitantly.

"It's so beautiful out here," I said, evading his question as I did mind but, then again, I wanted him next to me.

"Sure is. Are you enjoying yourself?" he asked, coming to stand next to me.

I laughed. "It's great. The aquaplaning thing was hilarious. I think it will be written into the archives that one."

He grinned. "It was so funny – I'd told all the boys about it from the start and so we just sat there and watched her growing more and more flustered when you girls couldn't find the word for her perfectly explained drawing of a plane landing on the sea."

I laughed with him then looked back towards the sea, enjoying the companionable silence that had fallen between us.

"It's nice to be able to chat like this again," I said truthfully, smiling towards him.

He smiled back, his eyes crinkling on the sides. Oh my, it still sent my heart into overdrive. Luckily Jake would be arriving tomorrow.

"You'll roll your eyes at me and probably walk away, but I'm dying to know if you've seen Sam lately and how things are going on his side."

He did roll his eyes at me then laughed. "Ok, I have to admit that I am tempted to walk away, but I'll be nice and answer your question." He looked serious. "Well, Sam is still having a hard time juggling between his work and the socialising it requires and his home life. He's letting himself be influenced by his single colleagues and I worry about him actually."

"He makes me so mad! What an idiot! I don't know if Vic will ever forgive him if he does mess around. She's barely hanging on as it is."

"It's sad isn't it? I really thought they were such a great couple and that they had it made. You just never know do you?" He looked pensively out to sea.

I cringed – thanks for nothing Sam! I had been counting on him to encourage Matt to get married and he had done exactly the opposite.

"My dad told me about Mr. Delano. You should have told me," he said quietly looking at me with concern.

"What? Call you up out of the blue to tell you every time he showed up?" I asked him, making a face and shaking my head.

He smiled sadly. "Well, I see your point. But I wish you would. I'm worried about you and I hate knowing that that guy keeps showing up like that. I should have told him where to go when I had the chance."

"Don't worry, Jake won't let him hurt me," I said quietly, knowing he wouldn't like to hear that too much.

"Are you happy with him Lucy?" he asked looking sad.

I sighed, thinking of the best way to answer as truthfully as I could. I looked at Matt before quickly looking away again. I just couldn't do this looking into his eyes.

"Yes, he makes me happy although he doesn't make me laugh like you do. But he's sweet and kind and cares about me."

"Ouch!" he said, putting his right hand over his heart and smiling desolately at me. "I guess I asked for that. Didn't realise it would hurt so much to hear it though..."

"You would like him you know," I said, not wanting to comment on his reaction. "He's a good guy."

"Yes, from the little I saw of him at the movies, he did seem like a genuinely nice guy." He smiled, then said dramatically, "I *hate* him!" making me laugh as our eyes locked and everything went silent around me.

I quickly tore my eyes away and told him we'd better get back inside as otherwise the others would talk. He laughed and grabbed my hand as I was turning to leave. He leaned in and gave me a gentle kiss on the cheek, making me hold my breath and close my eyes wishing it would go on and on. Then he turned and walked back inside.

I went to bed not long after that, just wanting to be alone. It was already almost 2 a.m. anyway. I tossed and turned for a while, thinking about the day. Matt seemed to have accepted that I was with Jake now. He hadn't hidden the fact that it was hard for him but at least he had been nice about it. In a way, I wish he would fight for me instead of just giving in so easily. But knowing him he was probably telling himself that Jake would make me happier than he ever could! Idiot!

Once again, my heart was in turmoil. Matt, Jake. Would I ever manage to forget the first and truly fall in love with the second?

Chapter Forty-Four

The next morning we all woke up rather late and had breakfast outside overlooking the sea. It was a beautiful day, the sea was pretty rough as the tide was high but the waves were majestic. I could just sit here and watch them break over the reef for hours. The beach was still deserted as there weren't many cottages along the long stretch of coast. The filao trees and palm trees dressed up the coastline and it was so refreshing to feel so lost in nature.

Jake would be arriving at around noon. I was looking forward to seeing him but had mixed feelings about finding myself with both Jake and Matt here. It was something else that I would have to get used to, so might as well start now. We all went for a swim but the sea was quite cold and the current a bit strong, so we didn't stay long. Everyone sort of flopped down in the sun like big Labradors, relaxing and talking. I hadn't talked to Matt all morning and it looked like he was avoiding me too.

Just then Rachel asked me if I wanted to play Scrabble with her and Josh.

"Sure, sounds like fun," I said absently, suddenly reminded of my idea to see whether I could do a course in writing or copywriting.

I really needed to get my act together and talk to John to see if there could eventually be any job openings for me in the creative field if I did a copywriting course. Copywriting was always fun, exciting, stressful but exhilarating and work was never routine as every new campaign, new ad, new radio or TV spot had to be original and creative. I would definitely start looking into that. I couldn't just keep floating along as I was, doing something that bored me to tears.

Just as we were about to start, Matt walked past and saw us. To my surprise, he sat on the empty chair opposite me and asked us if he could play. I grinned as I knew that unlike me, he wasn't much of a Scrabble player. Fifteen minutes later Matt had managed to put down PIG, HER, DOG, IT, CUT and now he had come up with ESTOMACH.

"That word so doesn't exist Matt!" I exclaimed, as Josh and Rachel laughed and agreed with me.

"What do you mean it doesn't exist? Have you guys read the new edition of the Oxford dictionary recently?" he said, deadpan.

That set me into a fit of giggles as Matt didn't even own a dictionary and he was acting all pompous as though he spent his days analyzing and reading the dictionary.

"What does it mean then?" I challenged him.

"I'm not actually sure but I know it has something to do with the upper stomach – it's derived from a French word."

As none of us were convinced by the word and we didn't have a dictionary, we ruled against it and told him to find another one.

"You guys are such cheats!" he said grumpily, as he placed SIT on the board making Rachel and I giggle some more. He looked like a frustrated little boy. After another round, Matt announced that he had the greatest word ever – AMATING!

"Amating?" Rachel cried.

"Haven't you ever heard people say "Look at those lions - they are amating!"

"No Matt, I can't say I have," Rachel replied.

"It means "to be mating!" he said with assurance, trying to suppress his laughter.

"Matt you are so full of it!" I giggled, as he grinned at me.

And the game continued with fits of laughter as Josh joined Matt in the search for unheard of words that only existed in the Matt Riley English dictionary.

Suddenly, I was distracted by voices coming from inside. I turned and saw that Jake had arrived. Matt followed my gaze and I saw his smile freeze on his face.

"Jake's here," I told the others, feeling shy. "Looks like Matt's definitively our big winner here guys!" I said grinning, trying to lighten the moment and I stood up to go and greet Jake.

His face lit up as he saw me heading towards him. I saw that Olivia had already introduced herself and could tell from her slightly flushed face that she found him hot! I grinned at her as she hid behind him and said "WOW!" I kissed Jake on the cheek, then taking his hand, I went around introducing him to all the others.

When we got to Matt, Jake held out his hand and with a genuine smile said, "Hi Matt, it's nice to see you again." He really was such a nice guy, I reminded myself.

We then headed to the kitchen to grab a drink and he went to change into his swimming shorts. He came back, bare chested, and boy did my insides go all hot! He could have been on the front page of a magazine. His chest was heavenly.

I saw Matt staring at him and felt sorry for him because he was obviously comparing himself to Jake, and with a body like Jake's, it was difficult to come out the winner.

Jake and I went to join the others and Jake quickly fell into conversation with everyone, taking the time to ask each person about themselves and drawing them into conversation. I noticed him and Matt talking like old friends. He really was a people person and was very much at ease with everyone. He seemed to be the type of person who didn't worry about whether or not he would be liked by others, because he probably always was.

Before lunch Jake and I went for a quick swim, the tide had gone down and the current was less strong. It was divine.

"How did it go with Matt?" he asked me softly.

"It was actually fine," I answered. "We didn't talk alone much but just through the others and acted like friends would. The more often I see him the more natural it will become. I can't lie and say that it's as if we never went out, but it's getting easier."

"I'm glad," he replied, with genuine warmth in his eyes. "Come here you." He pulled me into his arms and kissed me passionately. He was a great kisser and I loved feeling his body pressed to mine, and let's just say, I could tell he was pretty much enjoying it too – but I couldn't lose myself in the kiss as I was worried that Matt would see us. I know that I should want to stick it in Matt's face and say "Look what you're missing out on" but I didn't. I knew it would hurt him, and despite everything, it was the last thing I wanted to do.

As we finally headed back up to the house, having had to wait a little for Jake to "calm down" so to speak, I discretely tried to see where Matt was. But he was nowhere in sight. Maybe he was helping Olivia out in the kitchen. But there was still no sign of him when we sat down for lunch. I couldn't ask anyone as I didn't want Jake to realize that I cared. Lunch was a lot of fun and Jake seemed to be having a great time. I was happy that he fitted in with my friends. He was more reserved than them and didn't crack jokes every two minutes, but he laughed at their jokes and talked easily about any subject that was discussed.

I helped clear the table and joined Olivia in the kitchen.

"Where's Matt?" I couldn't stop myself from asking.

"He left. Said he had to go to lunch at Nadia's house," she replied, shrugging as she walked back out towards the table. I didn't say anything but just kept busy with the washing up.

"Jake is gorgeous Lucy!" she exclaimed as she came back with more dishes. "And he's a real gentleman," she said smiling dreamily.

"Are you lusting after my boyfriend Olivia?" I scolded her with a grin.

"Well, who wouldn't?"

I laughed.

"You look really cute together actually," she said, smiling. "I can tell that he really likes you. His eyes follow you everywhere."

"Somehow, I can smell a 'but...' coming up," I laughed, nudging her away.

"Well, he does look really smitten. You on the other hand aren't totally relaxed with him, you seem more reserved than when you were with Matt. Or maybe you just don't seem all 'there'," she explained, shrugging.

"Really?" I replied in surprise. "But you've only seen us together for a few hours."

"I know, but I know you so well Lucy and you're just not you," she said.

I hadn't realised that I wasn't totally me with him. I guess his 'Englishness' made me a bit more serious than I usually am. It's not that he's stuck up or anything, because he's not, but he's just a bit more formal than we are I guess.

But right now he was relaxed and talking away to all my friends as if he had known them forever. I sighed. I was sad that Matt had left. I missed having him around. It seemed that everything was more fun when he was around…

Just then Jake put his arm around my waist and kissed my cheek – I guiltily turned towards him, relieved that he didn't know what I had just been thinking about. Poor Jake, he didn't deserve this. I had to stop this obsession with Matt and find a way to get him out of my system.

"How about you show me your room and we have a little nap?" he said, grinning.

I laughed, took his hand and showed him the way. Maybe I couldn't get Matt out of my heart for now, but if anyone was going to manage to make me forget Matt, I knew Jake could. I locked the door behind us and let Jake lead me to the bed. I for one was more than willing to at least let him try…

Chapter Forty-Five

I had just finished putting on my eyeliner and was squirting perfume in all the right places, when the doorbell rang. Knowing it was Jake, I raced happily to the door and opened it with a big smile.

"Hi gorgeous," he said tenderly as he pulled me into his arms. "Are you ready?"

"You bet!" I replied grinning.

"That's a new one," he answered grinning, "Lucy Evans ready when I pick her up!"

I laughed realising that he definitely had a point there. I slapped him playfully on the arm, pushing him out the door. We headed to the pub where Olivia was having her going away party. She had been much more relaxed since the weekend at the beach and finally actually seemed quite excited at the prospect of going to Paris to meet Pierre.

Jake and I chatted away good-humoredly on the way and after spending ten minutes looking for a parking, we ended up getting one right in front of the pub.

"How's that for luck?" he said grinning at me.

As soon as we arrived, Jake said he'd go and get us drinks and I made my way through the crowd looking for Olivia. I finally spotted her talking to a group of people amongst whom I recognized two of her former work colleagues, and made my way towards them. She seemed overly jolly and I guessed that she'd already downed quite a few drinks.

"I'm going to Paris! I'm going to meet Pierre!" she exclaimed happily as soon as she saw me. "Can you believe it?"

I laughed and hugged her. "I'm so thrilled for you."

There were so many people, it being a Friday night. I saw Phoebe and Yann in a corner and decided to go and say hi to them. It was hard work squeezing past everyone without standing on peoples toes, spilling their drinks or bumping into them. As I avoided a glass of beer which suddenly sprung out in front of me, I bumped rather hard into a man's back. I excused myself into his back, which was still turned. As he heard me speak, he turned around and as soon as he saw me his face broke into a big grin.

"Hi you! Should have guessed it was you," he chuckled. "Once a klutz, always a klutz huh?" he laughed.

"What do you mean *I'm* a klutz? You're the one who put your back where it wasn't wanted!" I cried in fake indignation.

He laughed. "Actually it's my chat up line. I do it to all the pretty ladies so that they have to stop to talk to me."

"Charming," I said, rolling my eyes.

He laughed. "What can I say, I do my best."

I grinned. "I'll talk to you later, am just going to say hi to Phoebe and Yann."

"Ok! Nice having *you* bump into *me!*" he said winking, making me laugh as I walked off.

Olivia was steadily getting drunker and seemed to be having a great time. It was good for her to let out all the stress she'd been under over the past weeks. I saw her stagger towards me and grinned as I noticed her brow creased in concentration as she avoided stools and people on her way.

"Hey you! How are you feeling?" I asked as she finally reached me.

"Fa-bu-lous!" she exclaimed, slugging her wine. "I'm going to Paris to meet Pierre!" she chanted at the top of her lungs. "Ain't it grand!" she added as I laughed with her.

I was so apprehensive for her but impatient that she finally meet Pierre and see if their relationship would go any further. I didn't want her to stay in a dead end relationship and it would at least allow her to see if they really were compatible. Everything they had shared via emails and phone calls would now be put to the test. Would the chemistry be there? I hoped that she wouldn't be hurt or disappointed, but I was a bit skeptical of the outcome of a meeting on Match.com, no matter how close they had gotten and how often they had spoken on the phone.

Three days later I waved Olivia off at the airport. She was once again in a terrible state of panic. She couldn't even get a smile out.

"Relax and enjoy!" I shouted as she started walking into the airport lounge.

She waved, not turning back. I think she was scared

that if she looked back, she'd turn around and go running straight back out the door and forget about ever going to Paris.

"Good luck Olivia," I said under my breath, crossing thumbs for her. I headed back to the office having obtained special permission from John to drop Olivia off during work hours. So good of him! I thought sarcastically. I arrived at the office and fell on my chair, feeling Olivia's absence already. It would be pretty quiet around here without her. Not to mention that Sarah was still away on maternity leave. Well I guess there was Phoebe, but Phoebe being Phoebe… it wouldn't help too much as she was off on another planet most of the time.

I decided to ring Sarah up to cheer me up. I hadn't talked to her in a while and wanted to see how Leo was.

"Sarah hi, it's Lucy," I said as she answered the phone.

"Lucy! You won't believe how happy I am to hear another adult voice. I feel like a human cow these days – I feed Leo, feed myself, and sleep. My IQ has been reduced to goo-gooing and ga-gaaing."

I burst out laughing and we began chatting away as she told me all about Leo and how fast he was growing already. She loved being a mum and was finding it difficult to imagine heading back to work. Then she asked me about Olivia and me and wanted to hear all the details of our love lives. I told her about Pierre and Olivia having left for Paris today. I had told her all about Jake and was in the middle of telling her about the weekend at Olivia's aunt's place, when I saw John's car pull into the driveway.

"Oh-Oh, got to go – the big boss is back!" I said grimacing.

"Tell him I say hi, and thanks so much for calling," she said as I hung up quickly and pretended to be engrossed in typing my report.

"Who the hell were you talking to for the past 20 minutes Lucy?" he said angrily as soon as he set foot into the office. I glanced sideways. He didn't look too pleased. Oh well, nothing new, I thought, as I concentrated on my screen again, ignoring his bad temper. "Well, hello to you too!" I said sarcastically

He glared at me, clearly not amused by my insolence and waiting for an explanation.

"I haven't been on the phone but I don't know about the others," I lied, enjoying his anger.

"I've been trying to call you on your *private* line for the past 20 minutes!" he snapped.

"And it was engaged?" I asked innocently, feigning total surprise. "I probably didn't put the receiver back properly after my last call."

He looked towards the phone, which of course was perfectly well placed.

"Looks fine to me," he said curtly.

"I used it just before you arrived to call Mr. Johansson to confirm your meeting tomorrow," I continued smoothly.

He rolled his eyes at me, clearly not buying it, turned his back and marched into his office, slamming the door behind him.

I sighed. Things sure weren't going to be much fun around here without Olivia, I thought glumly.

Chapter Forty-Six

"Lucy! It's me Olivia. Can you hear me?"

"Olivia! Oh my God! Where are you?" I said, bolting up in my chair.

"I'm standing in my train cabin at the Gare du Nord in Paris and am about to get off to meet Pierre."

"Oh wow!" I replied, getting goose pimples for her. "Have you seen him yet?"

"He's right in front of me. Well at least I think it's him. He looks a bit older than in the photo. Poor thing, he's looking around everywhere, waiting for me," She said nervously. "He looks as nervous as I feel."

"Well go and put him out of his misery," I encouraged her.

"I can't! I'm so petrified my feet are glued to the floor and I just can't get myself to move. I think I might just wait here until the train leaves again!"

I couldn't help laughing but could feel the panic in her voice.

"He's looking at his watch! Oh shit! He's taking his mobile out of his pocket – he's going to call me! What do I do Lucy?"

"Olivia! GO AND MEET HIM – *NOW*" I said, trying to shake her up.

"He's quite cute actually… Lucy, I can't do this, I can't!" she said wailing.

"Of course you can!" I said reassuringly. "Just remember that you might not have physically met him before, but you know the guy well."

"I know, I know… but I'm shitting myself here. Oh no! Another call is coming in – it's obviously him. Will you hang on a sec?"

I waited a minute while she probably spoke to Pierre. Poor thing, my heart was beating so fast just thinking of her in the cabin of her train, looking out the window at the man she's been communicating with for the past months and who she had even said 'I love you' to, and seeing him in flesh for the first time. I was so glad not to be in her shoes!

"Lucy? Are you still there?" I heard Olivia come on again.

"Yes, so was it him?" I asked, curious.

"It was, and I must admit I feel a bit better now that I've spoken to him. I've got to go, he's waiting for me…"

"Good luck Olivia. Everything will go really well - I just know it."

"Thanks. I'll email you or skype soon because I don't think I can afford too many phone calls – and you know how much I hate texting!"

"Ok, but just make sure you keep in touch. And have a great time. Bye."

I was about to hang up when I heard her shouting my name in the phone.

"What now?" I asked her chuckling.

"What do I do when I see him? Do I hug him or shake hands?"

I laughed. "Just go with the flow Olivia. You'll feel what's right when you see him. And besides he might make the first move."

"Ok thanks, got to go. Bye!"

And she was gone.

I was dying to be there and watch the reunion. How it would go? How would they greet each other? What would they say?

The following week, I was deeply engrossed in a new strategy outline I was typing out for John, when my SMS chat popped up advising me that Olivia was online. Being the professional that I am, I threw my strategy aside and quickly logged on, hoping to catch her. My laptop at home had chosen now of all times to crash and as I was too broke to fix it, the only time I could communicate with her was at work, which made it a bit tricky.

Olivia: Are you there?

Lucy: "Comment aller vous?"

Olivia: Very good – that is for both your French and how I am.

Lucy: And? Give me details woman! Lots & lots of them!!!

Olivia: I'm laughing by the way.

Lucy: Don't laugh, just WRITE!!!

Olivia: What do you want to know first?

Lucy: The meeting – how did it go?

Olivia: Oh, it was a bit awkward but Ok. Basically we just said hi and we kissed.

Lucy: YOU KISSED?!? I mean, there and then, after two seconds of meeting each other?

Olivia: NOT FRENCH KISSING you twat ☺!!! Just a peck on the cheek as the French do! But it was embarrassing because we both put out the same cheek and almost ended up kissing on the mouth by mistake.

Lucy: Ooohh! Then what?

Olivia: Well, we walked to our train platform and talked about my trip to Paris.

Lucy: Olivia! You're really not TELLING me much here! I want details, details, details!

Lucy: Olivia?

Olivia: Hang on a sec Lucy, they're calling me.

As I waited for her to return, I bit my nails in impatience. It was so amazing to realise that this wasn't a movie I was watching but that Olivia was really experiencing it all.

Ooh! Goody, she was back! I mumbled happily as I saw that she was typing again.

Olivia: Sorry, but I have to go!

Lucy: Noooooooooooooooo!

Olivia: We'll chat tomorrow Ok?

Lucy: No, it's not Ok! You can't leave me like this! What if I die before tomorrow and I never get to know the rest of the story!

Olivia: Lucy, stop being such a drama queen!

Lucy: Fine! But it's not fair!

Olivia: You're hilarious. BYE!

Damn! Damn! Damn! I was dying of curiosity here. I wish she'd told me more. It was so frustrating being thousands of kilometers away and not being able to really gossip.

After a whole week of desperately trying to get into contact with Olivia, I was hanging out to hear from her. I had been really busy at work, and John had made me tidy up the whole office – I think he was taking his revenge on me for all my slack days - and so I was never able to just sit at my desk and write. Olivia had sent two emails just telling me that she'd be online at such and such a time, but I had never made it.

I had started searching the internet for Copywriting courses and saw that there were lots of options, both online and in colleges. I saw one from Australia which seemed really interesting and despite being by correspondence had a lot of interaction with the tutor. There was also another one which was an intensive 1 month course in Cape Town – the first two weeks being workshops from 9am to 5pm every day and the last two weeks would be work placements in Advertising Agencies where we would work side by side with the Copywriters and actually work on specific campaigns with them. It sounded so exciting but it was also quite expensive. But then again, I knew that my godmother, who lived in Cape Town, would be more than happy to have me stay with them if necessary, and I was sure that my parents would be willing to help me out with the course fees if I chose this option.

But I didn't know whether I wanted to leave Jake (and Matt…) or not. In a way it would definitively do me the world of good to just get away for a while and really get my head and heart back together. But anyway, before I could start thinking of that, I had to see if my parents could help me out with whatever option I chose and I also had to talk to John.

After lunch, seeing that John was out at a meeting, I logged on to chat with Olivia.

Olivia: Hi! Where have you been?

Lucy: Hi! John probably got wind that we were chatting because he's made sure that I was nowhere near my computer all week! But never mind that, tell me all!

Olivia: I'm soooo bored – a few photocopies and typing out a few faxes (in French!) is about as exciting as it gets!

Lucy: Gee, sounds about as thrilling as my job☺!

Olivia: I'm so used to being run off my feet that I just hate this idleness.

Lucy: So, how's the ol' Pierre doing?

Olivia: Good.

Lucy: Good? At what exactly?!!

Olivia: Lucy! You're terrible!

Lucy: What? What did I say?

Olivia: ha-ha!

Lucy: So how is he? I mean, in "that" department??

Olivia: LUCY!

Olivia: I can't believe you're being so indiscreet!

Lucy: It's my job to be indiscreet – it's written in the code book for best friends. So go on, spit it out!

Olivia: Well… nothing's really happened yet actually. It's only been 2 weeks anyway.

Lucy: I know, but since you've been corresponding for so long, it feels like you've been together ages.

Olivia: I know and it's actually strange because he sleeps next to me as naked as an earthworm, yet he doesn't try anything.

Lucy: Maybe he doesn't want to rush you?

Olivia: Yeah, but I think it's strange that he hasn't even tried to have sex with me yet. I mean the French are meant to be fantastic lovers aren't they?

Lucy: Yes, but they are also romantic and probably like to take their time...

Olivia: I guess you're right. It's just that I'm only here for 2 months so I hope he won't be too much of a gentleman about it for too long!!

Lucy: Oh no! Got to go!

I quickly logged out as I saw John head my way. I pretended to be typing out a report as he walked past me and went straight into his office.

It was strange, and a bit sad, because Olivia was so confident and assertive in her everyday life, her work and with her friends but as soon as she was involved with a guy, she lost all her back bone. She sort of just faded into the background and tried to be the person she thought the guy wanted her to be. She became unsure of herself and let them treat her any way they please. I just didn't get it. I had never told her that but maybe I should. It sounded like she was on the same road with Pierre. I mean, the Olivia I know would have sat him down and said, "Are you attracted to me physically or not? Why aren't you even trying to seduce me?" But by the sounds of it, she hadn't said a word to him and was just waiting to see what happened. It was just so unlike her.

The next day I finally decided to talk to John about the Copywriting course. He was really surprised when I knocked on his door and asked him if I could talk to him for a few minutes. I told him about my interest in writing, how much I loved the advertising world and that I was thinking of doing a Copywriting course. He looked really surprised and told me to go on. I told him that I had found two that seemed interesting – one by correspondence and one in Cape Town. He told me that if I could it would be much more interesting for me to do the intense course in Cape

Town. He explained that whether I did a course over 1 year or in one month, it didn't really matter, because it was all about creativity. Either you had it or you didn't.

Of course they would teach you techniques to help you find ideas and work on them and that was important, but on the whole he felt that I would be able to see in the one month intensive course whether I enjoyed it and if I was good at it. He told me that he definitely would be willing to take me on as a junior copywriter and train me if it was what I wanted to do. He told me that if I went to Cape Town he would find me a replacement and when I got back, we would see whether I wanted to keep my present job or start as a junior copywriter. I was so excited that I bounced off my chair and went around his desk, giving him a big hug. He was startled and laughed at my enthusiasm.

"Lucy Evans, I must say that you are full of surprises! Never a dull moment with you around – never know what you're going to do next!" he said, shaking his head in amusement.

I laughed and thanked him for his time. I told him I would let him know what I had decided for the course. I would now have to see whether my parents would lend me the money and if my godmother could have me at her place for a month. I was pretty sure that both would be Ok. I also needed to see when the next course was starting. I couldn't believe that I had finally done something about my unfulfilling work life. I was thrilled and very proud of myself.

What would happen when I went away for 1 month? Would Jake wait for me? Would Matt have moved on with his life by the time I got back?

Two days later, John was out and I logged on hoping that Olivia was online. I was dying to speak to her and find out if things had evolved since the other day.

Olivia: Hi!

Lucy: How are you?

Olivia: Still bored.

Lucy: Apart from that?

Olivia: Fine. In fact, can't chat for long because Pierre's about to pick me up - we're off to lunch somewhere along the Champs Elysée.

Lucy: That's sounds so romantic... but how are things with him?

Olivia: I haven't seen him much actually.

Lucy: What do you mean??

Olivia: Well, we only see each other twice a week because he has to work really late most of the time and when he gets home he just wants to sleep…

Lucy: You're joking surely?

Olivia: No, why?

Lucy: The guy has been waiting 6 months to meet you and now that you're there he's too tired to see you after work?!

Olivia: Well, he takes his job really seriously.

Lucy: Yeah, fair enough, but surely he can handle being with you afterwards?

Olivia: Oh, I don't know. You're making me feel uneasy! His career coach told him not to sleep late too many nights a week.

Lucy: CAREER COACH?

Olivia: Yes! He has a career coach to guide him. I think it's a bit like a psychologist but centered more on the business side of things.

Lucy: Oh, and you don't find that a bit weird?

Olivia: No! Well maybe a little, but nobody's perfect right?! He's here! Talk to you soon!

Lucy: Bye

Career coach! Early nights! How old was he for goodness sake? What about passion and love? Where did that fit in? I'd be so angry if I was in Paris for two months and the guy told me that we could only see each other twice a week because he had to focus on his work and get enough beauty sleep! I'd tell him where to go that's for sure! Is he really interested in her or not? I had my doubts...

I told Jake about my worries concerning Pierre over dinner that night. He had cooked me a roast chicken with vegetables and bought a bottle of wine which he had chilled for me. It was delicious. He was wonderful in that way and knew all the little things to do to make me feel special. I filled him in on what Olivia had told me. He agreed that Pierre's behaviour was rather strange, but thought that maybe he had his reasons. The most important thing was that Olivia was happy - and she did seem to be very happy. It just didn't feel right to me, but I guess this wasn't about me. It was Olivia's life and she was entitled to live it however, and with whomever, she chose.

Chapter Forty-Seven

Olivia: The deed is done!

Lucy: That's great! Are you happy then?

Olivia: Mixed feelings

Lucy: ?????

Olivia: Well, in a way I'm relieved, but then again I'm a bit disappointed…

Lucy: Why?

Olivia: You remember years ago there was that huge boxing match between Tyson and Halloway and we got up at five in the morning to watch it, all excited - then Tyson knocked him out in just a few seconds?

Lucy: Yes, I remember but what does that have to do with you and Pierre?

Olivia: That's what it was like last night! All this waiting and anticipation for it all to be finished in a few seconds!!

And to top it off, he asked me if it had been as wonderful for me as it was for him!

I burst out laughing, forgetting that I was in the office and that a client could walk in at any moment or that John could and would realise that instead of working on his urgent budget plan, that I was chatting with Olivia… I couldn't stop laughing - Olivia ended up asking me if I was still there, thinking that I had logged off. I told her that I couldn't stop laughing and she told me she was glad that her love life was a source of laughter for me! I giggled even more.

We chatted some more about Paris, how she loved going for walks along the Seine and strolling through Montmartre. She asked about Jake and if Mr Delano had showed up again. I told her what had happened and she was really surprised.

"That sounds scary Lucy! I didn't think it would get this bad."

I told her I had called Matt's dad and now we would just wait and see what he did next. I also told her my copywriting course idea to which she answered, "Finally!" She had been on my back for ages, trying to encourage me to find something that interested me instead of doing a job that bored me.

In the end she had to go as they were finally asking her to join them in a client meeting. She was really excited but then again it would all be in French and she wouldn't understand much of it.

Olivia: Never thought I could ever miss my work so much!

Lucy: You're such a nerd☺! Aurevoir!

I decided to go and visit Vic as Jake was busy preparing a report that was due in a few days and couldn't go out. I arrived and was greeted by the usual sound of mayhem.

"Are you sure the noise level is legal?" I asked Vic, wincing as I walked inside.

She laughed good-naturedly and hugged me.

"They're playing cops and robbers apparently. But they seem to think that it involves a lot of loud shooting and shouting!" she said smiling indulgently.

We went to sit outside. Sam was out yet again, at a conference this time. I asked her how things were and she seemed a bit resigned as she told me that things hadn't changed much and that he was hardly ever there and when he was, she still just felt like he was elsewhere, or at least that he wished he were.

"He's trying to be more affectionate but I just don't feel like his heart's in it..." she said sadly.

"Hey! Why don't you try to get a babysitter one night and come out with me for a change?"

"Oh! That would be heavenly," she sighed.

"Well do it! Next time Sam tells you he's working late, see if you can get a babysitter and I'll take you out on the town. Don't tell Sam, let him find out afterwards that you also have a life. Better yet, we can go where he hangs out and pretend we don't know he's there and see how he reacts when he sees you out having fun."

"That definitively sounds like an awesome plan Lucy! You're on!" she grinned wickedly at me as I laughed.

I was excited at the idea of taking Vic out and surprising Sam at one of his 'work dos'. I just hoped it wouldn't be one with any long legged brunettes present!

I hoped that it would stir Sam up enough for him to realise that he could lose Vic if he carried on like that. Maybe I could get Jake in on it and set up a fake pick up scene between Jake and Vic in front of Sam? That would teach him! I grinned happily, imagining the look on Sam's face!

I went over to see Jake the next day and we had lunch together before he had to get back to work on his report. I told him about my idea and he laughed telling me he couldn't believe I was actually planning on going through with an idea like that. I told him that of course I was, and that he was going to help me.

"You have got to be joking?" he said, eyes wide in surprise after I filled him in on the part he would have to play in my plan.

"Oh, go on, don't be such a bore! You have to help us out here. It's for a good cause."

I told him it would be perfect because Sam hadn't met him yet and that as he was gorgeous it would make Sam go crazy!

"Thanks for the compliment," He grinned. "You're pretty gorgeous yourself, but definitively on the crazy side!"

I punched him playfully on the arm and told him that I hadn't decided on the best course of action yet but that I would let him know as soon as had.

The next day at work, I saw Olivia pop up on my screen.

Olivia: Bonjour!

Lucy: hey you! So how is ze city of lurrve?

Olivia: Still luurvly ☺

Lucy: So how's your strange French man? Still only seeing him twice a week?

Olivia: He's not strange and actually this week I've slept over two nights already!

Lucy: Has his stamina improved?

Olivia: I can't believe you're so indiscreet! But if you really want to know, can't complain in that department anymore!! But just one little problem - he practically jumps out of bed to go and shower even before I realise that it's over!

I laughed but had no idea what to answer to that except maybe "get out of there *fast!*" This guy was a definite weirdo.

Olivia: Lucy? Are you still there?

Lucy: Yes, but I just don't know what to answer to that without being mean; how about we talk about your job instead?

Olivia: No! Tell me what you think.

Lucy: Ok, fine - he's weird.

Olivia: He's just different.

Lucy: Definitely weird!

Olivia: Well at least he lets me sleep over now, although...I have to sleep on a mattress next to his bed!!

I was surely reading this wrong – I shook my head and read it again; no, I had read it correctly. What kind of a man was he? First of all, he was far from being a gentleman making her sleep on a mattress on the floor! What a cheek! I'd tell him where to put his mattress that's for sure. In fact, I'd take his mattress and throw it out his apartment window! I couldn't believe Olivia was taking this so well and was so un-fussed by it all. She, an ardent feminist, seemed to be fading into the background, letting the incredible Pierre take over. I didn't like it one bit.

Olivia: Hello? You still there?

Lucy: Olivia! How can you let him treat you like that?

Olivia: It's not so bad, really.

Lucy: Open your eyes Olivia! It's not normal behaviour and you deserve better than that. Come home!

Olivia: You don't know him like I do that's why you feel like that. But he's really special, honestly.

I sure am glad I don't know him any better than I do, I muttered under my breath. I realised I'd had more than enough of hearing about Pierre for today and I would end up saying things that could affect our friendship, so I decided to pretend I had to go and logged off. I really needed to talk about this with someone, but although I had told Jake all about Pierre and Olivia and I knew I could trust him, today I realised that it was Matt that I really wanted to talk to because he knew Olivia really well and would be able to judge the situation better than Jake.

Hello-o? Lucy Evans, a little voice called me back to reality, you're no longer going out with Matt remember? I sighed, knowing full well I couldn't just call Matt and chat away about Olivia's love life but - boy would I love to be able to do that. I felt a huge sense of emptiness engulf me. I had lost my best friend, after Olivia, when we broke up. It wasn't a place that Jake could fill for the moment. It was something which we had built over four years together, mutual friends and shared experiences.

It was a pity life was like that, I thought as I shuffled a few papers around on my desk, not really motivated to do anything in particular. When you broke up it was the end of everything you had built over the time you'd spend together. From one day to the other, you lose love but you also lose friendship, and often a very strong one at that. It's a pity we couldn't keep the friendship even if the love was gone... But the problem, I thought sighing wearily, is that there's always one of the two who's still in love with the other, and it's just too hard playing at being friends afterwards.

I gazed out the window as the breeze swept through the trees and thought how much I'd love to be the one who just wanted to be friends. Wouldn't it make it all so much easier...?

Half an hour after I got home from work, the doorbell drilled, signaling the arrival of my grandmother - handbag under armpit, freshly painted lipstick and hair just brushed on the way up the stairs.

"Hi love," she said, coming in. "Just popping in to see how you are."

"I'm fine thanks. Come in, have a seat," I said leading her into the lounge, knowing that she would refuse.

"No, no, I won't sit down, I'm just about to leave," she said, but then sat down on the very edge of the sofa anyway, bag still firmly under her armpit. She asked me news of my family and I showed her my sister's postcard. We then chatted about this and that and five minutes later she got up to leave.

"What's the rush?" I asked, telling her to sit down again.

"Joan is picking me up in a little while as we're off to play scrabble at Sofia's," she answered, turning towards the door.

"Why don't you go in your car?" I asked knowing how much she liked being independent.

"Oh, it's at the garage. You know I've been having trouble with it for a while. As I was telling the mechanic this morning, there's a serious problem with my accelerator. Every time I put my foot down on it, before I know it I've reached 80km/hr! It's just not possible. So I asked him to take my car and see if he can readjust the accelerator for me," she explained.

I burst out laughing.

"Gran! Why don't you just press your foot less hard on the accelerator?" I exclaimed in mirth as she looked at me in surprise.

"Less hard? I didn't think of trying that!" she said, looking perplexed, as I tried to stop myself from giggling hysterically.

I accompanied her downstairs and as we waited for

Joan to arrive, she chatted away, telling me the latest health news of everyone she knew, and suddenly, out of the blue, she asked me how Matt was. My head swung around and I looked at her, completely surprised.

"I was just wondering as you never talk about him anymore and I really thought he'd come running back when you broke up…" She said, fumbling with the handle of the bag, still under her armpit. Although she talked a lot she didn't like directly probing into other people's personal affairs.

"Well, he hasn't Gran," I sighed.

"You still love him don't you?" she asked, patting my hand compassionately.

"I guess I do. I try not to, but it's so hard. There's also Jake now, but I guess I just don't feel for him what I feel for Matt. Do you think I'm a monster for leading Jake on?" I asked worried. I really valued her opinion as despite her age and funny ways, she was my family here.

"If Jake doesn't make you tingle all over when he touches you, you must… umm, how do you young people say it nowadays… Oh yes! 'Dump him'!" she exclaimed grinning - clearly very proud of her modern day language - as my eyes opened wide. She never ceased to surprise me.

I couldn't help grinning back at her. It was just such a funny picture - my grandmother telling me to 'dump' Jake if I didn't 'get tingles all over when he touched me'. I wonder what she meant exactly when she said 'touched'… I decided to test her and see how she'd react.

"Umm, Gran, just so I'm sure, do you mean that it should tingle when he touches my hand or my cheek or what?"

She shook her head and rolled her eyes at me, "Oh don't make me spell it out to you love. You know it's not your hand I'm talking about!"

I burst out laughing, not believing I was actually hearing that from my grandmother's mouth.

"Matt is such a nice man…" she continued, shaking her head, sighing. "But he's still acting like a little boy! A real pity. Of course I think Jake is also lovely too dear, but I must admit, that despite everything, I do have a little soft spot for Matt… Not that he deserves it mind you!" She added scowling. I laughed and waved her off.

I guess I had a soft spot for Matt too…

Chapter Forty-Eight

Jake and I were still cruising along, although we saw a bit less of each other as he was really busy at work. He was actually off to America in a week and would be gone for two weeks. I'd miss our little weekly rituals; movies, dinner, drinks at the pub, and the nights that followed at either Jake's place or mine. But then again, I wouldn't mind some time to think about our relationship. I felt really bad because I wasn't giving myself to him 100% and he deserved more than that. I really liked him a lot, but I knew that I couldn't be fully with him until I got Matt out of my system. And that hadn't happened yet.

I was beginning to think that I should probably break up with Jake. I felt sad at the thought of no longer being with him, but knew that it would be the right thing to do for Jake. It wasn't fair to treat him this way. I just didn't know what to do – I was so confused.

Olivia: Bonjour!

Lucy: Bonjour you! How are things?

Olivia: Really good. We went to Cassis, in the South of France, to meet his family during the weekend and it went really well. Except that he refused to introduce me as his 'petite amie' (girlfriend) and referred to me as his 'amie' (friend) who had come to Paris on holiday.

Lucy: But WHY?

Olivia: No idea. But you should see him with his little niece, Claire. Just watching them together made me go all gooey inside…

Lucy: Well at least that's one point for him!

Olivia: Lucy! That's low.

Lucy: Sorry, it slipped…

I felt bad but my fingers had been faster than my reason and I hadn't been able to control myself.

Olivia: I'm slowly learning about all the little things about him I didn't know – one thing which is just so cute and just cracks me up; he has an alarm clock in his bathroom which he switches on when he goes to brush his teeth and it rings every 30 seconds so that he knows exactly how long he spends brushing each part of his mouth. 30 seconds top left, 30 seconds top right etc.! So funny!

Hilarious! I thought it was more along the lines of "phobic" and "psycho" actually. Why not tell me he counts each square of toilet paper he uses so as to use the same amount every time! I was so glad Olivia couldn't see my face or hear my voice as I'd give myself away completely. Oh, the wonders of the internet, I mumbled under my breath, as I tried to think of something nice to reply.

Lucy: That's funny?

I doubted she'd realize how sarcastic I was being.

Olivia: The only thing is that he's still a bit on the express bus side with regards to 'doing it'. He doesn't take the time to stop at bus stops or take new routes…

I snorted with laughter at her analogy and suddenly she told me she had to go. In a way it was a relief as I no longer knew how to answer the increasingly weird stories about her dear Pierre. Jake couldn't possibly still think I was being too hard on him once he heard about all this.

I was sorry for Olivia but I would tell him every last detail – well, except for the express bus bit maybe – I had to know if it was just me overreacting or if this Pierre person was indeed really strange!

Chapter Forty-Nine

Vic turned up on my doorstep with dark circles under her eyes, looking utterly miserable. She didn't even make her usual grand entrance, but instead just walked in and sat down on the sofa not saying anything.

I went to get us some wine and sat down opposite her.

"What is it Vic?" I asked gently

She didn't answer at first, but then looked up at me, tears welling up in her eyes. I went and sat next to her as she cried and cried. As the tears subsided, she calmed down, hiccupped and suddenly started talking.

"Sam told me that when he went on business trips they always went to pubs and nightclubs after their daily work sessions but that I didn't have to worry because he loved me."

She stopped and looked in the distance again. Just when I thought she wouldn't say more, she continued, eyes lost in space.

"He was different when he came back from Singapore at the beginning of last week. He was too affectionate and too ready to please. He even came home early all week - I just knew something had happened. I asked him a few times but he kept saying that there was nothing the matter. I left it at that but, as they say, women have an intuition for that kind of thing, and I could feel it in my gut…"

Tears welled up in her eyes again and she stopped to wipe them away.

"On Saturday night we went to this party and he got really drunk. When we got home he started kissing me, and suddenly said, "I love you so much Vic. I don't know how I could have done something like that. I'm so sorry." I got such a shock as I realised that I had been right and it hurt so much, but then again, I was relieved that he'd finally confirmed what I had suspected all along. We had a big fight and I insisted that he give me all the details otherwise I would just leave him there and then."

"Oh my God, that's terrible…" I said in shock.

"Apparently he got completely plastered one night and at a nightclub this girl kept flirting with him and pressing herself against him as he danced. Before he knew it, she'd grabbed him and kissed him... At least he didn't dare say that he had no control over it. He said that he kissed her back and they snogged on the dance floor. Apparently she wanted to go back to his hotel room with him and they were waiting for a taxi to go, when he suddenly realised what he was doing and told her he couldn't go through with it..."

"Thank goodness," I said, relieved that I hadn't been completely wrong where Sam was concerned.

"Yes, I know. I felt relieved too - but what about next time? Will he say no again? What if the girl had insisted, would he have given in? Oh Lucy, it's just so humiliating. I feel so let down and I just don't know what to do. I can't just pack up and go with three little kids to look after. And besides, I love him to bits. But where do I go from here? What can I do? He loves me, I know that, but can I trust him when he goes off now? How can I live in constant fear of what he'll get up to? It's awful, and I'm so angry at him for doing this to us."

She stopped and gulped the rest of her wine down.

"It's so clichéd to say this Vic, but I think you need time to heal this wound. As you say, you can't leave. And besides, he does love you and you love him, he just made a mistake, an alcohol induced mistake, that's all. Maybe you should try to get him to leave his job, he might do it for you, you know."

"I know. I think that it's the only solution because, although it's a great challenge for him, it's tearing us apart. I hate it."

"Have you told him that?"

"Of course. He said he'll think about it and he'll talk to his boss to see what his options are."

"That's good. I really think you just need to try to forgive him. Just remind yourself that he had no reason to stop other than the fact that he loves you. He was far away, no one would have ever known. But still he couldn't do it. The trust will come back slowly but surely. Let yourself feel angry, sad, hurt and so on, and let all your feelings out so that you can get over it. It'll probably bring you and Sam much closer you know. And I know you're meant to be together..."

"We are... I know we are..." she said as she smiled sadly at me. "Thanks for the advice."

"I guess we won't have to go out and play tricks on him anymore then?" I said grinning.

She laughed. "Are you kidding? On the contrary, I was thinking of doing just that on Friday! Do you think Jake would agree?"

I told her that Jake didn't like the idea too much but that I was sure I could convince him. I was relieved to see her smiling again and looking so much more cheerful by the time she left. As I waved her goodbye, I just hoped that Jake was free on Friday and that he would agree to help us out...

"Oh come on Jake, pleeeease, please, pleeeeease," I begged.

"Lucy, I can't act to save my life. I'll give the game away straight away."

"You'll be great. Just smile and whisper sweet words into her ear, looking at her like she's the most beautiful woman you've ever seen."

He groaned. "Please don't make me do this."

"Oh, stop being such a bore! Plus, tell yourself it's for a good cause! You are helping to save Vic and Sam's marriage."

"Who says? Maybe Sam will be thrilled to see Vic with someone so that he can have a clean break."

"That's mean!" I said not amused in the least.

He laughed. "I'm only joking Lucy, but I really don't want to do this.""

"Please don't make me have to use emotional blackmail Jake."

He raised an eyebrow at me as if saying 'try me'.

"Ok, so maybe I'm not good at being threatening," I acknowledged as he grinned at me. "But I would be so grateful if you would do this for me…"

He raised his hands in surrender. "Fine, I'll do it Lucy. But I don't like it at all."

I jumped into his arms and hugged him hard. "Thank you! Thank you! Thank you!"

He laughed and asked me what my plan was. I told him that I was still working on the finer details which made him grin. I didn't have much time as Friday was only two days away.

The next day I told Jake the plan. He laughed and told me that I had watched too many movies, but luckily he was still going to play along. He didn't think for one moment that Sam would believe that he was really trying to seduce Vic, but he would try.

"Just imagine it's me," I said grinning, as he laughed.

I rang Vic up and excitedly told her my plan. She was much more responsive than Jake had been and we squealed in excitement as if we were fifteen again. I thought fleetingly of Matt and knew that he would have loved the idea and would have gladly played along, although of course it wouldn't have worked as Matt and Sam were best mates and Sam wouldn't have thought for a minute that Matt was chatting Vic up. I felt somewhat disappointed in Jake's lack of excitement and encouragement at my plan, but I was grateful that he was going along with it to please me though, even if he didn't see the funny side of it.

Friday night arrived and Vic came to join me at my apartment.

"Wow! You really went all out!" I said as she walked in. She looked stunning. Her long blond hair hung in soft shining curls down her back. She was wearing a tight fitting red dress which accentuated her curves and showed off her impressive cleavage. She wasn't wearing much make up but had accentuated her eyes with black eyeliner and blue eye shadow, making her blue eyes smoky and sexy.

Jake arrived a few minutes later and whistled when he saw Vic.

"I think I'm definitively going to enjoy this after all," he said grinning, making us laugh.

"It's great to see you again Jake. Thanks so much for doing this for me tonight."

Jake looked like a Greek God in his dark blue jeans and white linen shirt. He looked relaxed but chic. He gave me a hug and a kiss then held me at arm's length studying me.

"I think you forgot the black face paint for full effect there Lucy," he said chuckling.

I had dressed like a commando on a mission. Black close fitting jeans, black t-shirt and black sneakers. My hair was up in a French plait and I had just worn a bit of black eyeliner. I had removed all my jewellery so that I wouldn't shine too much!

"I want to blend into the crowd otherwise Sam will notice me straight away," I said blushing, thinking I might have gone slightly overboard.

"I think you may actually look more suspicious dressed like this than if you wore normal going out clothes!"

"You're such a killjoy," I said sulkily, making him laugh.

"Didn't I tell you she was wonderful?" Vic suddenly said looking at me then at Jake, grinning,

"You sure did – and thank you so much for being crazy enough to set your friend up with a stranger in a supermarket!" he said, grinning back at her as he pulled me back into his arms and hugged me.

"Let's get the show on the road guys!" Vic said, laughing and we headed out towards Jake's car.

Chapter Fifty

We went over the plan as we drove to the Waterfront. We would be connected at all times via our mobile phones and Vic and I would wear an earphone which we would hide under our hair. Jake and Vic would wait outside while I went inside to assess the situation, find out if Sam was there, where he was standing and then guide Jake and Vic on what action to take. I felt like Jack Bauer on a mission. We laughed imagining Sam's reaction when he spotted Vic and Jake cosily snuggled up together. I was hoping that there would be a band playing tonight so that they could get up on the dance floor and let Sam see them stuck together in a sexy slow dance.

At the Waterfront Hotel, we had a few drinks to relax a bit before the big event. We didn't really know how it would turn out and Vic wanted to have some fun before all hell broke loose for her. It was great to see her relaxed and laughing - and out of the house without any screeching kids around.

Finally it was 10 p.m. and we decided to head to the pub in case Sam left early for once. It wasn't likely, but we weren't going to take the risk. As we reached the door of the pub, Vic and I put our earphones in place: I would call her as soon as I was inside and from then on we would stay connected. I pushed the door open, my heart beating fast with adrenalin. The pub was packed which was a good thing as at least it was easier to go unnoticed.

I scanned the first bar but there was no sign of Sam. I was careful to stay hidden behind people as I made my way further inside to look for him at the terrace bar. I hid behind a pillar and tried to see above the crowd. I didn't want to get too close in case he saw me. If he saw me, then he would catch on that Vic was with me and the impact of seeing her with Jake wouldn't be as effective. He might even just assume that it was my new boyfriend she was dancing with. I didn't want to take the risk of ruining it in any way.

I pushed my way further towards the other bar, and saw him. He looked towards me and I quickly dropped down behind a big pot plant. I looked up to see a group of four women watching my bizarre behaviour curiously, clearly wondering what the hell I was doing. I gave them a distracted smile before standing up again once I was sure Sam was looking the other way, and headed towards a pillar which I could safely hide behind.

"Lucy calling Vic, testing-testing one-two-three! Can you hear me? Suspect has been spotted about 30m to the right of my position. Get ready to enter the scene, over and out, over and out," I reported into the phone to Vic in the same tone that I had heard so often in action movies.

"Is she for real?" I heard Jake say in disbelief as I snorted with laughter.

"You can come into the pub, he's standing with his back towards the entrance, so you'll be fine. The pub is really packed so he shouldn't notice you immediately. The band is playing which is great as I think it might be a nice touch if you sort of strolled up together on the dance floor and snuggled up in a slow dance" I said into the phone.

"This is so exciting!" screeched Vic. "Are you ready, Pretty Boy?"

"Please don't call me that – it sounds so gay!" Jake whined.

"How about Hunky-Dory then?" Vic asked laughing. "I heard that in a movie once and I've always wanted to use it – as in "you're so hunky-dory.""

"You need help lady!" Jake laughed. "Ok, let's do this."

I laughed at their exchange and stayed behind the pillar, watching them walk in and make their way towards the dance floor.

"Wait for me to tell you when to make your dance floor entrance," I said, keeping a close eye on Sam. His back was turned to me and he was standing sideways from the dance floor. "Ok, go now. He's not looking yet but I'll tell you when to give it your all."

I watched them stroll onto the dance floor and snuggle up in a slow dance. I kept my eyes on Sam, who hadn't noticed them yet as he wasn't looking their way. Go on Sam - just look at the dance floor will ya! I thought, getting impatient. The next song started and still nothing. Then suddenly, something caught his attention and he turned, looking at the band.

"Now! Now! Now! He's looking towards the band - give it everything you've got guys," I screeched excitedly into the phone.

I saw Vic grin and Jake whirled her in and out theatrically, as she laughed up into his face.

I watched Sam intently. He

hadn't noticed Vic yet. He was just watching people dance, then suddenly, his eyes stopped on her...

"He's staring at you Vic but he doesn't know it's you yet. He's probably just checking you out. Give it to him baby!" I said laughing. Suddenly I decided we needed to heat things up a bit. "Tell Jake to grab your butt!" I whispered to Vic, excitedly.

"What?" Vic said giggling.

"Just do it!" I giggled back.

"He says no way!" Vic laughed into the phone. "I asked him if he didn't think my butt was good enough to grab but he said that he just isn't a butt grabber!"

"Tell him he's boring!" I said grumpily.

"He grumbled that 'next thing you know she'll be telling me to grab your tits'!" she giggled into the phone.

I burst out laughing, keeping an eye on Sam who was talking to someone as he continued watching Vic, who still had her back to him and was holding tightly onto Jake. I must say that she looked really sexy from behind, her dress revealing the generous curves of her hips and her slim waist. Her legs were toned and looked super sexy in a pair of red high heels.

I was happy to see that Jake was trying to play along as his hands caressed Vic's back as they danced. He even pushed a stray lock of her long blond hair, and gently put it behind her ear. Ooh, he was pretty good at this! I turned back to stare at Sam – I was beginning to get very impatient.

"He's still watching you, turn sideways so that he realises it's you Vic."

I watched him intently waiting for the flicker of recognition…

"I think he's caught on!" I exclaimed elatedly into the phone as I saw him frown and then stare heatedly towards them. "Give him your back again, he's not sure yet but the look on his face is priceless!"

Sam's eyes were locked onto Vic and then I saw the blood drain from his face, his eyes widening with shock as his grip tightened on his glass. I quickly took a photo with my phone - Vic had to see this.

"He knows! He knows! Watch out, he's coming!" I screeched, barely able to contain my excitement.

I watched Sam making his way towards Vic and Jake.

"He looks furious, make that ballistic," I giggled, finding the whole thing hilarious, although I couldn't help feeling a tad worried as I watched him push his way to the dance floor, smoke in his wake. I wouldn't like to be in Jake's shoes I thought guiltily.

Oh no! I hoped he wouldn't hit Jake! He burst onto the dance floor and prodded Jake on the shoulder, looking really angry.

"What do you think you're doing?" Sam asked coldly, eyes wild.

"Dancing with this beautiful lady," Jake said calmly. "Do you have a problem with that?"

"I sure do mate!" Sam snapped. "It happens to be my wife!"

Jake pretended to be shocked at the revelation.

"Is that true Vic?" Jake asked, pretending to be hurt, and she nodded shyly mouthing, "I'm sorry."

"I should beat the shit out of you for trying to seduce my wife, but as she didn't seem to mind at all there's not much point," Sam said glaring angrily at Vic.

"Plus he's got way more muscles than you honey, so I don't think it would be a good idea," Vic said silkily, pouring oil onto the fire, as I snorted with laugher in my corner.

"That's it!" he shouted. "We're going home!"

"But I'm having fun Sam. Can't we stay a bit longer," she whined, winking towards me. I whispered, "Careful Vic" worried that Sam would do something stupid.

"NOW!" he said, grabbing her arm and leading her away.

"Ok, Ok, calm down - I'm coming," she said, as she grinned at Jake over her shoulder and mouthed 'thank you'.

He winked at her and looked around trying to find me. I waved to him but he couldn't see me. I stayed hidden until I was sure Vic and Sam had left, then I walked up to Jake and gave him a huge hug.

"Thank you! You were great. You should have seen the look on Sam's face when he suddenly realised that the sexy woman he was staring at was Vic!"

We laughed and made our way to the bar to get a well-earned drink.

"Well, that sure was something I've never done before!" Jake said grinning. "Quite an adventure!"

"So you're not much of a butt grabber then?" I teased him, giggling.

"Well, it depends on whose butt it is…" he replied, grinning wickedly, as his hand reached out to grab my butt, causing me to break into peals of laughter.

Vic rang me up the next morning sounding really happy.

"It worked!" she screeched into the phone, making me pull the phone away from my ear. "Thank you, thank you! And Jake was great; a born actor!"

"It was a lot of fun! I'm thinking of becoming a detective or a spy actually."

Apparently Sam had been sick with jealousy and screamed at her telling her that it wasn't a way to act when she was a married woman and what the hell was she doing going out by herself. She calmly told him that that's what he did almost every night and she'd had enough of sitting home alone with the kids. She was still young and also wanted to go out and have fun.

Apparently he'd seemed shell shocked by that, as if he expected her to want to wear slippers and watch TV every night. He asked her a thousand and one questions about Jake which she answered truthfully and mostly with "I have no idea". They had walked around the Waterfront until he had calmed down, and then they had sat in a café and talked for hours.

The long and the short of it was that seeing her dancing with Jake he had thought he had lost her. Facing the fact that she might be in love with another man made him realise how much he loved and needed her. He felt lost in the new life created by this new job and he was happy. He was going to start looking for another one immediately as he acknowledged that this just wasn't a job for a married man.

"And he intends to stay married to me so the job has to go. And…Oh my…!" she said theatrically into the phone. "The make up sex was *un-believable!*"

"Too much info Vic," I said laughing, bursting with happiness for her. I just hoped that Sam wouldn't go back to his old ways too fast. If so, we'd have to stage another date for Vic! I thought grinning.

"Did you tell him we set him up?"

"No way! I want him to keep thinking that a hunk like Jake found me sexy," she laughed. "He'll end up seeing Jake with you and probably figuring it out, but for the moment I'm savouring his jealousy."

I didn't get around to corresponding with Olivia at all

in the next few days, which in a way suited me fine as, although I would have loved to tell her about Sam, Vic and Jake, I couldn't handle much more of Pierre right now. She had sent me an email telling me that they were off to a friend of his in the country for four days. He had actually agreed to take 2 days off – his coach had said it was ok! Oh pl-ease! I thought impatiently. Anyway, I didn't have to reply and it was a relief. I was finding it harder and harder to be natural and pretend it was all wonderful when in fact I couldn't wait for her to get out of there.

On Wednesday afternoon, just after getting back from work, my doorbell rang. I knew it wasn't my grandmother as it was just a normal doorbell ring! Who would be visiting me at 5 o'clock on a Thursday?

I flung open the door and froze.

Mr. Delano was standing there - *on my doorstep!*

Chapter Fifty-One

"Hello, beautiful," he said silkily as my heart pounded in my ears.

"How did you find out where I lived?" I asked in shock.

"I looked in the phonebook and since I had seen you doing your grocery shopping around here, I knew it had to be an Evans living in this area."

"You're sick do you know that?" I replied, a shiver running through me. The creep just stood there, his eyes slurping over my body.

I didn't know what to do. I was petrified; did he plan to hurt me? I yanked the door to close it but he was too quick for me, pushing back against it. He was stronger than me and the door flew open again.

"Wait! Just give me a minute will you?" he exclaimed.

"Just GET OUT OF HERE!" I shouted as I saw him pull something from behind his back. I froze.

Was he going to shoot me right there on my doorstep, or pull a knife out and rape me? The scream was bubbling in my throat as his hand came out from behind his back.

"As you refused the flowers, I thought I would bring you some chocolates," he said with a flourish.

My heart was hammering in my chest - I didn't understand what he was doing here. Was he really just here to give me a box of chocolates? Did he have anything devious planned? I felt like my knees would buckle any minute but I didn't want to show him how scared I was. I grabbed the box of chocolates from his hand and threw it behind him.

"Playing hard to get again aren't we now?" he said with a smarmy smile. As he turned to pick up the chocolates, I seized the moment and slammed the door in his back. I fumbled frantically with the lock, my hands shaking uncontrollably, making it very tricky.

I heard him thud against the door as he tried to push it open again, but I had finally managed to get the safety lock in place and the door couldn't open more than an inch. We battled silently, him trying to push it open and me to close and lock it.

"Oh, come on now - don't be so difficult. Let me in

and we can just chat," he said through the door, trying to cajole me.

I raced to the phone and dialled the first number that came to mind.

"Hello… Lucy?" I felt my body sag in relief at the sound of Matt's voice.

"Matt, please, come quickly!" I said bursting into tears.

"Lucy, what's wrong, where are you?" he said sounding worried.

"At home. He's here behind my door. I'm so scared."

"Who is? You're not making any sense."

"Mr. Delano. Please, come quick!" I cried in fear as I heard him banging on my door again.

"I'll be there in 5 minutes - keep your phone with you and keep talking to me if it makes you feel better. I'm not far from your place. Just stay put and relax. He can't get in Luce."

Matt talked to me as he made his way over, driving like a maniac as I heard a lot of honking from other cars and swearing from him until he finally said, "I'm here."

In the meantime, I had pulled a small table in front of my door then had hidden in my room not wanting to listen to Mr. Delano still trying to get me to open the door for him. He was persistent, that much I would give him. Suddenly all became quiet. Then I heard Matt storm up the stairs and pound on my door.

"Lucy! Open up! It's me, Matt."

I stood up shakily and walked to the door, opening it slightly to make sure he was really there. Tears rolled down my cheeks when I saw his familiar face.

"Did you see him on your way up? He was still here just before you arrived," I said, my voice quivering as I let him in and fell into his arms, my body shaking uncontrollably.

"Don't worry Luce, I'm here. Relax - I'm not going to let anything happen to you," he whispered soothingly into my hair as he stroked my back reassuringly. "Ever," he added as he hugged me tightly.

"I didn't hear him leave," I whispered to him as my heartbeat slowly returned to normal. "I watched through my window but he hasn't left..."

"There's a blue Honda downstairs, is that his car?" he asked gently, frowning.

I nodded, eyes wide in panic.

"Lock the door behind me. I'll be right back."

I didn't want him to leave me but I wanted him to make sure Mr. Delano had left. Just as I heard Matt go down the stairs, I heard a car roar past my window and saw that it was Mr. Delano's blue Honda. I heaved a huge sigh of relief. He was gone.

A few seconds later I saw Matt's car scream past my window and realised he had gone after him. I waited impatiently for Matt to come back, still shaking uncontrollably. I hoped nothing would happen to Matt. After what seemed like hours, I heard Matt's car come back. I felt my body sag in relief. I ran to the door and pulled it open, racing into his arms, bursting into tears again.

"Shush…" he said comfortingly, as he held me in his arms. "It's Ok. Everything's fine."

He led me to the sofa and sat me down. "I'll be right back," he said, smiling, and I heard him moving around in the kitchen. I was still in shock and just sat there staring into space. I had never been so scared in my life. Thank God that Matt was close by and had managed to come.

"Drink this; it'll make you feel better," Matt said as he handed me a small shot glass filled with whisky.

I swallowed it in one gulp and grimaced as it burnt its way down my throat - but it had the desired effect and I felt it burn through my fear and help me to relax.

"Thanks," I said, looking at him gratefully and smiling for real this time.

"So I managed to catch up with him at the end of your street. I almost punched him there and then, I was so angry. But luckily I managed to calm down. I just grabbed him by the collar and I think I scared the living daylights out of him because he begged me not to hurt him. I then told him that my dad was a lawyer and that you were going to file a restraining order against him at the police station."

Matt told me that the blood had drained from Mr. Delano's face and that he had almost been in tears, telling Matt that he hadn't wanted to scare me, but that he was just trying desperately to get me to go out with him. He thought I was just being difficult and that I enjoyed bantering with him.

"I told him that if he ever came near you again that I would make sure that my dad put him behind bars," Matt said. "I'm pretty sure that the message was loud and clear! And he seemed genuinely upset and honest when he said he would leave you alone and that he was sorry to have upset you that way."

I was relieved to hear that, but I knew I would still be looking over my shoulder for a long time. It was a horrible feeling knowing that someone was watching you and following you. But I had to believe that what he said was true otherwise I would be living in fear and I didn't want that. He hadn't actually shown any signs of being violent or dangerous or ever given me the impression that he would hurt me, I suppose, but his constant harassment over the phone and turning up everywhere had made me paranoid.

"Thank you so much Matt," I said gratefully. "I don't know what I would have done if you hadn't been nearby. I've never been so scared in my life."

Matt stood up and came to hug me. "I'll never let anything happen to you Luce, I promise."

I hugged him back, enjoying the feel of his arms around me and his beloved smell. He pulled away and looked at me, seeming to hesitate before speaking.

"Maybe you should call Jake now…" he finally said softly.

Oh noooo! I had called Matt instead of Jake!

Jake arrived five minutes later. Matt greeted him at the door and they exchanged a few words which I couldn't make out before Matt waved at me and left. I felt my heart plummet as I watched him go.

Jake walked up to me and hugged me tightly. He looked at me sadly, I wasn't sure why, although I had a pretty good idea.

"You called Matt. You didn't call me…" he said, almost in a whisper, as my heart sank.

I looked up at Jake with remorse. "I'm so sorry. I guess it's just a force of habit. Four years is a long time you know," I said weakly.

He nodded but didn't reply. He then asked me to tell him what had happened in more detail and so I filled him in on everything.

"Can I stay over at your place tonight?" I asked. "I don't want to stay at home."

"Of course," he replied softly. Jake was caring and gentle with me but I could feel that he had withdrawn from me; he wasn't himself.

What a disaster. I had called Matt, not Jake, when I found myself in danger. And I guess that told Jake everything he needed to know and that I hadn't been telling him…

Chapter Fifty-Two

Thursday and Friday at work were a nightmare. I felt shaky with nerves. I kept glancing out the window expecting Mr. Delano to show up at any moment. I was also sad to have hurt Jake; I knew that he had been deeply disappointed. I hadn't heard from Matt again and was tempted to ring him to say thank you but I knew it wasn't a good idea. I had sent him a quick text message on Thursday morning just saying "Thank you" to which he'd replied, "I'm just so glad that you're Ok."

I tried to shake myself out of my dark mood and forget about Mr. Delano, Matt and Jake. To take my mind of things, I studied the course content of the Copywriting course. My parents had agreed to help me out and my Godmother was more than happy to have me stay with her. I was just waiting for the confirmation of my registration and then it would be all set. John had been great about it and told me that I could leave at any time. He had found a temporary secretary who could fill in while I was away and who was really flexible and could come at a week's notice.

It looked like the next course would be starting in 2 weeks. So if they accepted my registration, I would be flying off in less than 2 weeks! I was so excited and so proud of myself for finally taking control of my future. I really felt that it was something I could be good at. If they didn't confirm my registration in time, then I would have to wait until the start of the next session which was in 2 months' time. Either way, I would be going and if all went well, by the end of the year I would be a copywriter!

After work on Thursday, I went to visit my grandmother as I needed to be with my family. I didn't want to tell her about Mr. Delano, but just being with her made me feel at peace and helped me to relax. I watched an episode of *The Young and the Restless* with her and was treated to a non-stop commentary about the lives of each character and what had recently happened and what she thought of them. It was exactly what I needed to take my mind off everything.

I didn't really want to be alone in my apartment. Jake had told me to come over to his apartment if I didn't feel up to sleeping alone at my place and I accepted, relieved. I still felt like Mr. Delano would jump out from behind the door at any moment.

Jake was quiet all evening, telling me that he was tired, but I knew that he was still upset about me calling Matt - and I didn't blame him. I didn't push him to talk and just let him be as I wasn't ready to face 'the talk' yet. I knew it would come, and it had to, but I really didn't want to lose Jake. I knew I was being selfish but right now I didn't have the strength to be alone. He cuddled up to me in bed but didn't try anything else, which in itself said a lot. But I didn't take it to heart as I knew I had hurt him and he needed time to get over it.

By Saturday, he seemed himself again and even I felt cheerful again. We went shopping, had lunch in town and then I went home to relax and prepare for the big Gala Charity Ball in aid of cancer research that we were attending that night.

He told me that he would be picking me up at eight and had asked me not to be late as otherwise it would be really hard to find a parking. I had already found a dress – a long dark blue dress, with a low cut back, tight at the top and loosening from my waist down. It was really flattering in all the right places and I loved wearing it. I washed and blow-dried my hair, trying to make an effort. I put on some eyeliner and lipstick, a dab of perfume and I was ready! I smiled at my reflection, happy with the way I looked and feeling much more upbeat than I had all day. I loved dancing and it would be a wonderful way to forget everything else…

When Jake arrived, I grabbed my bag and raced to the door, shoes in hand.

"I'm ready!" I said, planting a kiss on his lips with a big smile. Shoes didn't count after all! "Let's go!"

He looked at me quizzically and I wondered if maybe he didn't like the dress or if he found my happy mood disconcerting. I didn't think so and preferred to gaze at him as he looked so handsome in his tux. He really was what you'd call 'drop dead gorgeous'. I looked back at his face and he was still looking at me, as if waiting for something. A grin suddenly spread across his face.

"You know," he said, obviously trying to suppress his laughter. "I've always dreamt of taking a woman with a gorgeous dress and a sexy shower cap to a ball."

My hand flew to my head and I burst out laughing as I took my ugly green shower cap off. I had put it on while applying my make up as my hair kept falling into my face and I couldn't find anything to put it up with. I had completely forgotten to take it off!

I was relieved that Jake seemed relaxed and in a good mood. The ball was taking place in an old Colonial house in the middle of the sugar cane fields near Flacq. The place was magical, with huge trees all around and flowers blooming everywhere you looked. Every sugar estate had its Colonial House which had been built during the colonial period by the plantation owners and had been kept until now. Most had been demolished and the few that remained where now used for receptions such as balls, weddings, cocktails and family reunions. As we drove through the big white wrought iron gates we saw the garden illuminated with candles - it looked like something out of a fairy tale.

There were lots of our friends attending the ball, and in fact there were many generations present which made it all the more enjoyable. Jake and I made our way in, greeting people as we passed them.

The evening was a lot of fun, with so many people of all ages I knew. I introduced Jake to everyone, and he was charming to them all. Matt waved to me from a distance; I waved back and smiled, my heart beating so fast I could hardly breathe. Otherwise he seemed to be avoiding us as we had managed not to bump into him so far. I was relieved, as I didn't want to hurt Jake any more than I already had. After a while, Jake got into conversation with a colleague of his, and I decided to leave them to it and head to the buffet. I was suddenly starving. The buffet was amazing with an endless array of food: salads, pastas, chicken, ham, salami, pâtés, cheeses, fruits, bread and the list went on. I was just leaning over to grab a piece of bread to spread some pâté on, when I felt goose bumps invading my body.

"Could I have this dance?" Matt said in my ear. I turned around and he was standing there, his blue eyes sparkling at me, his smile crinkling at the sides. My heart melted and everything around me disappeared. The effect he had on me never ceased to surprise me. All I could see was Matt in his tux holding out his hand to me. I almost let my guard down and accepted. But suddenly a little voice inside of me shouted 'snap out of it Lucy!' and I was jerked back to reality. Matt was still smiling at me, waiting.

"No, I can't Matt," I answered sadly.

"Please..." he insisted, smiling irresistibly.

"No. I am so grateful for what you did for me the other day, but the fact is that I'm going out with Jake now..."

"I'd really love to dance with you. Let's say it would be a way for you to say thank you," he smiled.

"Why don't you dance with your partner?' I asked, fishing for information.

"I didn't bring anyone," he answered quietly, looking into my eyes.

"Why?" I asked despite having firmly decided that I wouldn't ask.

"Because the only person I wanted to be with was already going with someone else..." he said not taking his eyes off me.

I was completely bewildered. What was he trying to say? Was I reading too much into what he was saying?

Was he really talking about me?

"Don't play games with me anymore Matt," I sighed.

"I'm not. I promise." He looked intense and I knew he was being honest, but I didn't know what to say.

"Dance with me Luce..." he whispered, taking my hand.

I let him lead me to the dance floor in a daze. I had a fleeting thought for Jake, wondering if he could see us and feeling bad, but as soon as Matt put his arms around me and we started moving slowly in time to *"Lady in Red"*, I was lost. We danced in silence, both lost in our thoughts, just enjoying being together.

Suddenly I felt Matt tighten his grip on me and looked up questioningly.

"I have never been as scared in my life as I was when you called me the other day," he said, his voice quaking.

I stared at him, surprised by his outburst and even more so at the intensity of his voice.

"If anything had happened to you, I don't know what I would have done," he whispered into my ear.

I didn't know what to say. But I knew that I had to get away from him. I started to pull away but he pulled me back. "Stay!" he said loudly, before whispering gently. "Please…"

I fell back against him and we carried on dancing in silence, my heart beating in my throat. I never wanted the song to end. Then I glanced to the side and was shaken back to reality as I saw Jake standing on the edge of the dance floor looking straight at us…

I pulled myself away from Matt, feeling incredibly guilty. He started to restrain me and then saw Jake too and let me go. My insides were in upheaval as I raced to Jake's side.

"Lucy, I think we need to talk…" Jake said flatly as I reached him, his eyes showing his inner turmoil. My heart sank.

"I know we do," I said wearily and followed him in a daze as he led me outside to one of the benches in the garden.

"When Matt came up to you to ask you to dance, I was opposite you because I was also making my way over to you. I caught the look in your eyes as you looked at him - I've never seen you look at me like that Lucy," he said sadly, looking away. "And the two of you on the dance floor…" he shook his head seeming to want to rid it of the image of us dancing.

I didn't know what to say, as I knew he was right. I couldn't handle the thought of hurting him anymore than he'd obviously been. He turned back to me and carried on.

"I'm not angry with you as I know how much you're hurting yourself. It's hard to love someone who doesn't love you back." He smiled desolately at me. "But then again, the way Matt looked when he held you in his arms… sure looked to me like he was in love! But that's not my business anyway."

"I'm so sorry Jake. You're really wonderful and it's been nothing but happiness being with you. I care so much about you and wish things could be different but you're right, I still love Matt and I've tried so hard to forget him, but I know that I'm not over him yet. I'm so sorry…" I said as tears fell down my cheeks.

He took my hand and nodded, brushing my tears away with his fingers. He smiled up at me looking so sad - it broke my heart. He squeezed my hand tightly in his, pulling him to me and hugging me tightly.

"I'm so sorry for not being honest with you from the start. I just liked you so much and loved being with you and truly thought that I would manage to put Matt behind me and move on with you."

"I forgive you Lucy. I know you didn't intend to hurt me. You're too much of a softy for that," he said tenderly, as I smiled sadly up at him.

"If you can handle being friends, I sure could use a friend like you," I said, honestly.

"Give me a little time to get used to the idea of not being with you anymore, and then I'd really love for us to be friends."

We spoke on for a while longer, both sad, yet knowing it was the only thing to do. After a while, Jake got up and told me he was leaving. I accompanied him to his car and watched him pull away, sure I would find a lift with someone without a problem. A part of me felt such a sense of loss, whereas the other part felt a huge sense of relief.

I jumped, startled as I felt a hand gently press my shoulder

"Is everything OK?" Matt asked gently.

"I guess so," I said, feeling so confused. Just too many things to deal with in one night…

"Do you want to talk about it?" he asked, putting his arm around my shoulder and guiding me back inside.

"Thanks, but no, not tonight," I answered realising that I wasn't prepared to open my heart to Matt again.

"I'm here for you, Luce," he whispered. "You know that don't you?"

"I can't do this Matt," I said, pulling away from him. "I can't become your good friend suddenly. It's still too hard. Just leave me alone. Please…" I pleaded and ran off before he could catch me. I raced to the ladies room knowing he wouldn't follow me there.

After ten minutes, I headed back inside and made sure I didn't bump into Matt again. I was on the verge of tears and couldn't face talking to anyone. Thankfully, half an hour later Alex said that he was tired and was leaving and offered to drop me home.

I was so relieved to be home and finally alone. I was so sad that it was finished with Jake as he really was amazing.

Matt's way of treating me puzzled me and sent mixed signals. I just didn't understand what he was trying to do. He didn't want to marry me, but he wanted me.

I couldn't go back to that. I had to be strong and not give in now that I no longer had Jake to fall back on. But it had been the only fair thing to do, at least until I got Matt out of my system… whenever that would be…

Chapter Fifty-Three

I couldn't believe it had already been a month since Olivia had left for Paris. So much had happened, and I was dying to speak to her. I needed to talk to someone about Matt and Jake. I wished I was in France right now too and that everything that had happened was in fact just a nightmare…

I decided to ring Vic up. She picked up the phone after it rang for hours and sounded half asleep.

"I'm sorry, did I wake you up?" I asked.

"No, not at all. I'm actually sitting on the veranda making Christopher do his reading homework," she answered as she yawned. "It's actually a perfect sleeping pill if you ever have any trouble getting to sleep."

I laughed and heard her tell Christopher to go and play for a little while. Needless to say that he didn't need to be told twice!

"So how are things with Sam?" I asked.

"They're really good actually," she replied as I heard her light a cigarette. "It's actually made us grow a lot closer so it hasn't all been bad."

"That's great," I answered honestly.

"He's actively looking for a new job and has an interview next week. The job won't be as challenging as the one he has now, but at least he'll work less hours and our family life will become normal again," she said taking a puff of her cigarette.

We chatted on about her kids and I waited for her to ask me about Jake. I knew it would come, sleepy or not sleepy, curiosity and her love of gossip always showed through. And five minutes later it came.

"So how's Jake?" she asked.

"Oh, umm… not so good," I said, hesitating, not sure whether I should tell her. Oh well, here goes, I thought. "We've broken up," I said trying to sound as casual as possible.

"Oh, that's good," she replied nonchalantly.

I frowned, confused. That was one reaction that I really hadn't expected from her and was about to say so when she suddenly exclaimed, *"What do you mean you've broken up! Whhhyyy?"*

That was more like it! I thought grinning to myself.

"Well, he told me that he couldn't compete with my feelings for Matt and it was no use trying," I said sadly.

"Matt! What do you mean your feelings for Matt? He's history remember?" she said, clearly frustrated.

"Not really…" I replied not sure whether I wanted to say more or not.

"Oh Lucy, what am I going to *do* with you?" she said, sighing dramatically. "I find you a wonderful man to make you forget Matt and you're still talking about him."

"I know. Jake is wonderful but it's not as easy as that. I'm in love with Matt and I can't help it," I replied, crestfallen.

"So you let Jake go?" she asked as if needing to be sure.

"Yes - I can't pretend to love him when it's Matt I'm still crazy about - I respect him too much for that."

"Lucy, Lucy, Lucy…" she said dramatically and I imagined her long golden locks swinging from side to side. "I just want you to be happy you know that don't you?" she added gently.

"I know Vic, and thanks..." I said touched.

After I had said my goodbyes to Vic, I threw myself on my bed feeling like screaming and breaking everything. I just wanted time to go by really fast so that last night would seem far away and that I could look back on it and laugh.

That evening, although I really wasn't in the mood, I showered and got dressed to go and visit my grandmother as it was her 76th birthday. I had gone to the bookshop and bought her a Cooking Book as she enjoyed making desserts and was extremely good at it. Her Tiramisu's were out of this world. I smiled as I remembered the Kama Sutra book I had bought Olivia as a joke, wanting to send it to her and tell her to give it to Pierre hoping to help his 'express bus' ways. I grabbed my grandmother's present, already wrapped up, the flowers and her card and went next door to her apartment.

I hugged her and wished her a happy birthday as she took the present and the flowers telling me I shouldn't have but quickly, and excitedly, un-wrapping the book while I went into the kitchen and helped myself to a glass of coke. I was pouring it into a glass when my hand froze midway.

"Kama Sutra? Oh, that's lovely dear. Is it a book

about India?" she called out innocently, looking at me as I raced into the lounge and stared at her, mortified, not knowing what to do. "Auntie Sue was telling me about this wonderful new book about a love story set in India. This must be it," she said, smiling happily down at the book.

I was about to grab the book from her and hide it when Uncle Jim and Aunty Peggy, my grandmother's youngest brother and his wife, walked in. I cringed realising that the book was still in my grandmother's hands.

She greeted them and thanked them for coming, all the while, shaking the book around in her hand as she talked. I wanted to snatch it from her and run out the apartment but couldn't quite get myself to do that! And then, to my utter mortification I heard her say to them, "Lucy is as darling as ever and has bought me a wonderful book, Kama Sutra it's called, and it's all about India. Have you heard of it?"

I turned crimson as, to her surprise, I grabbed the book out of her hand mumbling that I wanted to check if it was set in India all the while trying to avoid the horrified looks of Uncle Jim and Auntie Peggy, who obviously knew exactly what it was about! My grandmother was clearly oblivious to all this and continued chatting away happily offering them a drink and opening their present. I tried to pretend not to notice their dirty looks and was relieved when they announced that they had to go ten minutes later.

I excused myself and went into the bathroom not having the courage to face them as they left. I came out as I heard the door close behind them. I grabbed the book from the table and discretely slipped out, running back to my apartment.

When I returned I told my grandmother that in fact I had got mixed up and had given her the wrong present and that this was in fact the book I'd bought for her. She seemed confused but was really delighted by the cookery book.

"But I'm sure I would have really enjoyed the book on India too, love," she said. I couldn't help giggling, imaging her flipping through the book and looking at the illustrations!

The weekend was pretty depressing without either Jake or Olivia. I felt lost and couldn't stop thinking about Matt and the way he had held me as we danced. It had really felt as if he loved me. But he hadn't called since and I'm sure he knew that Jake and I had broken up, so I had obviously misread the signals again... He'd probably just had too much to drink and the Mr. Delano episode had given him a fright.

It was normal, as if it had happened to any of my close friends, I would have been in quite a state.

I went for a walk along the beach on Saturday afternoon as the sea always soothed me and made me feel a sense of peace when I was feeling upset. I ordered a Chinese Take Away and watched TV, desperately trying to distract myself from my thoughts.

As soon as I opened my eyes the next morning I saw the rays of sunlight filtering through my curtains, and I just wanted to cry. I felt miserable and couldn't bear the thought of spending the day alone, yet there was no one I wanted to spend it with either. Well, except for Matt, Jake, Olivia, Vic (but without her family) or my family and none of them was a possibility. I went out and bought some croissants and the newspapers and sat reading my horoscope. I hated reading the newspapers actually and I had no idea why I had bought them. Matt used to be exasperated with me when I did decide to skim through the newspaper because I always managed to mess up the order of the pages and hand it back to him in what he declared was 'an unreadable mess'. I chuckled quietly at the thought.

My horoscope read "Positive week ahead - Lots of love and sunshine." Great! If only these things were true. But how could a horoscope be applicable to the millions of Sagittarians alive in the world? It was so unrealistic. I threw the newspaper aside and moodily munched on my second croissant.

Just then the phone rang. It was my mum. I couldn't believe what great timing it was. Of course I didn't tell her what had happened with Matt but just told her that Jake and I had broken up because I wasn't over Matt yet. She was upset for me because she knew how hard I was trying to move on. It was so good talking to her and I felt much happier when I hung up.

I decided to clean up my apartment as it was always a good way to evacuate stress. I began in my bathroom, scrubbing and rubbing the shower, the bath, the floor, the curtains and anything else I could get my hands on. Then my room which I vacuumed, cleaned the windows, tidied my cupboard.

This was followed by the dining and living room, then I could bear it no more and fell on my bed, moaning as I felt aches and pains all over.

The phone woke me up an hour later. It was Vic.

"Lucy, what are you doing at home on a Sunday?" she asked.

"Where else do you want me to be?" I said, sounding depressed.

"Come over for tea if you like, we're also at home today."

"Thanks Vic, I really appreciate it but I need to be alone."

"Ok, fine. But it would do you good to have the children around you and relax, you know, change your ideas a bit," she said as I heard a lot of noise in the background, it sounded like hitting and banging against various things.

"How can you put 'children' and 'relax' in the same sentence Vic?" I said laughing.

"I'll pretend you didn't say that," she said. "And besides it's your loss, you'd have fun - the kids have just learnt how to make instruments with pots and pans, you should hear them, they're great."

I could hear them and I already had a headache!

"Thanks, but no thanks Vic, I don't think I can handle it right now."

"Oh well, I thought I'd try anyway."

"And I really appreciate it," I said honestly. "Thanks."

I actually considered changing my mind and going to join Vic and her family - for a whole fraction of a second! Coping with her monsters was the last thing I wanted to do. And I was proved right as we suddenly heard a loud shattering sound. Something had just broken.

"Oh no! I think Christopher thought the window was another good instrument to hit and he's just smashed a pan through the kitchen window!"

"Did anyone get hurt?" I asked thinking how dangerous that could be.

"No, no, but we are minus a kitchen window," she said matter-of-factly. "Oh these kids; aren't they something. You never know what they're going to get up to next."

Relieved that I was in fact quietly at home, I settled myself on the couch and zapped my way through endless series, documentaries and films until it was finally time to go to bed.

Over the following week, Olivia sent me daily accounts of Paris and Pierre, who hadn't gained any further points in my books. I didn't have the heart to explain about Matt and Jake as it seemed too much to say in a mail or during a chat. It was something I needed to talk about face to face.

On Tuesday I finally received the confirmation of my course registration. Excited, I raced into John's office to tell him. He grinned at me, equally thrilled. I seemed to have grown in his esteem since I told him I wanted to do the course. I sent an email to my parents and my godmother telling them the great news then went online to book my flights for the following week. I would arrive in Cape Town on Wednesday and the course was to start the following Monday. It would give me a few days to find my bearings, visit the college and discover the area. I couldn't believe that I was really flying off to Cape Town. It was exactly what I needed and couldn't have happened at a better time.

On Wednesday afternoon, I decided to try and chat with Olivia to tell her the news.

Lucy: How are things?

Olivia: He actually introduced me as his girlfriend the other night!

Lucy: Yeah? So? It's kind of normal usually isn't it?

Olivia: I know, but he just has hang-ups about relationships. Matt wasn't much better on the commitment thing was he?

Lucy: Ouch!

Olivia: No, but it's true. Everyone has hang ups and Pierre just happens to be scared of getting involved - that's why he's kept his distance so long.

Lucy: It just seems such a waste of time when you only have 2 months to be with the other person.

Olivia: I know and it's only now, when I'm just about to leave that he's all over me.

Lucy: Is he performing any better now?

Olivia: Lucy Evans you're really bad! I leave you alone for two months and you turn into a sex freak!

Lucy: You know I'm not, but I'm just worried about you – I actually bought you a present but never got around to sending it. It was for you to give to Pierre…The Kama Sutra book!!

Olivia: I could have never given him that!!

Lucy: Just wanted to help! I actually ended up giving it to my Grandmother for her birthday by mistake – thankfully she didn't have a clue what it was and thought it was a love story set in India. Was devastated when I took it back and gave her a cookery book instead!!!

Olivia: God, I miss you Luce!

Lucy: So is he???

Olivia: He's actually getting better every day. He even lets me sleep next to him all night sometimes.

Lucy: Well aren't you lucky!

Olivia: You really don't like him do you?

Lucy: I guess I just find his behavior towards you very strange.

Olivia: He's just different. Give him a chance and at least wait until you meet him before judging him. I know he's not my usual type of guy, but I care about him.

Lucy: Are you guys making any plans for the future?

Olivia: He's promised to come and visit me in 3 months as he won't be able to get time off before then.

Lucy: And then what?

Olivia: I really don't know. One day at a time... for the moment I'm just happy knowing that we'll soon be seeing each other again.

Lucy: Would you leave everything to go and settle in Paris?

Olivia: I'm not sure... I need to see if it's really serious or not first.

Lucy: I really can't wait for you to get back.

Then she asked me how Jake was and I told her all about Matt and Jake and what had happened. She wasn't too surprised as she knew I still loved Matt. I then told her about my Copywriting course which she was thrilled about. As we said our goodbyes I felt relieved that things finally seemed to be working out for Olivia with Pierre. I couldn't help being skeptical about it but then again, only time would tell and I just hoped that Olivia wouldn't get hurt.

I spent the weekend at my aunt's beach cottage just relaxing on the beach, reading and thinking of everything that had happened. Before I knew it, it was Tuesday night and I was leaving for Cape Town at 2pm the next day. I had said my goodbyes to everyone at the agency, and told them that I would see them soon. John told me to enjoy every minute of it and to 'go get them'.

He seemed to really believe in me. It's true that I had participated in brainstorming sessions in the past but I had never realised that John had seen any real potential in me. But the way he was encouraging me on and almost seemed proud of me, I had the feeling that maybe I had missed something.

Of course I was running late the next day and ended up arriving at the airport 1 hour before take-off instead of the recommended 3 hours! I put my luggage through registration and handed over my passport excusing myself profusely for being so late.

The lady took my passport and began doing whatever it is they do on their computer, then suddenly stopped and looked at me, "I'm sorry but there seems to be a problem. Nothing important but you'll have to come with me."

Oh my god! What had I done now? I ran through everything in my head; passport validity – checked; ticket; checked – visa; checked – proof of address; checked. What the hell was wrong? I started to panic as there wasn't much time left before take-off.

"Will I miss my flight Madam?" I asked worried.

"No, you'll be fine. They won't leave without you."

We finally reached what looked like airport waiting rooms or offices, and she led me to a door and knocked.

"Come in," I heard someone say from inside, as my heart raced in fear. What the hell was going on? Had they found drugs in my luggage? Was I going to be interrogated then arrested? I had often watched those real life documentaries on airport arrests and drug smuggling and started to feel faint. But then again, I realised that it was impossible as had only just arrived at the airport.

She pushed open the door and told me to go in before closing the door behind me. I didn't know if my legs would carry me in, but then I looked inside and saw Matt...

Chapter Fifty-Four

"Matt! What are you doing here! Oh my God! I thought I was going to be interrogated for drug trafficking and put into jail or something?" I cried hysterically.

"Why? Are you carrying drugs?" he asked deadpan.

"Of course not you idiot! But I had no idea what was happening! What are you doing here?" I exclaimed, still high on adrenalin.

"You didn't tell me you were leaving…" he said quietly, looking up at me.

"Well, it's not as though we talk every day and it happened kind of fast," I replied defensively, not really knowing why I felt I had to defend myself.

"This isn't how I planned to do this," he said, smiling up at me. "But then again, when it comes to you, nothing really happens in the way you think it will."

He laughed as I pulled my tongue out at him. He

always did bring out the child in me!

"What do you want Matt? I don't want to miss my flight!" I said, getting serious.

He stood up making his way towards me then suddenly got down on one knee. My knees almost gave way, a feeling I often seemed to be having lately, as I stared at him in a daze.

"Wh-wh-at are you doing?" I said in a barely audible whisper, really feeling faint this time.

"Luce, I love you with all my heart. Will you marry me?"

"What do you mean – WILL YOU MARRY ME!" I screeched.

Impervious to my violent outburst, he smiled tenderly at me and said, "Lucy Evans, you gorgeous, crazy woman, will you do me the honour of becoming my wife?"

My eyes popped out of their socket as I stared at him, still on his knee, but for once I couldn't find any words. I had lost the power of speech.

"Please… say something," he said pleadingly, as I looked into his anguished eyes.

Then a flicker of mischief spread through them and he grinned. "My knees are killing me here woman!"

A spurt of laughter rang out and I realised it had come out of me.

"Why now Matt? I don't understand," I finally managed to say.

"I've wanted to do this since the night Mr. Delano showed up at your place, but I couldn't decide how to propose to you! You know me and my indecision!" he said, grinning at me again as I laughed. He stood up then sat down on the bench, pulling me down next to him.

"Then suddenly this morning Sam rang me up to tell me that Vic had just told him that you were leaving today for a month. I thought I would go crazy with frustration - so I got into my car and drove here to catch you before you left."

I stared at him in disbelief as my heart sang a million songs. He loved me!

"But you being you, I arrived at least an hour before you! I should have known I didn't need to rush," he said chuckling. "And I've been sitting here sick with nerves waiting..."

I smiled tenderly at him but didn't know what to say.

"Why?" I finally asked.

"Why what?" he answered confused.

"Why do you want to marry me all of a sudden?" I insisted.

"I love you like crazy Luce. I always have. It's just that the whole for-ever thing scared me to bits, you know; with my parent's marriage, then Sam and Vic and just relationships breaking down all over basically. I didn't want to take the risk of having that kind of marriage or of getting hurt. But with us I know it'll never be like that... It'll be fire and sparks non-stop!"

I grinned. "But why now?"

"When Mr. Delano showed up at your house and you called me, I swear my life flashed before me when I thought he might hurt you. I knew then my life without you in it was empty. I had been feeling so lost without you all this time and it just finally made me snap out of my indecision and face up to the fact that *you* are my life Lucy. I need you... I want you by my side every day and every night. I want to love you and protect you always. I want to fight and make up with you. I want to have lots of little babies with you... I want you to be mine – heart, body and soul..."

Tears were running down my cheeks as I listened to him saying all the things that I had waited so long to hear. His eyes were also filled with tears as he tenderly brushed away my tears with his thumb.

Matt loved me. Matt wanted to marry me. Matt… my Matt.

"Matt… I can't," I answered, my voice breaking.

Matt's face drained of colour and he shook his head sadly, defeated.

"I'm too late aren't I?" he asked, as a lone tear rolled down his cheek.

"I've waited so long to hear you say those words… But now I'm the one who's scared. I love you Matt, more than anything and I've never stopped loving you, but I'm just so scared that you'll change your mind and break my heart all over again."

"I won't change my mind Lucy. I've never been so sure in my life," he pleaded desperately, holding my hands in his.

I shook my head, forcing myself to stay strong and not give in. I couldn't cope with another broken heart and I needed to be sure that Matt wouldn't change his mind.

"While I was waiting, I wrote a list of all the things I loved about you in case you asked me. I was scared that in the heat of the moment I wouldn't think straight. But it's all here," he said, getting up and picking up a pile of bits and pieces of paper of all shapes and sizes from the desk and handing them to me.

"I don't have time to read all this now, but thank you. I'll read them on the plane," I said with emotion. I was so touched and just wanted to throw caution to the wind and go home with him, but I couldn't. Not this time. Glancing at the bundle in my hands, I couldn't believe he had written all that. Tears welled up in my eyes.

"I have to go to Cape Town, Matt. I have to do this for me. I can't say yes today because I need to be sure that you're sure. I'm only going for a month so let's take this time to really think things through both of us and when I get back, if you still want to marry me, I'll give you an answer."

"Oh Luce, you're killing me here..." he said in anguish.

"I'm sorry Matt, but you hurt me too badly last time and my heart won't be able to take another hit like that if you suddenly get scared and go running."

"I will never leave you again Luce, ever…" He whispered as he pulled me up and hugged me tightly. I hugged him back and I felt like I had come home. He was my home… my everything.

But I had to go.

I kissed him tenderly on the cheek and told him to take care of himself and that I would see him soon.

"Lucy!" he called out as I started to leave. "*Please* come back to me…"

Tears rolled down my cheeks as I smiled, nodded and waved as I walked off, not looking back.

I was bursting with happiness but so scared that it would all go wrong again, that I didn't allow myself to dwell on the fact that MATT HAD ASKED ME TO MARRY HIM! MATT LOVED ME! Oh my god! I started hyperventilating as I made my way inside the immigration section. A lady next to me in line even asked me if I was OK. I told her not to worry that I would be fine in just a moment.

Matt had asked me to marry him! Matt loved me! I grinned happily and skipped inside.

But my reasonable self soon came rushing back telling me that it was probably just the fright he had had with the Mr. Delano incident that made him think that now, but that in a few weeks he would no longer be so sure.

As I sat down in the plane, I told myself that I had one month ahead of me to think things through and for him to do the same. Marriage was for a lifetime, and although I knew that I would love Matt forever, I couldn't go into it without being sure that he was 100% sure of himself. I didn't have to settle for someone who wasn't sure he loved me enough.

After all I had met Jake who was the living proof that I would be able to move on and find someone else in time. I might not want anyone else right now, but if push came to shove, I would be okay. I didn't want to settle for second best. I had to be Matt's first and only choice. And he needed to be sure that I was.

As the plane took off, I closed my eyes and realised that when I came back in a month I would be starting a whole new chapter in my life. I would finally be doing a job I enjoyed, one in which I could grow and learn. As for Matt, I had no idea what would happen – but whatever happened, it would be the start of something new for me...

Epilogue:

5 weeks later...

As the plane started its descent into Sir Seewosagur Ramgoolam Airport in Mauritius I smiled, thinking back to my month in Cape Town. The course had been fascinating, enthralling and I had never had so much fun working in my life. Every assignment was a blast and I had fit right in during the work experience in the two advertising agencies. I felt alive when I was writing and coming up with ideas and slogans. Every project was different and I thrived on the adrenalin of finding just the perfect word or idea for an ad. I had definitively found exactly what it was I was meant to have been doing all this time. I couldn't wait to get to work at Trends.

Most of the other students had been much younger than me but we had got along really well. I had felt like I was 20 years old again, just out of school and I had left all my problems behind me. I went out with them, got drunk, flirted and even indulged in a few drunken kisses with young and handsome University students who didn't realize that I was almost 6 years older than them! It was a blast. I had felt so alive again, so free - I had felt like I didn't have a care in the world.

Cape Town is beautiful. I went up to Table Mountain many times during my stay. It was so peaceful up at the top. It was my favourite place to think. I thought back to the time Matt and I were together, what had worked between us and what hadn't, our break up, Jake, the emptiness I had felt and still felt when Matt wasn't with me… I had tried to imagine my life without him and it was unbearable. But it was even more unbearable thinking of him marrying me but not truly loving me…

Of course there had been the typical Lucy incidents namely; me getting lost more times than I care to count, walking into the wrong meeting room at the first advertising agency I was sent to while there was a super important pitch underway, falling flat on my face as I got out at the top of Table Mountain, having my ice cream cone fall all over me… What can I say, that's all part of my life.

As I saw the coast of Mauritius appear, my heart started beating faster. I was already back. I wouldn't have minded staying on in Cape Town for a while longer but I knew that I had to come back to face my life, whether it would be easy or not.

I fumbled through my bag, which was full of all sorts of rubbish as usual, looking for my passport pouch. I found it right at the bottom. I pulled out my passport and the old boarding pass from when I had left came out with it and as it did, a bunch of bits and pieces of paper came flying out, falling all over me.

Oh my god! The papers Matt had given me when I had left! I had completely forgotten about them, it had all been such a blur. I had been so late to get through immigration and onto the plane that it had completely slipped my mind. I think I stayed in shock for a few days after that, remembering Matt on his knee in front of me asking me to marry him. So the papers had completely slipped my mind! I laughed to myself as I realised that he had written on the back of old receipts, obviously not having found anything else.

I love that you don't realise how beautiful you are.

I love that you let me snore all night just because you don't want to wake me up, even if it stops you from sleeping.

I love that your knickers and bra never match and that you have a pair of old and really BIG granny knickers that you wear even around me.

I love it that you write out a shopping list but then forget it at home or when you go to the shop to buy bread and milk and come back with chocolate, biscuits, toilet paper, soap, diet coke and juice but forget the bread and milk!

I love that you somehow always manage to come up with the craziest, and sometimes even plausible, excuses for being late.

I love fighting with you because it means that we get to make up afterwards…

I love how you absolutely have to kiss me one, three, five or any uneven number of times because 2, 4 or any even number of times just doesn't feel right.

I love how you twist a lock of hair round and around your finger when you're watching TV or when you're tired.

I love the chaos you bring to my life…

I love hearing you laugh and seeing you smile – it brightens up my life.

I LOVE YOU LUCY GRACE EVANS!
Pleeeeeeeeease, pleeeaasse, pleeessassse MARRY ME!

I was laughing and crying, shaking all over as tears rolled down my cheeks. The man sitting next to me was looking at me with concern.

"Are you alright love?" he asked kindly in an English accent.

I nodded, laughing.

"I sure am," I said happily.

After what seemed like the longest ride of my life, I had finally arrived!

I raced up the flights of stairs, exhausted and out of breath by the time I got to the fifth floor. As I reached the last step, I'm not sure what happened, but the next thing I knew I was flying through the air screaming *shhhhhiiiiiit!!* I fell flat on my stomach, my bag soaring through the air, hitting Matt's door with a bang.

His door flew open as he shouted, "What the..." and the rest of his sentence stuck in his throat as he saw me grinning up at him from the floor.

He was dumbstruck.

"Lucy?" he said, just staring at me in shock.

Finally, he snapped out of his trance and a huge smile spread across his face as he held his hand out to help me up. He was looking at me as if mesmerized. He pulled me up and grinned.

"Don't tell me, the step jumped out at you," he said laughing.

"Something like that," I replied, smiling as I brushed down my clothes and reached down for my bag whose contents were of course scattered all around the place.

Matt looked at the mess, shook his head and bent down to help me, smiling happily.

My heart skipped a beat as I looked at him so close to me. I could smell that delicious Matt smell that I loved so much. I had been dreaming of this moment for so long... well except that in my dreams I didn't end up sprawled out on the floor on his doorstep!

He looked towards me as a huge smile lit his face, his eyes reflecting all the happiness I felt too.

"You're back... *Finally!*" he exclaimed beaming, and

grabbed me and hugged me as I laughed and cried in his arms.

I couldn't find anything to say, so I took out the bundle of receipts on which he had written his notes to me and asked him, "Is this all true?"

He looked at the bunch of papers I was showing him and was confused at first, but then as recognition dawned, he smiled tenderly and stroked my face. He lifted my chin up so that we were looking at each other.

"Yes, definitely… I love you Lucy - with all my heart. *Please* will you marry me?"

And I knew. I had no more doubts. He loved me.

"YES!" I shouted, jumping into his arms, almost knocking us both to the ground as we both burst out laughing. He steadied himself then pulled me into his arms, his hands sliding up the sides of my neck to tenderly cradle my face.

"That was the longest 5 weeks of my life!" he whispered. "Thank you for coming back to me…"

Then his mouth covered mine in a kiss filled with tenderness. It was magical. We went from tender, to passionate in half a second, practically jumping each other right there on his doorstep. Finally, we came up for air, both dazed with lust.

"Wow!" he said, breathless.

I looked up at him and grinned. "Have you been practicing while we were apart?"

He looked at me not understanding what I was getting at. "Kissing I mean – I don't remember it being so... so... *amazing,*" I said, acting blown away.

"Sure did," he replied, winking mischievously at me and pulling me towards him again. "Every night since we broke up..." he whispered huskily, then kissed my forehead. "In my dreams..." he kissed my nose. "With you..." and he tenderly kissed my lips.

"Maaattt!" I exclaimed, snorting with laughter as I playfully slapped him on the arm.

Grinning widely, he said mischievously. "What? You mean that actually sounded as corny as I thought it had?"

I nodded and fell back into his arms as we both shook with laughter.

Lucy: I'M GETTING MARRIED !!!!!!!

Olivia: You're WHAT?

Lucy: I'm getting M-A-R-R-I-E-D!

Olivia: To whom!?!?

Lucy: MATT !!!!!

THE END...

ABOUT THE AUTHOR...

*Cassandra Piat is a part-time English teacher and a full-time disorganised mother and housewife who spends her life trying not to forget to do the endless things on her **Things-to-do-and-to-remember** lists... but fails spectacularly most of the time!!*

Cassandra lives in Mauritius with her husband and three children. This is her first novel which she really hopes you will enjoy.

A complete novice in all things technological, she hasn't yet figured out how to set up a blog or a web page – but she will get to it soon! In the meantime, she would love to hear from you on her Facebook page - Facebook.com/Cassandra Piat - and know your thoughts on her debut novel.